FRIENDS AND SPECTRES

Friends
and
Spectres

edited by

Robert Lloyd Parry

Swan River Press
Dublin, Ireland
MMXXIV

Friends and Spectres
edited by Robert Lloyd Parry

Published by
Swan River Press
at Æon House
Dublin, Ireland
in November MMXXIV

www.swanriverpress.ie
brian@swanriverpress.ie

M. R. James and F. Anstey photograph is courtesy of
Archive Centre, King's College, Cambridge:
Papers of M. R. James F/8/1

Cover design by Meggan Kehrli
from artwork by John Coulthart

Set in Garamond by Steve J. Shaw

Paperback Edition
ISBN 978-1-78380-783-3

Swan River Press published
a limited hardback edition of
Friends and Spectres in June 2024.

Contents

On the evening of 9 March 1883, as darkness settled over Cambridge, forty-three members of the King's College Debating Society crowded into Arthur Benson's rooms on staircase H in the Gibbs Building. It was an interesting and attractive venue. The tall sash windows of the front room commanded a close-up view of the south side of the great college chapel, with its snarling stone gargoyles and dark expanses of stained glass. Within, the cupboard doors were painted blue with designs reminiscent of William Blake. Inspiring, if enigmatic, mottoes were inscribed on the walls: "*Luce magistra*" ("with light as a teacher") above the bedroom door; and over the fireplace "*Fay bien, crains rien*" ("Do well, fear nothing").

That evening's meeting was the best attended in the history of the society to date. And such was the interest in the subject to be discussed, that a senior member of the college had even turned up to listen, and deliver an argument of his own. When it was clear that no more members were expected—or could be fitted in—the meeting was called to order and the second year Classicist, Goldsworthy Lowes Dickinson, stood up before the crowd to propose the motion: "That this House believes in Ghosts."

Participants in the debate probably treated it with varying degrees of seriousness; a report in *The Cambridge Review* the following week suggests that it was an occasion for tall story-telling as much as anything else. But fourteen men spoke that night, several of whom were to achieve serious recognition in later life. Lowes Dickinson himself became a noted political philosopher and pacifist, and was instrumental in the establishment of the League of Nations. Oscar Browning, the senior member mentioned above, who seconded the motion, was already well-known in Cambridge and beyond, as much for his indefatigable self-promotion as for his progressive theories of education. One of those who spoke in opposition was the future Dean of St. Paul's Cathedral, William Ralph Inge, who became known as "the gloomy Dean" for his pessimistic views of society, which found expression in the pulpit and the *London Evening Standard* where he had a regular column.

Two of the writers whose work appears in this book (Arthur Reed Ropes and Arthur Benson) argued, perhaps surprisingly, against the motion. But the last person to speak that night, in favour, was the twenty-year-old M. R. James, in only his second term at King's. And just before 8:30 PM, long after the meeting ought to have wound up, the belief of the King's College undergraduate body in the existence of ghosts was affirmed, by twenty-three votes to fourteen.

What MRJ had to say that night or how big a part his rhetoric played in winning the debate will probably never be known. But his subsequent influence upon the ghostly imaginations of his Cambridge contemporaries was extensive, as the following pages amply show.

Friends and Spectres is a companion volume to *Ghosts of the Chit-Chat* (Swan River Press, 2020), an anthology of supernatural tales written by men who had been members, alongside MRJ, of the Cambridge University Chit-Chat Club. Here the associations with MRJ are less formal, but stronger and more enduring, for it is the bonds of genuine friendship that tie the writers featured here to him. These bonds were formed in Cambridge, when most of the men were young, but they matured, went beyond the boundaries of the university and, in most cases, strengthened over a lifetime. Each of the writers was close enough to MRJ to read their stories to him, go on holiday with him, dedicate books to him.

The majority of pieces in *Friends and Spectres* were originally published under pseudonyms, and over half appeared first in amateur magazines or local newspapers. All deal with the supernatural, and several of the stories are themselves spectres—or perhaps more properly "revenants", only now re-emerging into the light after decades of neglect and oblivion. There are rediscoveries here of "lost" tales by Arthur Benson, Arthur Reed Ropes, and E. G. Swain. Some might fairly be described as minor works, but each contains within it something unique to its creator—a twist of the imagination; a verbal dexterity; the ability to spring a narrative surprise. And all attest, in some degree, to the beneficial influence of M. R. James.

Robert Lloyd Parry
Southport
February 2024

Friends and Spectres

For Alban and Carys Lloyd Parry.

M. R. James
(1862-1936)

Given that he spent nearly half his life there, it's perhaps surprising how little Cambridge features in the ghost stories of M. R. James. In "The Tractate Middoth" (1911) memorable scenes take place in the old University Library and at the railway station. And the openings of "Oh, Whistle, and I'll Come to You, My Lad" (1904), and "The Fenstanton Witch" (undated; first published 1990) offer vivid sketches of High Table life. But it's in the English countryside with its great houses, or on the east coast, or in mainland Europe, that MRJ's curious creatures are most likely to be encountered.

"A Night in King's College Chapel" is unique among his tales for being set entirely in a recognisable Cambridge location. Unpublished in his lifetime, it appeared first in *Ghost and Scholars* in 1985. A date of 1892 seems likely for its composition, as that was when MRJ published an article in the *Cambridge Review* about the windows in the chapel, which seems to be alluded to in the opening of the story. But there's a fragment of an alternative, probably earlier, version in the King's College archive, written on the notepaper of the University Pitt Club, and it's been suggested that MRJ might have first had the idea as early as the 1880s.

Certainly, the chapel loomed large in his life from his earliest days at King's. He went up in October 1882, and the following year moved into rooms on the ground floor of a staircase immediately adjacent to the south porch. As an undergraduate he was sometimes called upon to read the Lesson, but "often enough", he recalled, "I would go there uncompelled". The windows, in particular, grabbed his attention early on. In May 1883, he wrote to his father about a striking text he'd come across on one of these: "One of the angels—a delightful being in himself—holds a scroll with the following very unseraphic inscription '*Egredere egredere vir sanguinum et vir Belial*' ['Come out, come out, thou bloody man, and thou man of Belial']. It is of course apropos of the adjacent representation of Shimei cursing David, but it amused me."

MRJ's involvement with the chapel became official when he was appointed college Dean in 1889. An early proposal to have the windows photographed wasn't taken up, probably on the grounds of practical difficulty and expense. But between 1893 and 1906 fourteen of the great windows were restored by the stained-glass designer C. E. Kempe, under MRJ's supervision. The enormous Last Judgment that fills the west end dates from 1875, but most of the other glass was painted by Flemish artists between 1515 and 1531, and by the end of the nineteenth century it was in need of attention.

Under the magnificent fan vaulted stone ceiling, it's easy to admire the kaleidoscopic effect of the painted glass on the chapel's interior, an effect that changes according to the times of day and year. It's more challenging, however, for the casual viewer to follow the stories that the windows tell, or to appreciate the fine detail within them. Even the lowest registers are several feet above eye level, and the stone uprights that divide the scenes, and dark horizontal strips of metal that cross each pane every few inches to support its weight, make them harder still to read. As the narrator of MRJ's story concedes, "People complain that they are so hard to make anything of, and there is a certain amount of truth in this statement . . . "

Twenty-four windows dominate the north and south sides of the chapel, each of which consists of five "lights"— long vertical expanses of painted glass, divided into two registers. The central light of each window contains four "messengers"—prophets or angels—who hold scrolls inscribed with quotations that (usually) elucidate the scenes depicted beside them. Each window typically contains four different narrative scenes, and each scene is spread across two lights. The upper scene on each pair of lights usually depicts an event from the Old Testament that prefigures an episode from the New Testament shown beneath it.

So, for example, in window nine (which features in MRJ's story) a depiction of the wandering Israelites being fed with manna from heaven, appears directly above the scene of Christ feeding his disciples at The Last Supper. Next to the Israelites, the messenger's scroll reads, in Latin, "Thou didst give them bread from heaven", a verse from the apocryphal *Wisdom of Solomon*. The lower messenger's scroll quotes the Gospel of Luke: "With desire have I desired to eat this Passover with you before I suffer." The manna is therefore presented as a foreshadowing of the eucharistic meal, a "type". The Old Testament is shown to anticipate the New.

The Biblical imagery and quotations within the windows chimed perfectly with MRJ's academic interests, and their restoration gave him the thrilling opportunity to examine the scenes close up. "Great was the excitement," he remembered, "when a fresh window was . . . made accessible", and he recalled "curious discoveries [that] sometimes rewarded one's scrutiny". He found evidence, for instance, of a little-known glass-painting industry in England in the 1630s, and "that the original painters of some of the inscribed scrolls had

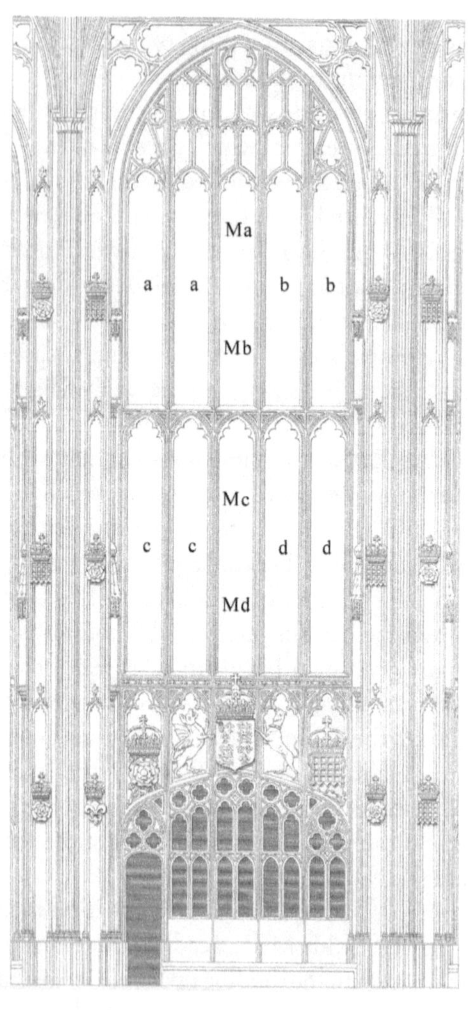

*Decorative arrangement of the twenty-four
Great Windows in King's College Chapel;
a & c: Old Testament scenes;
b & d: New Testament scenes;
Ma-Md: Messengers.*

been so lazy or stupid as to duplicate them, or put them in the wrong window"—a confusion that is alluded to in "A Night in King's College Chapel".

As well as stoking his scholarly interests, the windows also satisfied MRJ's enjoyment of the diabolical picturesque. A guidebook that he published in 1899 draws the viewer's attention to "some admirable demons" in The Harrowing of Hell, and the "two magnificent devils" who are scourging Job—one of whom speaks up on his victim's behalf in "A Night in King's College Chapel".

MRJ's close examination of the glass might also have fed into his most famous ghost story. The scroll of the lowest messenger on window twenty, which is partially hidden by the woodwork of the choir screen, reads "Quis est iste qui venit de Edom tinctis vestibus"—the first five words of which are used to such chilling effect in "Oh, Whistle, and I'll Come to You, My Lad". The quotation comes from the Latin translation of the Book of Isaiah, and means "Who is this that cometh from Edom with dyed garments?" The words relate to the Ascension of Christ, depicted on the lower left of the window: and they are quoted in the account of the Ascension in the thirteenth century devotional book *The Golden Legend*, where they are spoken by the astonished angels in heaven as they watch Christ ascend towards them.

There's no reason to think that MRJ ever intended "A Night in King's College Chapel" to be published, and it doesn't stand up particularly well beside the best of his later fiction. It suggests a rich imagination, certainly, but there's no terror in it, pleasing or otherwise. He would use the idea of a spectator looking on helplessly by moonlight, as strangely illuminated, inanimate objects move and interact, to much more fearful effect thirty years later, in "The Haunted Dolls' House" (1923).

The strongest link between the story and MRJ's later work is to be found in the characterisations. Reuben, for instance, is the direct stage-cockney ancestor of the tram drivers in "Casting the Runes". Echoes of Mrs. Job's nagging can be heard in "The Rose Garden" and "The Diary of Mr. Poynter". While Mrs. Tobit's confusion of "alligators" and "allegories" is the first of several malapropisms that enliven (or mar?) MRJ's tales. And in this, "A Night in King's College Chapel" draws attention to an important aspect of MRJ's character that is sometimes overlooked by those who revere him for his more horrible imaginings: he was a jester. He liked to be not only the most knowledgeable person in the room, but also the funniest.

Between 1886 and 1890 MRJ was a leading member of the Twice a Fortnight Club, the TAF, a group of ex-public schoolboys at Cambridge who would gather each Sunday night after chapel in their rooms, in King's or Trinity, to eat, talk and drink cider cup. In Cyril Alington's biography of another TAF member, *Lionel Ford* (1934), it was recalled that towards the end of these evenings " . . . one or other of us . . . sang, or played the piano, or launched into Handelian choruses, or conducted imaginary conversations between college characters, or all of these things one after another." MRJ was at the centre of this conviviality, and it was a custom of the TAF that whenever he won an academic prize, (and he won several), he would host a dinner and read out "an original composition". "I am not at all sure," recalled St. Clair Donaldson in Alington's book, "that [MRJ's] . . . bad habit of writing ghost stories was not fostered by the encouragement we gave him in those formative days."

Light-hearted but learned, short and college-orientated, "A Night in King's College Chapel" seems like perfect fodder for the TAF. Was it written as an after-dinner entertainment to celebrate an academic triumph? A piece of stand-up comedy directed at an audience well used to hearing the author talk about his scholarly obsessions and put on funny voices?

Of MRJ's later supernatural tales, it bears closest resemblance in tone, perhaps, to "After Dark in the Playing Fields", which was published in *College Days*, an Eton magazine, in June 1924, and was clearly also written to be read aloud. Closer to it in time, however, is another short, non-supernatural, piece of fiction, which displays something of the same learned silliness.

"Athens in the Fourteenth Century. An Inedited Supplement to Sir John Maundeville's Travels. Published from the Rhodes MS. No.17" was published as a short pamphlet in 1887. Attributed to one "Professor E. S. Merganser" (a merganser is a genus of duck), it is clearly the work of MRJ, and he is identified as the author in his friend J. W. Clark's copy of the pamphlet, now in Cambridge University Library. The work purports to be a lost chapter from the fourteenth century *Travels of John Mandeville*, and the main body of the text is written in a style authentic enough, apparently, to have convinced Charles Waldstein, then director of the Fitzwilliam Museum, of its genuineness: "The cite Atenes is treuli to seien a feyr place and a Cristeyne . . . "

No one, however, could have been taken in by the foreword, which is composed in a brilliantly strange, broken English: "I shall from the upset beg to excuse me," it begins, "for all these that through misluck and an over-weening foreknowledge of the English speech mistakenhoods may befall me, my good-heart readers . . . " After a paragraph of this we are told that "a temporary indisposition will not allow of Prof. Merganser completing this sentence . . . " and a more coherent editorial voice takes over, that of the owner of the manuscript, one George J. Barker—a comic alter ego that MRJ had invented during his Suffolk childhood.

The Merganser pamphlet was published by the Cambridge company MacMillan and Bowes in 1887, the same year that MRJ was appointed to a Fellowship at King's. His friend Arthur Reed Ropes had used the same company to self-publish his poems to celebrate his own King's Fellowship in 1884. Was MRJ marking his achievement in a similar way?

The literary motif of figures moving about and interacting within a work of art goes back at least as far as Homer. In the late nineteenth century W. S. Gilbert had used it to creepy, comic effect in *Ruddigore*; and "A Midnight Fantasy" (1888), by "Henry Doone" (Arthur Reed Ropes) reprinted in this volume, continues the tradition. But "A Night in King's College Chapel" also belongs to a tiny subset of writings about people who get locked inside churches at night.

Nodding off during a service is, of course, a hazard faced by even the most devout worshipper. Dim light, the drone of the organ, long sermons, enforced stillness: the inducements to sleep are manifold. MRJ makes good use of the tendency in "The Stalls of Barchester Cathedral" where Archdeacon Haynes's first intimation of the supernatural persecution he will suffer, occurs as he drifts off during the singing of the Magnificat. Funnier references to the habit occur in "An Episode of Cathedral History" where the Canons are concerned that the removal of the choir screen will expose them to public gaze during the sermons "when they found it helpful to listen in a posture that was liable to misconstruction."

Earlier in the same story, the verger, Mr. Worby, recalls his discovery of a drunken sailor locked in the cathedral after falling asleep during evening prayers.

MRJ himself had an experience close to that of the narrator of "A Night in King's College Chapel" when he was travelling in France in 1884. In Troyes he visited St. Nizier, "a largish, flamboyant church standing alone in the square . . . It has a good deal of sixteenth century glass in a mutilated condition . . . [but] my notes are incomplete, owing to a sudden fit of sleep which overtook me opposite to the martyrdom of St. Sebastian."

He doesn't seem to have been locked in on that occasion. But as a young apprentice at Winchester Cathedral, the Gothic Revival architect George Edmund Street (1824-1881) was only just rescued from such a fate, by a Worby-like verger. As his son, who was a few years above MRJ at Eton, related in 1888: "One evening, when the strains of the organ had made my father quite forgetful of the present, he suddenly awoke to the consciousness that the sound had ceased, and at the same moment heard the door clang and the key turn in the lock. He flew to the door, not relishing the idea of being imprisoned for the night, and by banging it managed to attract the attention of the verger. The old man seemed considerably astonished that my father should have been so anxious to attract his notice, and said, 'Lor' bless you, sir, if you'd rung one of the bells, we should have come soon enough.' "

The most striking fictional example of the motif, however, is found in "A Night in a Cathedral", a story that was published anonymously in May 1856, in the short-lived *Oxford and Cambridge Magazine*. This monthly journal of essays, reviews, poems and fiction had been established earlier that year by a group of Oxford and Cambridge undergraduates, including William Morris and Edward

Burne-Jones. And Morris is generally acknowledged today as the story's author.

The cathedral of the title is that of Amiens in northern France, which MRJ had himself seen and admired in 1884, on the same trip as his sleepy visit to Troyes. The story's narrator is immediately struck by the beauty of the building ("I had never seen such entire loveliness in all my life . . . ") and returning after sunset, his appreciation is intensified: " . . . in the deepening darkness, I saw farther and more truly; I saw it as a house of God, and all my pride was bowed down, and I was filled full of awe and humility." He finds himself unexpectedly locked in, and the rest of the story charts the fluctuating emotional responses to his plight as the night passes.

The tone is entirely different to that of MRJ's comic fantasy; Morris's tale is fretted with terror, awe, and spiritual agony. And while MRJ's wry narrator is the detached observer of the unthreatening, surreal events that unfold before him, Morris's is prone to nightmarish imaginings:

> . . . Now, all alone in darkness, in what seemed the dead of night . . . in a place so fearful as a church, with the dead beneath my feet, and with spirits appearing to hover all round me, all the old fear and horror rushed back upon me, and seized me wholly . . . The skeletons rose from beneath the stones— thin, white ghosts glided before me; the fiends in the tympanum, and from under the feet of the saints, thronged into the church . . . the gargoyles followed them, and played uncouth antics all about me, on the floor, in the triforium, in the stalls . . . I heard their hideous half-human cries distinctly, mingled with the rattling of the bones of the skeletons.

He waivers between reason and panic, until he experiences a vision of ultimate horror. Imagining the people who first built the church, he pictures a medieval sculptor,

> and next to him . . . a young man . . . placing a female saint on the back of a devil, which was already fixed up in the porch . . . but before the saint's feet could be set upon him, [the devil] leapt down from his place, and gambolled into the church; and, oh horror! he was followed by a host of devils and gargoyles; and the stern knights and sad priests rose from their graves, skeletons with armour and robes dangling and folding about them, making the night hideous beyond endurance.

As the dawn breaks, the narrator collapses in despair having "never in all my life felt such profound sadness . . . alone in a foreign country, shut up in a church, the ghostly twilight shimmering in through stained glass . . . "

The similarity in theme and title between "A Night in a Cathedral" and "A Night in King's College Chapel" might be a coincidence, but it's possible that MRJ's attention was drawn to the earlier story by his old Eton tutor and friend H. E. Luxmoore, who was an ardent admirer of Morris, and had done much to encouraged his one-time pupil's interest in old churches.

A Night in King's College Chapel

M. R. James

"It is curious how few people ever notice the painted glass in our Chapel—comparatively few, that is. One has heard enthusiastic worshippers sometimes remark on the extreme excellence of the West window. But these are generally the ones who would like to see some handsome gas standards in place of all those guttering candles, and would like the service brightened up a little by some hearty congregational singing—'Hark, hark my soul' or 'Dare to be a Daniel'. No, our windows are a sealed book to most visitors; and did anyone say all residents? People complain that they are so hard to make anything of, and there is a certain amount of truth in this statement. Indeed the object of this paper is to throw some little light on the erudition of these masterpieces of medieval art. I must remind you that in the year 1754 . . . "

I had written so much of an article on the windows intended for the *Cambridge Review*, sitting in one of the stalls of the chapel after an afternoon service, and at that point I stopped for a little and, gradually succumbing to the associations of my place, fell into a doze. You will guess the next sentence and I will not therefore pain you with the repetition of it. I was awaked by the south door banging to, and discovered that I was locked in. Under the circumstances there is no chance of making yourself heard except by ringing the bell, and for the moment I was too surprised and lazy to do anything at all. There I sat. The moon was shining and I could see some of the figures in the windows, which pleased me, and I fixed my attention on that which represents Reuben looking at the empty well where he expected to find Joseph. To my horror I saw him, distinctly, lower his arms (which had been raised over his head in surprise), retire to the edge of the well, and sit down on it. Then he yawned—I heard him—and began feeling about in his drapery. Then he began to say something in a somewhat metallic tone which became more natural as he went on.

"Well, I suppose that feller Joseph as took and gorn off on one of his larks. I thought he worn't in that pit. And now for a pipe."

Yes—he said a pipe. You may imagine my feelings when, apparently from the bosom of his red shirt, he produced an extraordinarily murky clay, filled it, struck a match on the stonework of the well and lit up, so that soon an odour as of the worst variety of shag stole over the sacred edifice. But Reuben was not destined to enjoy his evening smoke altogether undisturbed. Just opposite to him is a representation of the Manna falling—in the shape of large halfcrowns—and I was suddenly brought to a recollection of this by hearing a sharp rattling sound, and seeing Reuben start, draw up his leg and begin rubbing his shin, muttering execrations. Suddenly he put down his pipe on the edge of the well and advanced to the foreground in a sad state of anger.

"Moses," he said, "I've spoke about this time and again. If you can't keep them Children of Israel in better order I shall speak to the Guvnor to ave you took out of that and put in one of the broke windows. You knows right well it'll be done too. I will not ave them throwin of their Manner at me and, to my thinking, you want all the Manners you can git yourself. You aven't got none to spare. I may be only a Type, but I ain't goin to be put upon."

There was a dead silence at this, followed by a whispering in the Manna window. Then Moses (as well as I could make out for he was on the same side as I) stepped forward and apologised, saying that his attention had been diverted for the moment, and promising that the offense should not be repeated. This explanation, which seemed to satisfy Reuben, was followed by a smart application of Moses' rod to the backs and shoulders of some of Reuben's descendants—he even sent across one of the "Messengers" who occupy the middle lights to borrow the rod belonging to his double in the scene with the Golden Calf.

But you must not suppose that these were the only windows which assumed so new an aspect. There was a perfect buzz of conversation on all sides; voices male, female and animal. I noticed that all the New Testament lights remained dark and inanimate while the Types and Messengers and Pontius Pilate seemed to be lighted up from some internal source.

"Do get up," said Naomi from her position at the East end, to her deceased husband. "Who do you suppose is a going to set and cry over you all night as well as all day?" And Elimelech got up in a submissive manner and muttered something about going across to see Job.

Job's wife (who, you will remember, is scolding him, usually assisted by a hideous demon) was rather inclined to continue the process now, as I judged from her opening words: " . . . setting there as naked as Adam on that nasty filthy dunghill—in a perfect coat of dirt. You ought to be ashamed of yourself," etc, etc. But here even the demon interposed and said he wasn't going to stand by and see the gentleman put upon. If Mr. Job didn't choose to stand up for himself, and a more affable gent he never see, then it was time his friends stood up for him. And as to sitting on dunghills and having no clothes to wear, well, all he should like to know was, who brought him to it?

A new element was here introduced into the discussion by the arrival of Eve, who had unfortunately overheard the remarks made by Mrs. Job on Adam's scanty attire, and now came rapidly up accompanied by the serpent, to inquire precisely what was meant to be conveyed by those words. Here were the materials for a very pretty quarrel, which in fact lasted a considerable time. But I was glad to notice that Job and Elimelech were able to slip off and join Adam in the Garden of Eden where, I concluded, they were having a quiet cigar.

The gentlemen who occupy the centre lights and hold long scrolls seemed to be forming themselves into a kind of servants' club in the West window, which, as being modern glass, had entirely disappeared. Some of them left their scrolls behind, but most took them with them, and left them about on the ground of the window. They were dreadfully mixed next day in some cases. One or two, I noticed, tied them round their necks in a bow, and these, from having been treated in this way persistently for three centuries, are almost entirely illegible now. The only ones who would not join the party were the four exactly similar figures of St. Luke, which hurried off at once to the broken windows at the West end and dragged out Enoch, who, between the fact that he is being translated and that he is also very much mutilated, is in no condition to be roughly handled. However, the St. Lukes were not inclined to think much of that.

"Come out," they said. "We'll have you right tonight, old man. You shall be thoroughly set to rights. Just drink off this electuary and we'll have you to pieces."

"No, not the electuary yet," said the second. "The purge—you forget the purge. Galen saith, 'let a purge precede every incision'."

"Purge quotha?" said the third. "Galen? Drink your own filthy purge. His salt humours must be dispersed or we shall have trouble anon. Exhibit a solution of the dust from the altar, and frankincense and a fat chapel spider."

Enoch groaned. "I hate spiders," he said, "and the dust you gave me last night nearly made me burst, because it's a week-day and I can only cough when the organ's playing loud."

Nobody paid any attention. The fourth St. Luke, who had said nothing, but had been slowly dancing round and round to himself, as it were, and trying the edge of his penknife on his thumb, now advanced, and said slowly, "There's only a little ink on it. Come here. You've got a rush of blood to the head," (though as a fact, few people could have been paler than Enoch at this moment), "and what you want is a good blood-letting: and by Theophilus you shall have it." They closed in upon him and I heard a faint scream. I have since thought that every day I look at Enoch in his place, he seems more hopelessly confused, and should he be treated in this way for a much longer time, I fear he will be too far gone for the College ever to mend him.

Others of these distinguished personages had their troubles. Tobias' mother, a respectable old lady enough, was anxious to get over to the Shunammite to have a chat, but had several difficulties to contend with. First there was her own son's dog, a vicious little creature which kept barking and howling at her, to her extreme terror. Then she wasn't sure if "that young man with the lions," (meaning presumably Daniel), "was to be trusted": had he got the animals quite under his control, because she had heard of so many unfortunate accidents occurring in menageries and that, "not but what he didn't keep no menagerie, far from it."

These imputations Daniel indignantly repudiated, but there seemed some ground for them in as much as one of the curious breed of lions, which the two Daniels keep, had just made an ugly rush at King Darius, and this had so frightened the angel in the next window, who is carrying Habakkuk by the hair, that he let that unhappy seer fall right into the den, where the promptest action on the part of Daniel was required to avert destruction.

Besides the lion and the dog, Mrs. Tobit had another awkward neighbour in the shape of Jonah's whale, which (I heard her saying) was always flapping about the place, and splashing one's silk dress when one went out to tea with any lady, and "what a blessing it would be if some people as give themselves airs about being prophets could keep themselves to themselves a trifle more." An innuendo which so moved Jonah that he said, with some asperity, that he had yet to learn that a prophet, even though he might have only five chapters, wasn't a cut above an old woman out of the Apocrypha with half a dozen verses to bless herself with. Besides, wasn't it a trifle mean to complain of a harmless animal like that whale, which after all was very likely only an allegory? To which Mrs. Tobit, together with much other matter, retorted that if it was a whale it couldn't be an allegory. She hoped she'd learnt her geography better than that when she was a girl, and allegories didn't live at Ninevah but Egypt.

I saw and heard much more that night, but these were some of the more noteworthy incidents and, in selecting even these, I fear I have detained you too long.

A Night in King's College Chapel
(Early Fragment)

M. R. James

After this there was an interval of silence broken only by the quiet fall of the manna onto the top of the stalls—and I was able to look round and notice some of the changes that had taken place in the disposition of the windows since night had come on. Reuben was sitting on the edge of the well, peering curiously into its depths, and I heard him muttering. "Well for three hundred years I've been put up here to look at this old hole and blowed if I won't find out whether there's something in it after all." So saying he craned over further and further, till at last there came a sudden splash, and several shouts which roused the keenest interest in the other Old Testament characters, who rushed to the edge of their windows, though the New Testament ones succeeded well in preserving the calm composure on which they prided themselves. Presently Reuben crawled out, very wet and draggled, into the middle light occupied by the messengers, who both protested loudly but vainly against the intrusion. Reuben not only refused to quit the usurped position but insisted on borrowing the messenger's cloak and scroll to dry himself with, remarking at the same time in sulky tones, "Well, it says distinctly in Genesis that there was no water in the pit, and of course that was in summer,

but they must mind and alter it in the Revised Version".
With which emendation he wrapped the cloak round the
head of the shivering messenger and retired to his place

F. Anstey
(1856-1934)

"From a fairly early age I was possessed by a devil of burlesque whose humour was very far from subtle."

– A Long Retrospect (1936)

At his best, F. Anstey could be a very funny man. Reviewing his debut novel, *Vice Versa* (1882), Andrew Lang wrote that it "make[s] us laugh with almost dangerous freedom and frequency". And that danger was not entirely exaggerated: it's said that the stroke that killed the great Victorian novelist Anthony Trollope was brought on by a fit of laughter provoked by an after-dinner reading of the book. But, as Anstey himself came to recognise, as the decades passed, his jests and fantasies—rooted as they were in Victorian society— too often failed to amuse; and *Vice Versa*, begun when he was an undergraduate at Cambridge in the 1870s, was his greatest hit in an uneven literary career that lasted nearly half a century.

Born Thomas Anstey Guthrie, he had gone up to Trinity Hall to study Law in October 1875, spurred on by his father's ambition for him to become a barrister, a career for which he himself had scant enthusiasm. His real interests lay in comic writing and illustration and, in emulation of his hero W. S. Gilbert, he became a sought-after contributor of light verse and "burlesques" to undergraduate journals. In 1878, while still at Cambridge, two of his stories—"Accompanied on the Flute" and "The Return of Agamemnon"—were published in *Mirth*, a new London magazine. This "Miscellany of Wit and Humour" went bankrupt after twelve issues, before it could pay the author his fee, but the editor inadvertently rewarded him with a valuable trademark: his byline was misprinted as "F. Anstey", a name which so well evoked his fanciful, imaginative storytelling, that he published under it for the rest of his life.

Pleased by this modest break into the world of letters, Anstey nevertheless returned to Cambridge determined to repay his father's support, and settled down to prepare for his Law Finals. "I went through my text-books and lecture notes," he recalled, "and felt that I knew my subjects well enough to afford to indulge in just one last literary orgy. So I wrote a comic story, which I called 'The Wraith of Barnjum' and sent it to the editor of *Temple Bar*, then one of the leading magazines."

This release of pent-up comic energy had an undesirable side effect, however, for, as his exams approached, Anstey realised with growing panic that in the excitement of writing "The Wraith of Barnjum", he'd forgotten all the Law that he'd previously reviewed. In one paper he found himself so at a loss that he quit the exam hall after half an hour, having handed in an almost blank sheet of paper. His stupefaction and despair, as he wandered the Cambridgeshire countryside afterwards, were relieved only by a chance meeting with a kindly vicar, who persuaded him to return to college and see through the rest of his exams. He was eventually awarded a third-class degree and returned to the family home chastened, and determined that henceforth there should be no more "philandering with the comic muse . . ."

Two months later *Temple Bar* published "The Wraith of Barnjum", paid him £4 10s, and F. Anstey's professional career began.

The story's two puerile antagonists, the narrator's relentlessly waggish tone of voice, the awkward ending: all perhaps mark "The Wraith of Barnjum" out as an undergraduate work. Yet it already has several of those winning ingredients that characterise the best of what was to become known as "Ansteyan Fantasy": farcical situations brought about by the invasion of the supernatural into everyday life; a hapless anti-hero who suffers (usually well-deserved) social and financial embarrassment; a dead-pan acceptance of the miraculous. Anstey's jokes can be ponderous at times, but there are plenty of absurdities to enjoy here too (the doomed stage show in Tenby is a highlight). And the anti-hero's preposterous spectral adversary does a good job of satirising other, more celebrated, literary nemeses. Is there a deliberate echo of "Green Tea" (1869) in the wraith's tantalising habit of disappearing every so often, and of glowing in the dark? Anstey was an avowed admirer of Joseph Sheridan Le Fanu (1814-1873) from his schooldays.

Anstey's legal training sputtered on in London after he left Cambridge, but more stories found their way into *Temple Bar* and other outlets, and his literary career progressed steadily until *Vice Versa* was published in the summer of 1882. By September, this inventive tale of a father and son who swap bodies, was entering its sixth edition, and Anstey was basking in warm reviews, excellent sales and a greatly enhanced social life. In April 1883, a stage adaptation of the novel opened in the West End, and when the undergraduate MRJ delivered his first address to the Chit-Chat Club in his room in King's College in May that year, he cited *Vice Versa* as a work which, while having no high intellectual or moral purpose, is one "without which our literature would be very much poorer". Over twenty years later Anstey and MRJ became good friends.

They were brought in touch initially by the aspirant humourist and illustrator, James McBryde (1874-1904), who after befriending MRJ as an undergraduate at King's in the 1890s, had left Cambridge to study medicine in London. Like the undergraduate Anstey, McBryde was reluctantly following his father's professional ambitions for him rather than his own, and he found himself bored and frustrated by a curriculum that allowed little time to pursue his real interests.

These interests were encapsulated in *The Story of a Troll Hunt*, a richly illustrated fantasy on which McBryde had been working, with MRJ's encouragement, since the summer of 1899 when they'd travelled together in Denmark. It's a whimsical tale about three Cambridge friends who visit Jutland to capture a Troll for the Fitzwilliam Museum. Successful in their quest, they bring the creature back to London where, at a black-tie dinner, it steals several magnums of champagne, climbs Nelson's column and explodes as the sun rises over Trafalgar Square.

McBryde seems to have seen *The Story of a Troll Hunt* as a ticket out of the drudgery of his medical studies, and he was keen for encouragement and advice about how to pursue the life of the comic illustrator. Anstey was by this time well established on the staff of *Punch* and, with his record of producing stories in which legendary creatures upset the staidness of Victorian London—*The Tinted Venus* (1885), *The Talking Horse* (1891), *The Brass Bottle* (1900)—he was an obvious person to consult. At a meeting with Anstey, McBryde seems to have been advised to see through his medical studies before pursuing his artistic ambitions. Deflated, he enlisted MRJ's help: "As far as Anstey is concerned," he wrote to him in February 1901, "I think a tactful letter such as you could write finding out what the prospects are would be useful and certainly could do no harm as far as his taking an interest . . . "

The rough draft of a letter about McBryde, written in MRJ's hand and held in Cambridge University Library, was probably the result of this pressure from his young friend: "My dear sir, I am venturing to trouble you with a letter—though I am not personally known to you—on the subject of Mr. McBryde with whom you had an interview quite recently. I hope you will forgive me . . . McBryde is a person in whom I have always taken a particular interest; & you have evidently dealt kindly with him . . . "

The Story of a Troll Hunt finally appeared in print in late 1904, too late for its author to enjoy the praise that it earned from its readers. McBryde had died suddenly in June that year from complications following an operation on his appendix, and MRJ oversaw the private publication of the book as a tribute to his friend. A copy was sent to Anstey who wrote to MRJ that December to thank him and commend the book's "Doyle-like humour and fancy":

> I remember so well [McBryde] . . . showing me the
> originals of these drawings when I first met him . . .
> He was one of the few people who could follow advice
> which must have been unpalatable & only a very
> rare degree of concentration & firmness could have
> enabled him to put aside work he loved & was meant
> to do until he had passed his last medical exam.

MRJ finally met Anstey face to face in early 1905, and in March that year Anstey went to stay with him at King's. There his host showed him the glass in the chapel, the treasures of the Fitzwilliam Museum, and introduced him to various friends, among them E. G. Swain—"a fresh coloured youngish clergyman with thinning grizzled hair and a pleasant mouth," as Anstey described him in his diary, now in the British Library (13 March).

The two men clearly liked each other and in August 1906, Anstey joined MRJ on a trip to Denmark, during which they visited some of the locations from *The Story of a Troll Hunt*. This was the first of several cycling holidays in Europe that they took together. A photograph taken on 13 August 1911, shows them, along with Allen Ramsey and Alfred Coneybeare, in the garden of what Anstey described as "a delightfully comfortable" guesthouse in Pressburg (modern Bratislava, then in Hungary).

Reading their respective memoirs—Anstey's *A Long Retrospect* (1936, published posthumously) and MRJ's *Eton and Kings* (1926)—one can see why the two men got on so well. It's clear that their schooldays remained of vivid importance to both of them throughout their lives and, for all their grown-up achievements and responsibilities, like the central character in *Vice Versa*, their adult bodies were the lifelong hosts to playful schoolboys. On that Danish trip of 1906 they stayed in Viborg, the setting of James's ghost story "Number 13" (1904), and Anstey's diary records the subjects of conversation that kept the companions amused over breakfast:

> M.R.J. at school a bully. [The boy] . . . whose arms they used to twist. delicate skin. arms black and blue. M's parents sent for. The boy at Eton who said "Don't look at me or I shall scream" "So of course we did look at him" . . . [another] boy who cut out his tongue to be sent home. lots drawn to kill headmaster, falling on his son who accepted

A rose garden in Pressburg
Unknown, MRJ, A. E. Conybeare, F. Anstey,
and A. B. Ramsay (13 August 1911).

cheerfully, and stunned his father with the poker in class one day, then fled across fields (14 August 1906).

But they also shared more refined, antiquarian interests. Anstey was an avid collector of mediaeval painted glass, and one senses that in him MRJ found someone who could appreciate and enjoy his store of "useless knowledge". In August 1907 they visited Säckingen in Germany where, Anstey recalled, they saw

> a statue of St. Fridolin with Count Hugo whom he miraculously restored from death to the bosom of his family. Unfortunately, the saint seems to have resuscitated him as a living skeleton, so that his intervention might have been more tactful . . . Very likely Count Hugo's family were glad to have him back in any shape and soon got used to his appearance. Still, I think the general opinion must have been that if you must perform miracles it is just as well to do the thing thoroughly.

The words are from Anstey's memoir, but the droll tone could easily be MRJ's, and it must have been he who interpreted the statue for Anstey.

The two also shared a growing feeling that they were anachronisms; that, as the twentieth century went on, society and the currents of contemporary thought were leaving them stranded. They were both Victorians by birth and education, and as MRJ says in "A Neighbour's Landmark" (1924), "the Victorian tree may not unreasonably be expected to bear Victorian fruit." On the whole MRJ seems to have been content with this. Looking back in 1926 on his pre-war Christmas gatherings at King's he described them as "all very pedestrian and Anglican and Victorian and everything else that it ought not to be: but I should like well enough to have it over again." And when he realised that the First World War had changed Cambridge University for ever, he found a pleasant, nostalgic refuge in Eton, becoming its Provost in 1918 until his death eighteen years later.

For Anstey this obsolescence was more of a problem. MRJ's ghost stories were a sideline to an unusually successful academic career; he was doubtless pleased by any popularity they enjoyed, but he didn't rely upon them for professional or personal validation. He didn't need to cultivate a following. Anstey's writing was his sole occupation and chief source of income, and his inability—or refusal—to move with the times was a cause of increasing discomfort. In 1932 he wrote to Mrs. Kenneth Graham, thanking her for her interest in his work "which I doubt would be shared by the bright young things of the present day, for whom Victorianism is a synonym for stuffiness."

Anstey's last trip with MRJ, to France in 1922, ended sadly. While staying in Uzerche, and after recording some innocuous sounding events in his diary (losing at Jacobi, sketching a bridge, an evening stroll), Anstey abruptly notes, on 30 August: "Fit of depression and silence all the evening. Shall be rather glad when this tour is over and doubt I shall ever come on another." Two days later he was "Still very depressed and hopeless about future."

Anstey records no reason for this sudden gloom. MRJ himself put it down to his taking offence at a clumsy joke that had been made at his expense—an anonymous postcard sent to him at the hotel by his travelling companions showing a pig eating truffles. But whatever lay behind it, this was the last holiday that MRJ and Anstey took together, and the friendship seems to have cooled.

Anstey's memoirs suggest that there always was a streak of melancholy running through him, though this only occasionally found its way into his fiction. His 1896 novel *The Statement of Stella Maberly*, which was originally published without his name attached, purports to be an eyewitness account of a satanic possession and/or mental disintegration. A Gothic melodrama, it won the admiration of Arthur Conan Doyle, but the public at large ignored it. "The Breaking-Point", reprinted here, is perhaps Anstey's most successful attempt at a weightier supernatural short story. It originally appeared in *The Strand Magazine* in December 1919 and was reprinted in his final short story collection *The Last Load* in 1925. Like "The Wraith of Barnjum", it deals with apparent vengeance from beyond the grave, but it's much more tense, and much more gloomy.

The initial image of a man pursued by pieces of discarded wastepaper which carry messages directed at him, is found in a note in Anstey's diary from January 1889, long before he met MRJ. But there are incidents in the finished story that suggest the latter's influence—the message in the programme at the theatre, the mysterious handbill in the street: both recall the supernatural goading of Dunning by Karswell in "Casting the Runes". More pronounced is the resemblance to Le Fanu's "The Familiar" (1872)—a favourite of MRJ's—with the nocturnal pursuit by "something subtly malevolent"; the brusque, apparently posthumous, messages addressed to the protagonist; the doomed romantic attachment; and the fluctuating hopes and gradual despair.

But though initially conceived in the late 1880s, the story, as it was written, could only be set in post-WWI England, and in this sense it is unusually modern for Anstey. "The invisible enemy" that the protagonist Richard Alston faces—the memory of dead comrades, of explosions and wounds suffered, the guilt of survival—was the same that confronted countless others on their return from the trenches.

Anstey himself, like MRJ, was too old to serve in the regular army when war broke out, though he enrolled in the Inns of Court Reserve Corps and did his duty digging trenches along the south coast and guarding Hyde Park Corner and Grosvenor Bridge. But one wonders whether there isn't some of Anstey's own professional and personal frustrations expressed in the story. As Richard Alston's apparent persecution progresses, "His chief feeling . . . was irritation; this kind of thing was becoming grotesque; in fact, there was a ludicrous side to all these incidents, if he could only bring his sense of humour to bear on them; he might do so later, but not quite yet." The theme of being thwarted by fate and one's own limitations, and the struggle to laugh through it all, recurs throughout Anstey's memoirs.

Though they never travelled together again, that last 1922 holiday in France didn't entirely draw a line under the friendship between MRJ and Anstey. In *A Long Retrospect* he writes warmly, proudly even, of his trips abroad with the Provost of King's and Eton. And in 1928 Anstey published an article in an Eton College magazine *The Burning Bush* entitled "My First Book" in which he described the writing of *Vice Versa*, "[to] afford encouragement, or warning—I am not really very sure which—to such readers of *The Burning Bush* as may be thinking of Literature as their profession."

Ultimately MRJ and Anstey had much in common, and the latter's assessment of his own literary abilities in

A Long Retrospect could, with only a little tinkering, be applied to MRJ himself: "I was not a profound thinker; I had no message to deliver, no theories to propound, no cause to advocate. My only assets were a sense of humour, and some powers of observation and description . . ."

The Wraith of Barnjum

F. Anstey

I frankly admit, whatever may be the consequences of doing so, that I was not fond of Barnjum; in fact, I detested him. Everything that fellow said and did jarred upon me to an absolutely indescribable extent, although I did not discover for some time that he regarded me with a strange and unreasonable aversion.

We were so essentially unlike in almost every particular—I, with my innate refinement and high culture, my over-fastidious exclusiveness in the choice of associates; and he, a big, red, coarse brute, with neither sweetness nor light, who knew himself a Philistine, and seemed to like it—we were so unlike, that I often asked him, with a genuine desire for information, what had I in common with him?

And yet it will scarcely be believed, perhaps, that with such good reasons for keeping apart, we were continually seeking one another's company with a zest that knew no satiety. The only explanation I can offer for such a phenomenon is, that our mutual antipathy had become so much a part of ourselves, that we could not let it perish for lack of nourishment.

Perhaps we were not conscious of this at the time, and when we agreed to go on a walking tour together in North Wales, I think it was chiefly because we knew that we could devise no surer means of annoying one another; but, however that may be, in an ill-starred day for my own peace of mind, we started upon a journey from which but one of us was fated to return.

I pass by the painful experiences of the first few days of that unhappy tour. I will say nothing of Barnjum's grovelling animalism, of his consummate selfishness, his more than bucolic indifference to the charms of Nature, nor even of the mean and sordid way in which he contrived to let me in for railway tickets and hotel bills.

I wish to tell my melancholy story with perfect impartiality, and I am sure that I am not reduced to exciting any prejudice to secure the sympathies of all readers.

I shall pass, then, to the memorable day when my disgust, so long pent up, so imperfectly concealed, culminated in one grand outburst of a not ignoble indignation, to the hour when I summoned up moral courage to sever the bonds which linked us so unequally.

I remember it so well, that brilliant morning in June when we left the Temperance Hotel, Doldwyddlm, and scaled in sulky silence the craggy heights of Cader Idris, which, I presume, still overhang that picturesque village, while, as we ascended, an ever-changing and ever-improving panorama unrolled itself before my delighted eyes.

The air up there was keen and bracing, and I recollect that I could not repress an æsthetic shudder at the crude and primitive tone which Barnjum's nose had assumed under atmospheric influences. I mentioned this (for we still maintained the outward forms of friendship), when he retorted, with the brutal personality which formed so strong an ingredient of his character, that if I could only see myself in that suit of mine, and that hat (referring to the dress I was then wearing), I should feel the propriety of letting his nose alone. To which I replied, with a sarcasm that I feel now was a little too crushing, that I had every intention of doing so, as it was quite painful enough to merely contemplate such a spectacle; and he, evidently meaning to be offensive, remarked, that no one could help his nose getting red, but that any man in my position could at least *dress* like a gentleman.

I took no notice of this insult; a Bunting (I don't think I mentioned before that my name is Philibert Bunting)—a Bunting can afford to pass such insinuations by; indeed, I find it actually cheaper to do so, and I flattered myself that my dress was distinguished by a sort of studied looseness, that would appeal at once to a cultivated and artistic eye, though of course Barnjum's hard and shallow organs could not be expected to appreciate it.

I overlooked it, then, and presently we found ourselves skirting the edge of a huge chasm, whose steep sides sloped sheer down into the slate-blue waters of the lake below.

How can I hope to give an idea of the magnificent view which met our eyes as we stood there—a view of which, as far as I am aware, no description has ever yet been attempted?

To our right towered the Peaks of Dolgelly, with their saw-like outline cutting the blue sky with a faint grating sound, while the shreds of white cloud lay below in drifts. At our feet were the sun-lit waters of the lake, upon which danced a fleet of brown-sailed herring-boats; beyond was the plain of Capel Curig, and there, over on the left, sparkled the falls of Y-Dydd.

As I took all this in I felt a longing to say something worthy of the occasion. Being possessed of a considerable fund of carefully-dried and selected humour, I frequently amuse myself by a species of intellectual exercise, which consists in so framing a remark that a word or more therein may bear two entirely opposite constructions; and some of the quaint names of the vicinity seemed to me just then admirably adapted for this purpose.

I was about to gauge my dull-witted companion's capacity by some such test, when he forestalled me.

"You ought to live up here, Bunting," said he; "you were made for this identical old mountain."

I was not displeased, for, Londoner as I am, I have the nerve and steadiness of a practised mountaineer.

"Perhaps I was," I said good-humouredly; "but how did *you* find it out?"

"I'll tell you," he replied, with one of his odious grins. "This is Cader Idris, ain't it? well, and you're a *cad awry dressed*, ain't you? Cader Idrissed, see?" (he was dastard enough to explain) "That's how I get at it!"

He must have been laboriously leading up to that for the last ten minutes!

I solemnly declare that it was not the personal outrage that roused me; I simply felt that a paltry verbal quibble of that description, emitted amidst such scenery and at that altitude, required a protest in the name of indignant Nature, and I protested accordingly, although with an impetuosity which I afterwards regretted, and of which I cannot even now entirely approve.

He happened to be standing on the brink of an abyss, and had just turned his back upon me, as, with a vigorous thrust of my right foot, I launched him into the blue æther, with the chuckle at his unhallowed jest still hovering upon his lips.

I am aware that by such an act I took a liberty which, under ordinary circumstances, even the licence of a life-long friendship would scarcely have justified; but I thought it only due to myself to let him see plainly that I desired our acquaintanceship to cease from that instant, and

Barnjum was the kind of man upon whom a more delicate hint would have been distinctly thrown away.

I watched his progress with some interest as he rebounded from point to point during his descent. I waited—punctiliously, perhaps, until the echoes he had aroused had died away on the breeze, and then, slowly and thoughtfully, I retraced my steps, and left a spot which was already becoming associated for me with memories the reverse of pleasurable.

I took the next up-train, and before I reached town had succeeded in dismissing the incident from my mind, or if I thought of it at all, it was only to indulge relief at the reflection that I had shaken off Barnjum for ever.

But when I had paid my cab, and was taking out my latch-key, a curious thing happened—the driver called me back.

"Beg pardon, sir," he said hoarsely, "but I think you've bin and left something white in my cab!"

I turned and looked in: there, grinning at me from the interior of the hansom, over the folding-doors, was the wraith of Barnjum!

I had presence of mind enough to thank the man for his honesty, and go upstairs to my rooms with as little noise as possible. Barnjum's ghost, as I expected, followed me in, and sat down coolly before the fire, in my arm-chair, thus giving me an opportunity of subjecting the apparition to a thorough examination.

It was quite the conventional ghost, filmy, transparent, and, though wanting firmness in outline, a really passable likeness of Barnjum. Before I retired to rest I had thrown both my boots and the contents of my bookcase completely through the thing, without appearing to cause it more than a temporary inconvenience—which convinced me that it was indeed a being from another world.

Its choice of garments struck me even then as decidedly unusual. I am not narrow; I cheerfully allow that, assuming the necessity for apparitions at all, it is well that they should be clothed in robes of some kind; but Barnjum's ghost delighted in a combination of costume which set the fitness of things at defiance.

It wore that evening, for instance, to the best of my recollection, striped pantaloons, a surplice, and an immense cocked hat; but on subsequent occasions its changes of costume were so rapid and eccentric, that I ceased to pay much attention to them, and could only explain them on the supposition that somewhere in space there exists a supernatural store in the nature of a theatrical wardrobe, and that Barnjum's ghost had the run of it.

I had not been in very long before my landlady came up to see if I wanted anything, and of course as soon as she came in, she saw the wraith. At first she objected to it very strongly, declaring that she would not have such nasty things in her house, and if I wanted to keep ghosts, I had better go somewhere else; but I pacified her at last by representing that it would give her no extra trouble, and that I was only taking care of it for a friend.

When she had gone, however, I sat up till late, thinking calmly over my position, and the complications which might be expected to ensue from it.

It would be very easy to harrow the reader's feelings and work upon his sympathies here by a telling description of my terror and my guilty confusion at the unforeseen consequences of what I had done. But I think, in relating an experience of this kind, the straightforward way is always the best, and I do not care to heighten the effect by attributing to myself a variety of sensations which I do not remember to have actually felt at the time.

My first impression had not unnaturally been that the spectre was merely the product of overwrought nerves or indigestion, but it seemed improbable that a cabman should be plagued by a morbid activity of imagination, and that a landlady's digestion could be delicate sufficiently to evolve a thing so far removed from the merely commonplace; and, reluctantly enough, I was forced to the conclusion that it was a real ghost, and would probably continue to haunt me to the end of my days.

Of course I was disgusted by this exhibition of petty revenge and low malice on the part of Barnjum, which might be tolerated perhaps in a Christmas annual, with a full-page illustration, but which, in real life and the height of summer, was a glaring anachronism.

Still, it was of no use to repine then; I resolved to look at the thing in a common-sense light—I told myself that I had made my ghost, and would have to live with it. And after all, I had much to be thankful for: Barnjum in the spirit was a decided improvement upon Barnjum in the flesh; and as the spirit did not appear to be gifted with speech, it was unlikely to tell tales.

Luckily for me, too, Barnjum was absolutely unknown about town: his only relative was an aunt resident at Camberwell, and so there was no danger of any suspicion being excited by chance recognition in the circles to which I belonged.

It would have been folly to shut one's eyes to the fact that it might require considerable nerve to re-enter society closely attended by an obscure and fancifully-attired apparition.

Society would sneer considerably at first and make remarks, but I was full of tact and knowledge of the world, and I knew, too, that men have overcome far more formidable obstacles to social success than any against which I should be called upon to contend.

And so, instead of weakly giving way to unreasonable panic, I took the more manly course of determining to live it down, with what success I shall have presently to show.

When I went out after breakfast the next morning, Barnjum's ghost insisted upon coming too, and followed me, to my intense annoyance, all down St. James's Street; in fact, for many weeks it was almost constantly by my side, and rendered me the innocent victim of mingled curiosity and aversion.

I thought it best to affect to be unaware of the presence of anything of a ghostly nature, and when taxed with it, ascribed it to the diseased fancy of my interlocutor; but, by-and-by, as the whole town began to ring with the story, I found it impossible to pretend ignorance any longer.

So I gave out that it was an artfully-contrived piece of spectral mechanism, of which I was the inventor, and for which I contemplated taking out a patent; and this would have earned for me a high reputation in the scientific world if Messrs. Maskelyne and Cooke had not grown envious of my fame, declaring that they had long since anticipated the secret of my machine, and could manufacture one in every way superior to it, which they presently did.

Then I was obliged to confide (in the strictest secrecy) to two members of the Peerage (both persons of irreproachable breeding, with whom I was at that time exceedingly intimate) that it was indeed a *bonâ fide* apparition, and that I rather liked such things about me. I cannot explain how it happened, but in a very short time the story had gone the round of the clubs and drawing-rooms, and I found myself launched as a lion of the largest size—if it is strictly correct to speak of launching a lion.

I received invitations everywhere, on the tacit understanding that I was to bring my ghost, and the wraith of Barnjum, as some who read this may remember, was to be seen at all the best houses in town for the remainder of the season; while in the following autumn, I was asked down for the shooting by several wealthy parvenus, with a secret hope, unless I am greatly mistaken, that the ghost might conceive the idea of remaining with them permanently, thereby imparting to their brand-new palaces the necessary flavour of legend and mystery; but of course it never did.

To tell the truth, whatever novelty there was about it soon wore off—too soon, in fact, for, fickle as society is, I have no hesitation in asserting that we ought to have lasted it at least a second season, if only Barnjum's ghost had not persisted in making itself so ridiculously cheap that, in little more than a fortnight, society was as sick of it as I was myself.

And then the inconveniences which attached to my situation began to assert themselves more and more emphatically.

I began to stay at home sometimes in the evening, when I observed that the phantom had an unpleasant trick of illuminating itself at the approach of darkness with a bilious green light, which, as it was not nearly strong enough to enable me to dispense with a reading lamp, merely served to depress me.

And then it began to absent itself occasionally for days together, and though at first I was rather glad not to see so much of it, I grew uneasy at last. I was always fancying that the Psychical Society, who are credited with understanding the proper treatment of spectres in health and disease, from the tomb upwards, might have got hold of it and be teaching it to talk and compromise me. I heard afterwards that one of their most prominent members did happen to come across it, but, with a scepticism which I cannot but think was somewhat wanting in discernment, rejected it as a palpable imposition.

I had to leave the rooms where I had been so comfortable, for my landlady complained that the street was blocked up by a mob of the lowest description from seven till twelve every evening, and she really could not put up with it any longer.

On inquiry I found that this was owing to Barnjum's ghost getting out upon the roof almost every night after dark, and playing the fool among the chimney-pots, causing me, as its apparent owner, to be indicted five times for committing a common nuisance by obstructing the thoroughfare, and once for collecting an unlawful assembly: I spent all my spare cash in fines.

I believe there were portraits of us both in the *Illustrated Police News*, but the distinction implied in this was more than outweighed by the fact that Barnjum's wraith was slowly but surely undermining both my fortune and my reputation.

It followed me one day to one of the underground railway stations, and would get into a compartment with me, which led to a lawsuit that made a nine days' sensation in the legal world. I need only mention the celebrated case of "The Metropolitan District Railway v. Bunting", in which the important principle was once for all laid down that a railway company by the terms of its contract is entitled to refuse to carry ghosts, spectres, or any other supernatural baggage, and can moreover exact a heavy penalty from passengers who infringe its bye-laws in this respect.

This was, of course, a decision against me, and carried heavy costs, which my private fortune was just sufficient to meet.

But Barnjum's ghost was bent upon alienating me from society also, for at one of the best dances of the season, at a house where I had with infinite pains just succeeded in establishing a precarious footing, that miserable phantom disgraced me for ever by executing a shadowy but decidedly objectionable species of cancan between the dances!

Feeling indirectly responsible for its behaviour, I apologised profusely to my hostess, but the affair found its way into the society journals, and she never either forgave or recognised me again.

Shortly after that, the committee of my club (one of the most exclusive in London) invited me to resign, intimating that, by introducing an acquaintance of questionable antecedents and disreputable exterior into the smoking-room, I had abused the privileges of membership.

I had been afraid of this when I saw it following me into the building, arrayed in Highland costume and a tall hat; but I was quite unable to drive it away.

Up to that time I had been at the bar, where I was doing pretty well, but now no respectable firm of solicitors would employ a man who had such an unprofessional thing as a phantom about his chambers. I threw up my practice, and had no sooner changed my last sovereign than I was summoned for keeping a ghost without a licence!

Some men, no doubt, would have given up there and then in despair—but I am made of sterner stuff, and, besides, an idea had already occurred to me of turning the table upon my shadowy persecutor.

Barnjum's ghost had ruined me: why should I not endeavour to turn an honest penny out of Barnjum's ghost? It was genuine—as I well knew; it was, in some respects, original; it was eminently calculated to delight the young and instruct the old; there was even a moral or two to be got out of it, and though it had long failed to attract in town, I saw no reason why it should not make a great hit in the provinces.

I borrowed the necessary funds and had soon made all preliminary arrangements for running the wraith of Barnjum on a short tour in the provinces, deciding to open at Tenby, in South Wales.

I took every precaution, travelling by night and keeping within doors all day, lest the shade (which was deplorably destitute of the commonest professional pride) should get about and exhibit itself beforehand for nothing; and so successful was I, that when it first burst upon a Welsh audience, from the platform of the Assembly Rooms, Tenby, no ghost could have wished for a more enthusiastic reception, and—for the first and last time—I felt positively proud of it!

But the applause gradually subsided, and was succeeded by an awkward pause. It had not struck me till that moment that it would be necessary to do or say anything in particular during the exhibition, beyond showing the spectators round the phantom, and making the customary assurance that there was no deception and no concealed machinery, which I could do with a clear conscience. But a terrible conviction struck me as I stood there bowing repeatedly, that the audience had come prepared for a comic duologue, with incidental music and dances.

This was quite out of the question, even supposing that Barnjum's ghost would have helped me to entertain them, which, perhaps, I could scarcely expect. As it was, it did nothing at all, except grimace at the audience and make an idiotic fool of itself and me—an exhibition of which they soon wearied. I am perfectly certain that an ordinary magic lantern would have made a far deeper impression upon them.

Whether the wraith managed in some covert way, when my attention was diverted, to insult the national prejudices of that sensitive and hot-blooded nation, I cannot say. All I know is, that after sitting still for some time they suddenly rose as one man; chairs were hurled at me through the ghost, and the stage was completely wrecked before the audience could be induced to go away.

It was all over. I was hopelessly ruined now! My weak fancy that even a spectre would have some remnants of common decency and good-feeling hanging about it, had put the finishing touch to my misfortunes!

I paid for the smashed platform and windows with the money that had been taken at the doors, and then I travelled back to London, third class, that night, with the feeling that everything was against me.

It was Christmas, and I was sitting gloomily in my shabby Bloomsbury lodgings, watching with a miserable, apathetic interest Barnjum's wraith as, clad in a Roman toga, topboots, and a turban, it flitted about the horsehair furniture.

I was wondering if they would admit me into any workhouse while the spectre continued my attendant; I was utterly and completely wretched, and now, for the first time, I really repented my conduct in having parted with Barnjum so abruptly by the bleak cliff side, that bright June morning.

I had heard no more of him—I knew he must have reached the bottom after his fall, because I heard the splash he made—but no tidings had come of the discovery of his body; the lake kept its dark secret well.

If I could only hope that this insidious shade, now that it had hounded me down to poverty, would consider this as a sufficient expiation of my error and go away and leave me in peace! But I felt, only too keenly, that it was one of those one-idea'd apparitions, which never know when they have had enough of a good thing—it would be sure to stay and see the very last of me!

All at once there came a sharp tap at my door, and another figure strode solemnly in. This, too, wore the semblance of Barnjum, but was cast in a more substantial mould, and possessed the power of speech, as I gathered from its addressing me instantly as a cowardly villain.

I started back, and stood behind an arm-chair, facing those two forms, the shadow and the solid, with a feeling of sick despair. "Listen to me," I said, "both of you: so long as your—your original proprietor was content with a single wraith, I put up with it; I did not enjoy myself—but I endured it. But a brace of apparitions is really carrying the thing too far; it's more than any one man's fair allowance, and I won't stand it. I defy the pair of you. I will find means to escape you. I will leave the world! Other people can be ghosts as well as you—it's not a monopoly! If you don't go directly, I shall blow my brains out!"

There was no firearm of any description in the house, but I was too excited for perfect accuracy.

"Blow your brains out by all means!" said the solid figure; "I don't know what all this nonsense you're talking is about. I'm not a ghost that I'm aware of; I'm alive (no thanks to you); and, to come back to the point—scoundrel!"

"Barnjum—and alive!" I cried, almost with relief. "If that is so," I added, feeling that I had been imposed upon in a very unworthy and ungentlemanly manner, "will you have the goodness to tell me what right you have to this ridiculous apparition here?"

He did not seem to have noticed it particularly till then. "Hullo!" he said, looking at it with some curiosity, "what d'ye call that thing?"

"I call it a beastly nuisance!" I said. "Ever since—since I last saw you, it's been following me about everywhere in a—in a very annoying manner!"

Will it be believed that the unfeeling brute only chuckled at this? "I don't know anything about it," he said, "but all I can say is that it serves you jolly well right, and I hope it will go on annoying you."

"This is ungenerous," I said, determined to appeal to any better feelings he might have; "we did not part on—on the best of terms perhaps—"

"Considering that you kicked me over a precipice when I wasn't looking," he retorted brutally, "we may take that as admitted."

"But, at all events," I argued, "it is ridiculous to cherish an old grudge all this time; you must see the absurdity of it yourself."

"No, I don't," he said.

I determined to make a last effort to move him. "It is Christmas Eve, Barnjum," I said earnestly, "Christmas Eve. Think of it. At this hour, thousands of throbbing human hearts are speeding the cheap but genial Christmas card to such of their relations as they consider at all likely to respond with a turkey. The costermonger, imaginative for the nonce, is investing damaged evergreens with a purely fictitious value, and the cheery publican is sending the member of his village goose-club back to his cottage home, rich in the possession of a shot-distended bird and a bottle of poisonous port. Hear my appeal. If I was hasty with you, I have been punished. That detestable thing on the hearthrug there has dogged my path to misery and ruin; you cannot be without some responsibility for its conduct. I ask you now, as a man—nay, as an individual—to call it off. You can do it well enough if you only choose; you know you can."

But Barnjum wouldn't; he only looked at his own wraith with a grim satisfaction as it capered in an imbecile fashion upon the rug.

"Do," I implored him; "I would do it for you, Barnjum. I've had it about me for six months, and I am so sick of it."

Still he hesitated. Some waits outside were playing one of those pathetic American melodies—I forget now whether it was "Silver Threads among the Gold", or "In the Sweet By-and-By"—but, at all events, they struck some sympathetic chord in Barnjum's rough bosom, for his face began to twitch, and presently he burst unexpectedly into tears.

"You don't deserve it," he said between his sobs, "but be it so"; then, turning to the ghost, he added: Here, you, what's your name? avaunt! D'ye hear, hook it!"

It wavered for an instant, and then, to my joy, it suddenly "gave" all over, and, shrivelling up into a sort of cobweb, was drawn by the draught into the fireplace, and carried up the chimney, and I never saw it again.

Barnjum's escape was very simple; he had fallen upon one of the herring-boats in the lake, and the heap of freshly-caught fish lying on the deck had merely broken his fall instead of his neck. As soon as he had recovered from the effects, he was called away from this country upon urgent business, and found himself unable to return for months.

But to this day the appearance of the wraith is a mystery to me. If Barnjum had been the kind of man to be an "esoteric Buddhist", it might be accounted for as an "astral shape"; but esoteric Buddhism requires an exemplary character and years of abstract meditation—both of which conditions were far beyond Barnjum's attainment.

The shape may have been one of those subtle emanations which we are told some people are constantly shedding, like the coats of an onion, and which certain conditions of the atmosphere, and the extreme activity of Barnjum's mind under sudden excitement, possibly contributed to materialise in this particular instance.

Or, perhaps, it was merely a caprice of one of those vagrant poltergeists, or supernatural buffoons, which took upon itself, very officiously, the duty of avenging my behaviour to Barnjum.

Upon one point I am clear: the whole of this system of deliberate persecution being undertaken directly on Barnjum's account, he is morally and legally bound to reimburse me for the heavy expense and damage which have resulted therefrom.

Hitherto I have been unable to impress Barnjum with this principle, and so my wrongs are still without redress.

I may be asked why I do not make them the basis of an action at law; but persons of any refinement will understand my reluctance to resort to legal proceedings against one with whom I have at least lived on a footing of friendship. I would fain persuade, and shrink from appealing to force; and, besides, I have not succeeded as yet in persuading any solicitor—even a shady one—to take up my case.

The Breaking-Point

F. Anstey

Richard Alston, late first lieutenant in the West Marlshires, was walking home from Hampstead on a night in mid-December, 1918, with a lighter heart than he had known for the last three years, than he had ever hoped would be his again. Even now he could scarcely believe that anything so wonderful had happened as that he was engaged to Cynthia Royle.

His thoughts went back to his first meeting with her. She and her mother had come to see him in the private hospital for officers to which he had been taken. All they knew of him then was that he was in the same regiment as Cynthia's brother Nugent, and that he had been severely wounded in a reconnaissance they had been ordered to make together, in which Royle had been killed. Alston remembered how he had shrunk from seeing them; they would want to talk to him about the son and brother they had lost and he hated thinking of anybody or anything connected with the war.

But they had understood all that, and had spoken no more of Royle than was unavoidable. And Cynthia had been so fair and sweet that he could have wished she had never come, since it was not to be expected that hers was more than a duty-visit which would be her only one. There he had misjudged her; she had come to see him regularly during his long convalescence, and each time she had left him with a bitterer sense that it was only interest in him as her brother's friend that bought her there at all.

As a matter of fact, Royle and he had not been on any intimate terms. Royle had been in the Service before the war, and was his senior in rank as well as age. Alston had always had an uneasy impression that the other rather tolerated than liked him, while he himself admired and looked up to Royle and would have been proud to be admitted to his friendship.

However, there was no need to tell Cynthia that, and at least he could praise him to her without insincerity. He thought of the day when he had received his Military Cross at Buckingham Palace; Nugent's cross had been given to his mother the same day, and Alston was invited for the first time to the house at Hampstead. They had asked him often since that, and Cynthia had always seemed glad to see him, though there were times when he had felt it would be wiser if he went there no more.

It was not till this evening that he had had any hope that she felt more than friendship for him, and on that hope he had spoken, because he could not help himself, though he knew he was risking all by speaking so soon.

He had risked everything, and won. Fortune, not for the first time, had shown him favour when he least expected it. For, on the whole, his luck had been amazing. If he had been told, when, three years ago, he had at last decided to apply for a commission, that he would come through the war, not only without mutilation or disfigurement, but actually with distinction, it would have seemed incredible enough. Yet here he was, safe and free, released by his last Board from all further soldiering, able to return whenever he chose to the literary work in which, before the war, he had begun to make a name. He had felt too slack to take up writing again as yet. Now he would set to work for Cynthia's sake and do something worthy of her.

What a long way he had come without noticing; he was nearly at the end of Finchley Road already! It was amusing now to remember that not very long ago, as he had walked down that broad and commonplace thoroughfare, illuminated along its centre by cones of dim light, with its prim two-storeyed houses standing back behind their walled gardens, he had had a vague fear as of something hostile that was following with a kind of stealthy rustle. He had been afraid to turn his head lest he should see— what, he did not know precisely. It showed how shaken his nerves must have been, for now, though he heard the rustling again, he knew perfectly well what was causing it—simply a few fallen leaves drifting in the night-breeze.

And yet—there were none on the pavement in front of him. The trees along the kerbstone were bare now— most of their leaves must have been swept away or trodden into the mire by this time. It was strange, but that former sensation of being pursued by something subtly malevolent had begun to return. Alston quickened his pace, but without escaping from the sound. It was not until he was in Wellington Road, where the lamps were on the side-path and gave a stronger light, that he could bring himself to stop and look back.

And then he laughed aloud at his own folly, as he saw what had been scaring him. It was nothing but a piece of paper, which naturally made a scraping sound as it moved; he could still hear it after he had turned down Grove End Road, but it no longer gave him any uneasiness. He turned another corner, at right angles this time into St. John's Wood Road, and now, as the rustle continued to follow him, he became uneasy once more. It was hardly possible that— but when he looked back again he was relieved to see that it was only the same crumpled paper—or, more probably another—which had been caught by a cross-gust and carried after him. As he stood there, it was borne on till it stopped at his feet, and seized by a sudden curiosity of which he was slightly ashamed, he picked it up and unfolded it.

There was a nearly full moon sailing through a ragged gap edged with faint orange in a sky of greenish-black, but it was not bright enough to tell him more than that there was writing of some sort on the paper. He had to take it under the next street-lamp before he could read the words. After reading them he crushed the paper into a ball and flung it away as though it had stung him—as indeed it had.

The words he had read were these: "*I forbid you to see her again. You know why.*"

Only one person could have the right or the knowledge to have written thus to him. And that person was dead.

Alston walked on, shaken to his soul. He could not help looking over his shoulder once, but the ball of paper lay where he had thrown it, as if its mission were fulfilled. He was trembling still when he let himself into his flat in some Maida Vale mansions, but once back in his comfortable study and able to think calmly, he soon saw how absurdly he had exaggerated what might be, after all, a mere coincidence.

So far as he recollected, the handwriting was unknown to him. Why should the message not have been meant for another? Or, more probable still, it might have been a rough note for a line in a novel or play which some author had, as he himself had often done, hastily jotted down on the first available scrap of paper—and lost or thrown away. It was ridiculous to have been so upset by such a trifle—especially when he had everything now to make him happy. He would be a fool if he allowed himself to be seriously worried by a purely imaginary trouble.

And when he awoke the next morning, after a dreamless night, every trace of trouble or worry had disappeared, and all he thought of was how to get through the hours that must pass before he was to see Cynthia again. He got through them agreeably enough by revising the opening chapters of the novel he had left unfinished, and finding that his lost enthusiasm and confidence had come back to him.

It had been arranged over-night that he was to call for Cynthia that afternoon at a *depôt* in Kensington Square, where she was working for wounded soldiers. For the greater part of the war she had been a V.A.D. at a hospital, but had been compelled to give this up, and lighter and more occasional duties were all that she had since been allowed to undertake.

Alston was a little before his time, and was standing outside the old William and Mary houses in the gathering dusk, waiting for Cynthia to join him, when he saw something which revived the terror of the previous night. In itself it was nothing—just a crumpled piece of paper like the other, which was swerving across the road from the Square railings. Was he mistaken, or was it really making slowly toward him? He watched it spellbound, till presently it came within his reach, and at first he did not dare to touch it.

But he must, he knew, get the mastery of his nerves— or they would master him. It was a million to one that this paper was either blank or bore nothing of the least significance; he had only to satisfy himself of that to set his mind at rest for ever, and with this expectation he picked up the paper. Like the previous one, it had been written upon, and he could scarcely believe his own eyes as he read the lines: *"You have been warned once. You are unworthy of her and must give her up. – N.R."*

He was still unable to identify the handwriting, but the words, to say nothing of the initials confirmed his wildest fears. This at least could be no mere coincidence. Nugent Royle was dead beyond all doubt—but his spirit survived. It had been striving, longer than he knew perhaps, to establish communication with him. Now it had succeeded, and he would never be free again from this sinister and implacable persecution! The horror of it stunned him for the moment. Then he tore the paper into shreds, and, just as he had done so, saw Cynthia coming smiling down the steps. "Have I kept you waiting very long, Dick?" she had begun, and then, as she saw his face, her smile vanished. "Tell me," she asked, anxiously. "You're not in any pain again, dearest? I'd been hoping all that was over."

Alston said that he had had a slight return of it—nothing to speak of—he was all right again now.

"You poor old thing!" she said, affectionately. "You've been overtiring yourself. It's time you had *somebody* to take care of you—but you've got *me* now."

He was ordered to take her to tea at a shop she knew of close by, and was thankful that her animated description of her experiences during the day relieved him from all efforts of his own. But Cynthia had set herself to distract his thoughts from the pain he was evidently suffering, and was not so exacting as to expect him to entertain her just then.

There was something restful and almost homelike about the room they were in, with its subdued light, pleasant wallpaper, and pretty china. Alston, as he sat with Cynthia at one of the little tiled tables, near a glowing fire, gradually yielded to the sense of well-being and security. He felt he was somehow in sanctuary—his invisible enemy would not assail him so long as he was with Cynthia.

And as he grew more collected he began to see that he might have taken too serious a view of his position. Those messages were directed to him, and to him alone. If their inspirer had had the power to do more, surely it would have been used before now.

As for himself, he had a very obvious protection; he had merely to refrain from reading any further messages of this kind, and they could disturb him no more.

And at that his spirits rose, till, to Cynthia's delight, and rather to his own surprise, he was able to talk and laugh as gaily as though no malign influence had ever threatened his happiness.

On leaving the tea-shop he would have taken a taxi if he could have found one, but, none being available, they travelled to Hampstead by the District and Tube. A fitful wind was blowing as they mounted Holly Hill, and again there was that ominous rustle behind him, but, well as he knew what was dogging his footsteps, he steeled himself to bear it. So long as Cynthia noticed nothing unusual, he thought, he was safe enough. But his nerves were on the rack nevertheless, and he was less and less conscious of what he was saying.

They had come to more open ground facing the terrace of stately old houses, one of which was Cynthia's home, when a sudden blast whirled something above their heads and deposited it on the road before her feet—a sheet of paper which glided slowly on in advance, and stopped occasionally, in a manner that could not fail to attract her attention.

Yes, this time the message was to her, not him; if she read it, all was over! "For Heaven's sake, don't touch it, Cynthia, don't touch it!" he cried, losing all self-control as he stamped the paper into the earth under his heel.

"*Dick!*" she exclaimed, and laughed. "As if I was *dreaming* of touching it! What *are* you so afraid of? Not infection, surely?"

Even as the words passed his lips he had seen the folly of them. He could hardly have said or done anything more certain to excite her curiosity.

"There—there's always a risk," he said, determined to guard against it yet, if possible. "Don't think me fussy, darling, but I want you to promise me faithfully never to pick up any stray piece of paper that may come in your way. You will promise me that, won't you?"

"If it will relieve your mind," she said, "I promise faithfully that I'll never touch the dirtiest scrap of paper I see in the street, however much I'm tempted. There—are you satisfied *now?*"

"Yes," he said. "I know you'll keep your word." And he was satisfied, for, if she was a little astonished, it was evident that she suspected nothing. Yes, on the whole, it was better that this should have happened, or he might not have thought of exacting that promise from her.

At dinner that evening Mrs. Royle, attached as she was to Alston, saw nothing unusual in his manner. Cynthia was not quite happy about him, however, though she was careful not to let him see it. When they were alone together afterwards she led him to talk about his work, and he told her of the novel, of an idea he had for a comedy, and other projects, but it struck her that, for the time at all events, he had lost something of his belief and interest in them.

She was neither anxious nor alarmed—her hospital experience was sufficient to prevent that—but she could see that he was farther from complete recovery than she had been hoping. It was no wonder, she thought, if his poor nerves were still all ajar after the horrors he had been through. He must be induced to forget them; she would give up her work at the *depôt* and devote herself entirely to him. So, before they parted, she represented that she was longing to see a play again, and persuaded him to try to get seats for a matinée of one of them next day. He was to let her know on the telephone if he succeeded, and she would come up and meet him at the theatre.

The wind had gone down when Alston left the house, and though both on his way down the hill to the station and along St. John's Wood Road his ears were alert to catch the rustle he dreaded, he heard nothing. Might it not be that he never would hear it again—that his tormentor had shot his last bolt and could no longer molest him? He began to feel reassured.

Nor did anything happen to destroy this feeling all the next morning, most of which was occupied in making a round of the principal box-offices before he could get seats for one of the plays Cynthia had named. Then he had to ring her up and tell her the theatre and time at which they were to meet, and the rest of the time he passed at his club, which he had not visited since he had left for the Front. At the club he was glad to come across some old friends and find that they had not forgotten him; he lunched with them, but from some half-superstitious instinct did not mention his engagement to Cynthia. And then he went on to the theatre, and waited for her in the lobby.

He had not to wait long; the curtain had not risen when they were shown to their seats— and then the next blow fell and found Alston utterly unprepared.

He had broken the seal that fastened his programme and was about to pass it to Cynthia, when written across the two pages he saw the words: *"If she could know what you are she would have no more to do with you. – N.R."*

And at the same instant, before he could do anything to prevent it, she had taken the programme from his hand. But what could he have done?

When she had seen those terrible words, what would she think, what would be her next words to him? He dared not look at her as she read them; he sat rigid, setting his jaw hard, his eyes fixed on the drop-curtain a few yards in front, for what seemed an age, until she spoke.

And when she did, it was only to make a casual remark about the cast. He was saved: the words that had burnt into his brain were mercifully invisible to her, and, indeed, when he found courage to glance at the page again they were no longer there.

How near he had been to betraying himself by some mad appeal! Even now, if she saw his face, she might—but fortunately the curtain had already risen; he could recover his self-command unobserved.

And as his mind cleared he recognised that in what had just happened there was something rather encouraging than otherwise. For since these denunciations seemed to be visible to none but himself, they lost most of their terror; they would always be galling reminders of what he had hoped to forget, but never again would he let himself be outwardly affected by them. If he did he would surely end by alarming and estranging Cynthia—that was the only way in which he could possibly lose her.

He had been unconscious till then of everything on the stage, but now he was able to give his attention to the play, and even laugh without an effort, so that Cynthia congratulated herself on the success of her treatment. She was glad when he suggested, after dinner at Hampstead that evening, that she should dine alone with him the next night at a restaurant, and go on afterwards to see the Russian Ballet at the Coliseum. The next day was to be her last at the *depôt*, and she had promised to go to tea with some friends afterwards, but as it was not necessary to go home and change her frock, she could join him at the restaurant.

And again nothing happened to disquiet him till the following afternoon. He was going to his club, where he meant to have tea and see the evening papers till he was due at the restaurant, when a man in some fantastic costume suddenly offered him a handbill.

Alston accepted it mechanically, saw that it was headed in large letters: "READ THIS. IT CONCERNS YOU!" and threw it away, but not in time to avoid the words in writing that were below: *"I have not done with you yet. – N.R."*

His chief feeling, however, on this occasion was irritation; this kind of thing was becoming grotesque; in fact, there was a ludicrous side to all these incidents, if he could only bring his sense of humour to bear on them; he might do so later, but not quite yet.

By the time he was inside the club he had forgotten this latest warning, and it was not till later that he remembered it. He got to the restaurant some minutes before the appointed time, but the minutes passed, and more and more minutes after them, without bringing Cynthia.

Why had she not come? Was it because—she knew? Would he have a wire presently to tell him that she was not coming?

And, just as he was trying to prepare himself for this, Cynthia arrived, looking more radiantly lovely than ever in her furs, and apparently unaware that she had kept him waiting at all. With unspeakable relief he entered the restaurant with her, and led the way to the table he had reserved.

The restaurant was in one of the streets behind Piccadilly, a quiet little establishment which had a prestige and distinction of its own, together with the double recommendation of an excellent *cuisine* and no orchestra.

They had sat down and a French waiter had deferentially handed him the menu. As Alston took it he could not, for all his late resolutions, refrain from starting violently. For across it was scrawled another of those grim messages, more peremptory and menacing than any of the others.

"*You must tell her to-night,*" it ran, "*while you have the chance. In any case, she shall know. – N.R.*"

He felt a deadly chill strike his heart, and the card which he held to screen his face from Cynthia shook in his hand. But only for an instant; why, after all, should he let such things disturb him? Royle could threaten but he could do no more. As for telling Cynthia, it was unthinkable that he should ever be such a madman as to do that of his own accord. And no one, living or dead, could compel him. No, he had nothing really to fear. Already the writing had flickered out on the page, and his voice was quite steady as he read the items on the menu for Cynthia to choose from.

She was as frankly pleased as a child, declaring that it was so long since she had dined in a restaurant that she had almost forgotten what it was like. She approved of everything, from his choice of a table to the room, with its white walls, panels of old-rose satin, and discreetly tempered lights.

How enchanting she was, he thought, and how dear! Every now and then, amidst her lightest talk, some expression in her charming eyes, some inflection of her gay voice, revealed how deeply she loved him, how intensely proud she was of her lover.

And, by Heaven, he vowed to himself, she should have more reason to be proud of him some day! Soon they would be together like this for all their lives. For—and he must never forget this in future—there was no one but himself who could ever really destroy her love.

So for the remainder of the dinner he gave himself up to the bliss of being with Cynthia, and the terror that had haunted him seemed to have taken its final flight.

Dinner was over; the people at the adjoining tables had already taken their departure, and others were leaving. Alston had paid his bill, but he still sat on with Cynthia. There was no occasion for hurry—time for another cigarette at all events. It was pleasanter and quieter here, listening to her, than being in a noisy theatre where they couldn't talk so well. She was telling him of her plan for his spending Christmas with them—not at Hampstead, but at a delightful hotel in the pine-woods near Bournemouth. And he had welcomed the plan—not that he cared where he spent Christmas, so long as it was with her, but it was delicious to feel that she had arranged it all on his account. He was thinking when he would give her the ring he had bought that morning—in the taxi as they went to the Coliseum—or better, perhaps, on their way home.

And the next instant these pleasant thoughts of his fled, routed by a fear of something so infinitely more appalling than had happened yet, that he tried desperately to persuade himself that there was no real foundation for it.

The table he had chosen was by an archway which divided the restaurant, and he sat facing the inner room of the two. This was now deserted, and the waiters had retired, after switching off all the lights but one above a table at the extreme end, where a solitary figure was seated, apparently, though Alston could only see its back, in the act of writing. The figure was that of an officer in uniform, but there was of course nothing strange in that there had been several in the restaurant that evening. What had aroused Alston's fear was a growing conviction that the writer was one whom he had firmly believed dead, who could not in the nature of things be alive. The set of the shapely head on the square shoulders, the well-groomed auburn hair with a slight wave in it, were strangely like—but it could not be— it must be a delusion! The head was bent, and the mirror in front of it was hung too high to reflect even the forehead; perhaps when the writer looked up—but he did not, he went on writing, as one whose time was short.

Cynthia was still talking of their holiday, how they would golf and walk and dance together, and how soon he would get perfectly well, and go back to do more brilliant work than ever, and he was answering at random, watching feverishly for the moment when the writer would raise his head and end the suspense.

And at last it came—and Alston was in doubt no longer. Only the upper part of the face was visible in the glass, but the high, tanned forehead and the steel-blue eyes were these of Nugent Royle.

They met Alston's for a second or two with a stem inquiry, and then the head was bent once more.

Alston's brain was whirling in a rush of confused thoughts. This, then, was the meaning of that last message! If he did not tell Cynthia himself, Royle would; and Alston could guess how damning and merciless his indictment would be. Whether Royle were alive or had been permitted to simulate life was equally incredible—why trouble about that, when so many scarcely less credible things had happened? He was there in some form; there was no escape from him; if Alston attempted to leave this place with his story untold, Cynthia would hear it at once. Royle would find the means of reaching her—that at least was certain now.

Anything was better than that. By telling her himself, Alston thought, he would be able to present his conduct with such redeeming features as there were; he would anticipate his accuser—perhaps even Nugent might have mercy then, and the worst be spared him . . . Yes, there was no other course for him; he must speak now while there was yet time.

"Cynthia," he heard himself saying abruptly, in a voice that scarcely sounded like his own, "there's—there's something I've got to tell you."

"Not *here*, Dick," she protested, with a lightness that was only assumed, for she had been alarmed by the change in his face and manner. "It must be very nearly time for the Russian Ballet."

"When I've done," he said, "I doubt if you'll be in the humour for the Russian Ballet. It's about that night, Cynthia—the night Nugent and—I—"

"If you'd rather not go to the Coliseum, darling, we'll go home, and you can tell me on the way."

The figure of the officer in the inner room had stopped writing, and appeared to be watching him intently.

"I must tell you now," said Alston. "You—you don't know all yet."

"I know that you and dear Nugent went out together, a long way round behind the enemy's front-line," she said, seeing that it was best to humour him just then, "to find out—wasn't it whether some place was fortified or not?"

"A ruined farm, yes. An offensive had been planned, and we were sent out to discover if we could how strongly the place was held, whether the Boche had enough machine-guns to hold up our attack, and so forth. We got through their wire all right—our guns had put up a barrage and cut gaps in different places for us first, you see—and then we gradually worked round to the farm and found out all we wanted."

"And had to fight your way back, and Nugent was killed and you badly wounded, and I don't know which of the two I'm prouder of," she said. "But wouldn't it be better not to think of all that just now, Dick? I hoped you were beginning to forget it."

"I've tried," he said. "But I'm not allowed to. It isn't that—it's what happened on our way back."

Was it his fancy, or did the eyes in the mirror look less hard? They were lowered again, and from the writer's action it seemed that he was tearing up whatever he had begun.

"We were trying to make for the gap we got in by," Alston went on, "but a thick fog came on. We had luminous compasses, but it delayed us, of course, and we may have lost our direction a bit. Anyway, before we had a chance of putting up a fight, we were seized from behind and made prisoners."

"How frightfully hard to bear—just when you—!"

"I don't know. I think I was glad—to be out of it all. You see, Cynthia, it isn't as if I'd been a soldier from choice. I knew I should loathe it when I applied for a commission, though I'd no rest till I did. And when I got out to the front, it was worse than I thought even. I—I was in almost constant fear—I don't mean that I showed it—I didn't. But it never left me for long."

"Dearest," she said, and laid her hand lightly on his, "you *don't* suppose you were the only one to feel it, do you? Why, that's the truest courage—to fear death, and yet face it!"

"It wasn't being killed outright that I was afraid of," he said. "That got to be the best I expected. It was *pain*, Cynthia; the ghastly pain I'd seen so many poor fellows going through. I—I funked that."

"And you got the Military Cross!" she put. "You absurd dear! And was *this* all you've been worrying about?"

Could he not leave her to think so? The eyes he dreaded were on him still; he read contempt in their fixed stare; and then, with a gesture of sudden determination that Alston remembered as characteristic of Royle, the head was bent once more and the writing began again, slowly, relentlessly.

Alston felt that no evasion could save him—he must go on now, to the end.

"No, Cynthia," he said, "that isn't all. There—there's worse to come."

"But, Dick dear," she pleaded, "why distress yourself—and me—by telling me now?"

"Why?" he replied, almost roughly. "Because I must. Do you suppose that, if I could help it—But let me go on with it . . . After we were captured we were hustled down their trenches—how far I don't know, but it must have been a longish way. Then we were taken back to the Company Commander's dug out in their support-trench. He questioned us: about our strength, and when our offensive was coming off, and where. You can guess what we said to him. He was an evil-tempered brute—threatened to have us shot. When that failed, he told us he had other means of forcing us to speak, and—and—what they were."

"*Dick!*" she cried, "don't tell me that you and poor Nugent were—"

"Tortured?" he said. "No, no. It—it never came to that."

"Thank God!" she said, under her breath. "But what saved you from it, Dick?"

"I told you just now that what I feared most was pain. I knew I shouldn't be able to stand it. So—so I took the fellow aside, and said—I speak German fairly well, you know—that, on conditions, I was willing to—to tell him all I knew."

She looked at him with wide, indignant eyes. "And Nugent stood by and consented? No, nothing will ever make me believe that!"

"He didn't know enough German to understand. One of my conditions was that he shouldn't be told. But that sneering devil told him afterwards, all the same, and congratulated him on owing his life to me, provided my information turned out to be correct. If Nugent could have got at me I believe he would have killed me then."

"I have no doubt he would," she said, in a low voice. "But—he was killed, and you were set free."

"Not by them," he said. "The moment after, a shell from one of our own trench mortars—they were firing to cover our return; there was no idea that we could be up in that part at all—a shell burst right in the middle of us. Nugent, the Boche officer, and all the men who were there were killed on the spot. If I'd been standing a little nearer I should have been killed too. I wished to God I had been! And then it suddenly came to me that I was no traitor after all!"

"No traitor!" she repeated, and covered her eyes with her hands. "You could think that?"

"Wasn't it true?" he said. "I'd betrayed no one, now the only man I had told was dead. I'd still a chance of making good. There was no one about to stop me. I knew I'd been hit, but I didn't feel it much at first. The fog had lifted by that time, and I managed to crawl out to a shell-hole some way off. I lay there all the rest of the night, but at dawn our men started a raid on that part of the Hun line, and brought me in with the other wounded. I was just able to give in my report, and I remember no more till I found myself in a base hospital . . . Now I've told you, Cynthia. And I suppose it's made you hate me?"

As he spoke he saw that the figure in the inner room had again ceased writing.

Cynthia removed her hands from her eyes, tragic eyes which sought to avoid his. "If it had only been anything else," she said, lifelessly, "I could have—But I don't hate you. I think I'm sorry for you—a little sorry. I—I dare say you couldn't help being—like that. Only—it's made everything different. It was another man I loved—the man I thought you were!"

"And you—can't care for me any more?"

"I shall always care," she said. "But, if you mean, as I did before—before I knew this, I'm sorry, Dick, but that's impossible—quite impossible. At least, so far as I can think about it at all yet. If, some day, I should come to feel differently, I will tell you so . . . And now you must let me go home, please—alone."

Alston stood by as she got into the taxi he had ordered, knowing that he must let her go alone; and then he went back to the restaurant, impelled by the hope that Royle would be there no longer.

But there he still sat, waiting. Well, Alston thought, they were alone together—he would have it out with him, alive or dead! He entered the inner room, and as he drew near the mirror he saw the other's full face for the first time, and stopped petrified. For, if in the eyes and upper part of the face there was a rough resemblance to Nugent Royle, it was in all other respects as unlike him as possible.

"Here, you!" said the stranger, holding out a letter to a waiter who had just come in. "Just find someone to take this round at once, will you? He's to bring me the answer here, if there is one. And tell him to go to the stage-door, mind!" Then after the waiter had gone the officer turned to Alston. "Well, sir," he said, "you seem to know me all right, from the way you've been starin' for the last half-hour, but I'm afraid I can't for the life of me—"

"I'm sorry," said Alston, dully. "I—I mistook you for—for a friend of mine."

He turned abruptly and made his way out, passing the table where Cynthia had been talking happily to him so short a time—and yet such an age—ago. He might be with her now, if his overwrought nerves had not tricked him into exaggerating a chance resemblance. But that he could never have done if he had not first been almost harried out of his mind by those secret and terrifying messages. And they were real; it was inconceivable to him that he could have imagined them.

Whether they would continue, or cease, now their end had been gained, was a matter of indifference to Alston, as, stunned almost to insensibility, he went on his way. He had walked some distance before he remembered that he was still carrying the engagement-ring he had intended for Cynthia. That must be got rid of at once; the irony of it was more poignant than he could endure.

And then, in the very act of throwing it away, he checked himself as certain words of hers came back to him—words that implied, or seemed to imply, a possibility that, some day, she would relent.

It might be that she had merely tried to soften the blow, that the thought of Nugent would always be an impassable barrier between them. Still, she had left him with just a faint gleam of hope—would it not be like abandoning even that if he threw away the ring?

Yes, he decided, he would keep it—so long as any hope remained to him.

Arthur Reed Ropes
(1859-1933)

Arthur Reed Ropes published under a number of different names during his long literary career. A series of French and German texts that he edited for schools in the 1900s were credited to the dependable sounding "Arthur R. Ropes, M.A., Late Fellow of King's College, Cambridge". Undergraduate poems in *The Cambridge Review* were more modestly attributed to "A.R.R.", or sometimes simply "R." The libretto for a comic opera, *Faddimir or the Triumph of Orthodoxy*—an early, poorly reviewed attempt to crack the London stage in 1889—was advertised as the work of "Arthur Reed". But it was as "Adrian Ross" that he found his widest, most appreciative audience, and between 1891 and 1930, he contributed lyrics under that name to many of the most successful musical comedies in the West End.

There was another pen name, however, which Ropes used early in his career, and then only for a short time. Between his becoming a Fellow of King's College in 1884 and his forsaking academia for theatreland in 1890, he published a handful of poems, letters and ghost stories in magazines under the name "Henry Doone".

The name first appears in print in *The Cambridge Review*, on 27 October 1886, beneath the first of two "Notes from Normandy", a pair of amiable but unexceptional essays describing events and sites around the town of Avranches, in northern France. Ropes knew the area well; his parents had moved to Avranches in 1878, the same year that he had gone up to Cambridge, and he often stayed with them during university vacations. It was while convalescing in Normandy in the mid-1880s, having caught a chill at the Oxford and Cambridge boat-race, that he later claimed to have made his first serious attempt at writing musical comedy.

In November 1886, Henry Doone was briefly mentioned in *The Academy*, ("A Weekly Review of Literature, Science and Art"), as the author of the libretto for *The Ring*, a new opera that was being composed by Bertrand Luard-Selby based on "the story of the bridegroom who gave his ring to Venus". Luard-Selby would later collaborate with "Adrian Ross" on *Weather or No*, a short comic opera which was used as a curtain raiser for Gilbert and Sullivan's *The Mikado* in 1896.

In February 1887, the literary magazine *The Athenaeum* published a letter in which Doone introduced himself as a "young and not (as yet) celebrated writer of fiction", and lamented the difficulties faced by aspiring authors when sending out work to publishers. He complained particularly about the state in which rejected manuscripts were in the habit of being returned: "soiled and battered, and with the edges bruised and crumpled and torn". His persistence with editors seems to have paid off, however, because 1888 saw a flurry of pieces published in magazines with the name Henry Doone attached.

The title that carried most of his words was *The Reflector*, a weekly offering of essays, letters, verse and fiction, edited and produced almost single-handedly by its founder, J. K. Stephen (1859-1892; for more on Stephen, see *Ghosts of the Chit-Chat*). And it's in a bound volume of *The Reflector*'s complete run, that once belonged to Stephen's brother, Harry, and is now held in the University Library at Cambridge, that Doone's true identity is revealed.

At least half of *The Reflector*'s contents were written by Stephen himself, but he also published work by friends. F. Anstey, for instance, contributed "A Four-Legged Ishmael", a sentimental tale about a misunderstood dog. MRJ wrote an account of an archaeological excavation that he was involved in at the time in Cyprus. This latter was signed simply "Your obedient servant, M.", and most of the magazine's content appeared under initials or pseudonyms. But in Harry Stephen's copy, the identities of many of these contributors have been handwritten in, and beneath each occurrence of Henry Doone's printed name we read "A. R. Ropes."

"A Midnight Fantasy", reprinted here, first appeared in issue number five of *The Reflector*, on 29 January 1888. Poetry had been Ropes's chief literary pursuit as an undergraduate; he had won The Chancellor's Gold Medal for 1881 for his poem "Temple Bar". And in 1884, to celebrate his elevation to a Fellowship at Kings, he had privately published a selection of his own verse "written between the ages of fifteen and twenty-five".

With its eerie, animated sculptures and paintings, "A Midnight Fantasy" might owe something to Ropes's heroes Gilbert and Sullivan, whose *Ruddigore* had premiered exactly a year before the poem was published. This comic opera includes a scene in which portraits in a gallery come to life and sing: "Painted emblems of a race / All accurst in days of yore / Each from his accustomed place / Steps into the world once more." But with its Biblical heroes frolicking by moonlight in a locked church, it also anticipates MRJ's prose fantasy "A Night in King's College Chapel" which was written a few years later, around 1892. Had James read the poem? As a fellow contributor to *The*

Reflector and a long-standing friend of J. K. Stephen, it's more than likely.

Ropes was four years MRJ's senior at King's, but it was a small college (there were only fifteen undergraduates admitted, for instance, in 1882, MRJ's first, and Ropes's final undergraduate year) and their paths must have crossed often. Both were present, for instance, at the college debate on the existence of ghosts held in Arthur Benson's rooms in college on 9 March 1883, though they spoke on opposing sides (MRJ was a believer, Ropes a sceptic—see the Preface). And in 1914, Ropes—writing as "Adrian Ross"— dedicated his short horror novel *The Hole of the Pit* to "Montague Rhodes James, Provost of King's and Teller of Ghost Stories".

The Hole of the Pit is too long to reproduce here, but it is by some distance Ropes's best piece of supernatural writing. A tense, claustrophobic tale set during the English Civil War, it tells of a group of reprobate Royalists besieged in a bleak fenland fortress by an indescribable thing of slime. It's an impressively inventive work, and unlike other writers in this volume who dedicated their work to MRJ, Ropes never seeks to ape his plots or mimic his techniques. Perhaps the most Jamesian thing about the book is its title, which is taken from the Book of Isaiah: "Hearken to me, ye that follow after righteousness, ye that seek the Lord; look unto the rock whence ye are hewn, and to the hole of the pit whence ye are digged."

"Seraphita: The Story of a Spook" by Henry Doone, published here for the first time since its appearance in *The Cambridge Review* in May 1888, predates the earliest of MRJ's ghost stories by five years and has nothing notable in common with any of them (though MRJ could well have read it, having returned to Cambridge from Cyprus in April). It might originally have been intended for

The Reflector, but Stephen's magazine folded after only seventeen issues in April 1888.

Like Doone's other ghost stories ("Aaron and Son", which appeared in *The Reflector* on 19 February 1888; and "The Yellow Shadow", which is set in contemporary Cambridge but was published in the American *Lippincott's Monthly Magazine* in June 1888) "Seraphita" involves intimate and (largely) non-threatening interactions between the living and the dead. And if, like *Faddimir* (1889), Ropes's earliest, flawed attempt at light opera, they betray the inexperience of their author, they also give a good indication of his wit, imagination and potential. (All three, also, contrast sharply with Ropes's only other known supernatural work from the 1880s, "By One, By Two and By Three", a bloody tale of demonic murder, which appeared anonymously in *Temple Bar* in 1887).

"Seraphita" paints a vivid and amusing picture of contemporary séance culture: the high society attendees; the fashionable scepticism; the hackneyed tricks of the workaday medium: "divining and answering messages, writing on a locked slate, summoning spirits to rap and write, playing little instruments when tied up in the cabinet, and so forth." But it also touches intriguingly upon another, related, contemporary interest: the existence of higher spatial dimensions.

The spook Seraphita, exists, she explains, in four dimensions, and as such "can get out of a room without opening the door just as easily as you can walk out of a circle chalked on the floor, by stepping over it without touching it". The "Professor Cayley of Trinity" referred to was a real Cambridge mathematician; Arthur Cayley (1821-1895) had been the Sadlerian Professor of Mathematics since 1863, and was indeed celebrated for his pioneering work on the geometry of dimensions beyond the third. In a poem written by the physicist James Clerk Maxwell to encourage the commissioning of a new portrait of the Professor in 1874, Cayley was praised as "him whose soul, / too large for vulgar space, / In n-dimensions flourished unrestricted". And, unlike the story's protagonist, Ropes, who first entered King's in 1878 as a Mathematical Scholar, must have studied Cayley's work and likely attended his lectures.

But there was popular, as well as academic, interest in the fourth dimension at the time, too. Ropes might have come across speculation about multiple dimensions as a schoolboy: his headmaster at the City of London School, which he attended until 1878, was Edwin A. Abbott (1838-1926), author of the remarkable satirical science fiction novel *Flatland: A Romance in Many Dimensions* (1884). And in 1880, the English mathematician and author of "scientific romances", Charles H. Hinton (1852-1907) published an article entitled "What is the Fourth Dimension?" in the *Dublin University Magazine*. This was reissued as a pamphlet in 1884 aimed at a wider audience, with the alluring subtitle: "Ghosts Explained".

The idea that ghosts, or related spiritual beings, were the ever-present occupants of an imperceptible fourth dimension, enjoyed serious consideration by spiritualists and certain religious thinkers towards the end of the nineteenth century. In 1888, the same year "Seraphita" appeared, the Harley Steet physician and popular Christian author A. T. Schofield (1846-1929), published *Another World; or, The Fourth Dimension*, in which he reached the conclusion "[firstly] that a higher world than ours is not only conceivably possible, but probable; secondly, that such a world may be considered as a world of four dimensions; and thirdly, that the spiritual world agrees largely in its mysterious laws, in its language which is foolishness to us, in its miraculous appearances and interpositions, in its high and lofty claims of omniscience, omnividence, etc., and in other particulars, with what by analogy would be the laws, language, and claims of a fourth dimension . . . " In "Seraphita" Ropes examines such speculation to comic and romantic effect.

But the story and author go further than imagining ghosts as our mysterious, but ultimately harmless, dimensional neighbours. Seraphita reveals to her earthbound lover the existence of "five-dimension spooks" to whom she is herself subservient: the ineffably powerful Pentarchs. And Ropes's story is ultimately most remarkable for the effectiveness and unheralded horror of its climax, when one of these unmentionables makes itself manifest. "I seemed encircled by vague ghastly shapes," the narrator recalls, "writhing, slimy, phosphorescent, unspeakably loathsome, coiling, and lashing round me like the tentacles of a Kraken."

Giant, multi-limbed, indescribable beings emerging from non-Euclidean space, over a year before H. P. Lovecraft was even born . . . It's a vision of viscous, inchoate, ruinous horror that Ropes would return to at greater length in *The Hole of the Pit*.

Henry Doone was last heard of in December 1891 when *The Musical Times* carried an advertisement for "Books for Christmas Presents" published by J. & J. Hopkinson. These included a "New Charade Operetta. *Count Carlo*. In three acts. C. Vincent. Libretto by Henry Doone". This minor work is given a fuller title in the British Library Catalogue, *Count Carlo of Allegrettomanontroppo*, where the author's name is given as "A. Reed", the name under which Ropes had first tried his hand at writing for the stage.

There was already another Reed (Alfred, a theatre manager) and another Doone (Neville, an actor and librettist) working in London theatre in the 1890s and that may explain why Adrian Ross eventually rose above his fellow *noms de plume*.

A Midnight Fantasy

Arthur Reed Ropes

The great cathedral slumbers
Out in its grassy square;
Lulled by the bell that numbers
The holy hours of prayer.

In niche and painted casement
Rest saints and pious kings,
And in sculptured interlacement
Slumber the serpent's rings.

And down where the shades are deeper,
In the pillared crypt's retreat,
Lies many a knightly sleeper,
With a sleeping hound at his feet.

And ever in blue and amber
The sunbeam strikes the walls,
Till the glowing colours clamber,
And fade as the daylight falls.

And the candles shine at the altar,
And the notes of the evening hymn
Echo aloft, and falter,
And die in the vaulting dim;

And the church is dark and lonely,
As the last foot passes the door;
And a ghostly moonbeam only
Creeps on the marble floor,

Till midnight sounds from the steeple,
And ere the bell has ceased,
There comes a marvellous people
To a mass without a priest.

An echo goes through the arches,
Like a ghostly bugle blown;
Out of the crypt there marches
The troop of the knights of stone.

And the carven foliage clashes
As the pillars break in bloom;
A thousand sounds and flashes
Burst from the silent gloom.

Virgin and saint and devil,
Bishop, baron and dame,
The statues flock to the revel,
Each window leaves its frame.

St. Cecily sits sedately
Up in organ loft;
And a measure broad and stately
She plays so low and soft;

And then, as the tune grows faster,
And louder and wilder still,
King David, the ancient master,
Twangs on his harp with a will,

And Samson strains at the bellows,
And with a thundering din,
Gabriel and his fellows
Blow for the dance to begin.

But the cock-crow gives a warning
That the daylight comes full soon,
And the gradual grey of the morning
Creeps after the haggard moon;

And the figures flock to their places,
Hurried, afraid, aghast
But stony calm are their faces,
Now that the dance is past.

They find their places early,
And stand as still as before,
When the sacristan, old and surly,
Opens the heavy door.

And the saints all look so saintly,
Men pray for their help with tears;
And if they laugh, it is faintly,
So that nobody ever hears.

Seraphita
The Story of a Spook

Arthur Reed Ropes

If there is anything about which the present generation is bewilderingly well-informed it is the subject of spooks. Theories as to their nature are as plentiful as blackberries; instances of their appearing are as the sand of the seashore for multitudes. It will soon become an honour not to have seen a spook, and the summit of distinction not to possess a grandmother who has seen one; while he who shall chronicle a new apparition will meet with the scorn due to one who should bring coals to Newcastle, owls to Athens, patriots to Ireland, or fools anywhere. I do not propose, therefore, to tell my simple tale because of any singularity in the spook with whom I was for a time in close relations; the most interesting part of the story relates to myself. Most people have seen spirits; it is not everyone, however, who has been on the point of marrying one, or who has been deterred from doing so in the way that I was. But I am anticipating; I will go on to tell my story in regular order.

It was about two years ago that I first saw Seraphita. That was not her real name, indeed; but I am anticipating again. I was living in London, after having taken my degree at Cambridge, and devoting myself nominally to law and really to literature. College life had been so pleasant to me that I had very nearly reproduced my college quarters in the set of chambers in which I lived, and by a similar imitation of my former customs I had at command the absolute seclusion and quietude necessary to my work, and attainable in full perfection only when one is "sported". Then, whenever I wanted society, I had my club and a wide circle of friends; and so my existence had gone on in quiet prosperity for some years, when the event happened which threw me off my balance for a time, and perhaps permanently.

It was the afternoon of a bright autumn day that my lively friend and former fellow-student, Willett, bounced into my room as I sat writing. Without a word he seized my hat from a peg and jammed it on my head; then, hauling me out of my chair by the collar, he inserted my arms into the sleeves of a light overcoat, and pulled it on with a jerk that brought tears to my eyes. He next thrust my umbrella into one hand and my gloves into the other, and began to drag me to the door. Not till then was I able to collect my senses enough to ask him where he wanted me to go. As for resisting him, I had long given up that.

"Where are we going?" he echoed, "We're going a-spooking, my boy! No heel-taps, no knee-raps and Slade-pencils, but the real article, above proof, appearing and vanishing. No deception at all—look at that!" and he thrust a bill into my hands. It was a small and modest announcement that Baron Patchoulitchine would show his power over the spirits to a small and select company of friends at a "Penumbral" *séance*. The tickets of admission were very expensive, I believe; but this was a detail that I usually left to Willett in such cases. The wonders announced seemed at first glance to be of the common type, and even the special attraction, the "materialised" spook, which was to appear, seemed to be sufficiently well worn. I was returning the bill to Willett, with a strong expression of my disgust that he should drag me off to such an ordinary affair, when he called my attention to something that I had not read. The obliging spirit, "Seraphita" by name, was to manifest herself out of a vacancy in full view of the company, the medium being in another part of the room, and, after performing whatever was required of her, she would vanish not only out of sight, but out of the hold of any person selected by those present. Here certainly was something new, and either the spirit was genuine or the exhibitor had got hold of resources denied to ordinary conjurors. My mind was made up at once; I would go and either see something very unusual, or unmask a peculiarly impudent impostor.

We strode off together through the streets, Willett chattering away as usually about everything, and I racking my brains to think of some possible mechanical contrivance by which the disappearance of a material body in full view could be effected out of the hands of a person of ordinary intelligence. I could not think of anything, try as I might. No arrangement of mirrors could loosen one's hold, nor could a stuffed glove deceive the eyes in full light. My mind was still running on this idea when Willett twisted me into the door of a large restaurant, pulled me up the stairs, and ushered me into the secluded drawing-room, which "Baron" Patchoulitchine had hired for his performance.

The company was certainly both small and select, about fifty in all, seated on chairs round the room. I noticed, besides some literary ladies and gentlemen of my acquaintance, a Countess who I knew slightly, and her companion, a pretty, bright girl whom I knew much better, also a Bishop and one or two M.P.'s. In the centre of the room was the usual cabinet of the medium, a cupboard raised from the ground, of which the doors were open, disclosing a wooden chair. A small table with tambourines, slates and other necessary paraphernalia, was placed before the cabinet. All this I could see quite distinctly; for the twilight of the "penumbral" *séance* was only caused by the use of semi-transparent blinds of soft tints, admitting a tender light that suggested mystery, but did not leave anything in obscurity.

The *soi-disant* Baron was standing by the table ready to begin. He was a small wiry man, with heavy black hair and eyebrows, and piercing black eyes. He seemed intensely nervous, twitching all over from time to time and casting his eyes restlessly round the room. When the last of the company had arrived, Patchoulitchine drew himself up and began his preliminary address. He spoke excellent English, and impressed me favourably by not allowing himself to drop into the nauseous sentimentality and inane floweriness of language that Spiritualism so often seems to entail. Truth and sincerity may go with no taste or style at all, but seldom with a thoroughly bad taste and vicious style—at least, I have always thought so.

The Baron's address was brief; and he then proceeded to the business of the *séance*. The first marvels were of the usual kind, divining and answering messages, writing on a locked slate, summoning spirits to rap and write, playing little instruments when tied up in the cabinet, and so forth. I took little interest in this, for I had seen it all before, and could have done some of it myself; but he was certainly very clever, and surpassed most of the mediums and conjurors that I had ever seen. The company were evidently well acquainted with this part of the *séance*, and seemed rather inclined to be bored; but several times they were surprised into applause.

There was a brief interval after the first part of the exhibition was over, and we got up and walked round, chatting with our friends and stretching our legs in preparation for the next period of sitting. Then we all took our places again, and Patchoulitchine reappeared. I was struck by the change in his manner. Hitherto, he had been tremulously nervous, indeed, but cheerful and confident, as if what he were doing were mere child's play, with no risk of failure. Now, however, his nerves seemed to have been mastered by a powerful effort of will; he was unnaturally calm and solemn, and even had an apprehensive air about him, which made me prepared for something unusual. He was not acting now; evidently he himself believed in what he was about to show us.

He began, as before, by briefly describing the nature of Seraphita, his apparition. He explained the arrangement of that hierarchy of unseen beings to which she belonged, and of which she was (according to him) one of the most distinguished members; he dwelt on his own labours and risks in acquiring the moral eminence which enabled him to control such exalted personages—and finally he invited the company, as a precaution against deceit, to choose where the spirit was to be materialised, and to hold the medium and secure him in any way they thought proper. After some discussion it was decided that Seraphita should appear in the centre of the room, the cabinet having been wheeled to one side; and two of the gentlemen present were to hold the hands of the medium in the corner of the room as soon as he had made the necessary passes. Willett and I were chosen for this duty. We placed ourselves on either side of Patchoulitchine, and I watched him closely as he sat in his corner. As I looked at him, I saw the nervous trembling come over him violently—his black hair bristled, and his eyes gazed wildly out into vacancy. Then he began to utter some incantation or charm, like nothing I had ever heard. Never did such uncouth sounds issue from human lips before; I could not imagine how the fellow's throat held out. It was no known language, certainly, that he spoke. Then he made strange gestures, as of one beckoning, entreating, commanding—and lastly, after one cry of "Seraphita!" he dropped his hands at his side and we took hold of him.

Grasping the Baron firmly, I looked out into the room. The Countess was just opposite me, and she wore a very incredulous expression. A minute passed, and another. I could feel that the medium was growing uneasy. Suppose he should have failed? His hands were nerveless and damp in mine, and he shivered; and partly for pity of him, partly from my own curiosity, I set my own mind hard to will that the spirit should appear. Whether I had any share in the result, I do not know; but as I looked at the Countess, a sort of mist or silvery vapour seemed to be passing in front of her. It grew and thickened as I gazed, hiding objects beyond it, and seemed to outline itself and fall in folds. Then the mist was touched with a cloudy gold and faint rose; and then, in a moment, the cloud took shape and was the figure of a woman, and Seraphita was before us. I seem to see her now, for she was always the same. She had the pure profile of an antique statue, in which forehead and nose form one line, hardly deviating from straightness. A mass of golden hair was loosely coiled behind her head. She was dressed in a loose robe of lustrous white with long hanging sleeves, falling in fine folds around her; her feet, as I noticed, were bare, and exceedingly delicate of form, as if unused to touch the ground. There was a faint flush on her cheeks, and her large grey eyes looked with something of wonder and something of appeal around our circle. She turned her head till her eyes met the medium's and mine, and then she was still; but I fancied that she was looking rather at me than at Patchoulitchine, though perhaps this was only my vanity.

Willett and I now released our captive and left him to continue his performance. He began by asking Seraphita, in a very humble tone, whether she was willing to help him, and when she bowed her head in answer, he told her to do certain trivial things, such as carrying a book across the room, striking a tambourine, &c., chiefly, I fancy, to impress the company with a sense of her substantiality, and convince them that she was no mere Pepper's ghost. These commonplace actions also served to accustom the spectators to the novel intruder; for at first they had been sitting with eyes and mouths wide open, some frightened, and all too much astonished to speak. When the Baron saw that his audience was once more capable of appreciating a higher flight, he asked Seraphita to give answers to messages handed up by anyone who chose. Willett, ever ready to break the ice, called for the winner of the next University boat race. The spirit-woman extended her arm and beckoned, and suddenly, we could not see how, a sealed envelope dropped at our feet. Willett opened it, and out fell a pretty little bow of dark blue ribbon. There was a general laugh at his crest-fallen look, for he was well known as overzealous for the athletic honour of his University. Other questions followed, some verbal, some written on folded slips of paper, to which sealed and directed answers were returned. Only not a word would our fair spook utter, and when I asked Patchoulitchine if we could have a song from her, he shook his head with an apprehensive air. "I cannot ask it," he said in a low and serious tone, "it is beyond my power."

We had now almost all preferred our requests, and received answers of some sort. I felt it at first rather disappointing that the spirit was so unsupernatural, so unappalling; but after all this was only to be expected from a materialised spook. She could not abdicate her special character and yet retain it. It was now the turn of the Countess to ask her for some service or answer, and after some hesitation, she demanded that the spirit should conform to the old forfeit rule, to "kneel before the prettiest, bow to the wittiest, and kiss the one that you love best." She was soon to repent of her boldness. She had expected, no doubt, to secure (as Willett would have put it) at least two of the events; but a little reflection would have shown her that it was dangerous to require flattery from a spook—especially from one of her own sex. Seraphita gave a quick glance round the expectant ring, and then, moving noiselessly forward, she knelt for a moment in front of the lady companion, who cast a frightened, deprecating look at the Countess. Then she rose, glided round the circle, paused and inclined herself before the Bishop—and as she did so, the Countess grew yellow. Once more the white figure stood erect, hesitating, while the pure colour deepened in her cheeks; then with noiseless feet she passed on and came towards the medium, who still sat between my friend and myself. Doubtless she must acknowledge the superior attractions of her master and exhibitor. But no—she paused in front of me and bent forward, and as I sat powerless, trembling all over with emotion I could not describe, there came a touch of soft warm lips on my forehead.

I felt myself flush hotly, and I did not dare to look round. Seraphita also seemed embarrassed, if a spirit can be embarrassed; and nobody was sorry when the Baron arose and announced that the spook had done all that could be demanded, and would now vanish. But the manner of her vanishing was to be the greatest feat of all. Two persons chosen by the company were to hold or fasten the spirit in any way they chose; two others would secure the medium in the cabinet, and Seraphita would then vanish out of the ken and the very grasp of her captors. The votes for the spook's guardians fell on the Countess (since we wished to make some amends for her late disappointment) and the Bishop, as the most paternal and proper; and Willett and I, as before, had the custody of the medium. While we arranged his chair in the cabinet, and secured him to it, the other custodians settled, after a brief debate, that they would bind the materialised spirit with a cord of which each would hold an end, and thus prevent all trickery. Seraphita assented by a contemptuous nod; and the Bishop thereupon held her slender wrists, while the Countess, with much gusto, proceeded to tie them together. Being in a thoroughly bad temper, she drew the cord as tight as she could; and when the Bishop remonstrated that she was hurting her prisoner, she replied crossly that she did not believe "it" could feel anything, and that in any case she did not mean to let "it" get away by any acrobat's tricks. The Bishop appealed to Seraphita. I could see her lips part as if to protest; but suddenly she closed them again, and bent her head with a wicked smile, from which I drew the conclusion that she was meditating a little surprise for the Countess. After tugging at the last knot to her satisfaction, the lady jailer fastened the loose ends of the cords together, and took hold with both hands of the loops, as did also the Bishop; and we, having secured Patchoulitchine to his chair, closed the doors of the cabinet on him and retired to our seats. Then he began the usual ringing of bells, banging of drums, and shewing of hands at the window of the cabinet. I kept my eyes still on Seraphita, who was standing motionless between her captors. Suddenly the doors of the cabinet flew open, and a large tambourine was hurled clashing into our midst. Everyone started and looked at it; I started too, but did not take my eyes off the spook. I saw a shiver run up her dress and her whole form. Her robe became misty and undefined, her feet disappeared from the carpet; her flushed cheeks and golden hair were like a vague sunset cloudlet for a moment, and then were gone. Simultaneously there came the sound of two ringing slaps, and the Countess screamed and put her hands to her face—or would have done so, had it been possible. But though the ends of the cord were still knotted, and the loop remained in the Bishop's hands, by some occult power or trick, Seraphita, in freeing herself, had also bound her captor, and the Countess's wrists were, if anything, more tightly fettered than her prisoner's had been. She stood, the picture of helpless rage, misery and confusion, while we flocked round to examine this curious instance of spookical revenge; and when at length the Bishop tried to untie his colleague, so hard were the knots that he had finally to borrow a knife and cut her loose. Once released, she hastily drew her gloves over the blue marks on her wrists, put down her veil to hide her burning cheeks, and simply plunged out of the room, followed by her companion. The girl was evidently frightened at the coming storm with her employer, but she could not help saying in an undertone as she passed me, "For the Spook *was* a Boojum, you see." The Countess heard it, as people always do hear what they ought not to, and it proved the last straw. I heard afterwards that she dismissed her companion as soon as they reached home. Willett meanwhile had untied Patchoulitchine, who seemed much exhausted; and after warmly congratulating him, we took our leave.

A few days after, I proposed to Willett that we should go and see Patchoulitchine and his spook again; but I heard from him that the Baron had given up the really original part of his entertainment, and was now exhibiting merely the same tricks as any common Mr. Sludge. His mysterious power over his spirit, whatever it might be, seemed to have gone from him; and I was left with a feeling of disappointment and loss, which frightened me by its intensity. Whenever I let my thoughts rove, I found myself recalling the brief hour for which I had seen Seraphita; her classic profile came between me and my manuscript, till I took to drawing Greek heads on the margin of my paper, as Théophile Gautier used to draw steeples. Gradually, however, the impressions wore off, and my old way of life took me again, and ruled my thoughts as well as my actions. I made up my mind that Seraphita was nothing to me, and I should never see her again. Here I was entirely wrong—but I will not anticipate.

One winter's day, when I came into my rooms in the evening, I was surprised to find my lamp burning, and not only burning, but smoking. I was greatly annoyed, for I had expressly charged the housekeeper, Mrs. Perrin (who alone, besides myself, had a key to my apartments), never to light the lamp before I came back, when I was out, as I might at any time be kept late. So, after turning down the flame, I rang and asked her rather crossly why she had lit my lamp. To my great surprise she denied having done so; and even when I showed her that the lamp had been smoking for some time, she persisted in her denial. I did not know what to think, for I have always found her scrupulously truthful; so I merely dismissed her with a strong recommendation not to let this occur again.

A few days after, as I was coming in, the housekeeper met me on the stairs, and at once announced in a low voice, "If you please, Sir, a lady has called to see you and she is waiting in your room." I was surprised, for I had no female relatives, so far as I knew, within reach, and it was a singular thing for anyone but a relation to call alone. "Who is she, and what is she like?" I asked.

"A tall young lady, very fine looking, in a white dress, and with no bonnet on, which she never gave her name at all," she answered; "and I told her you was out, she said she would wait in your room, and I showed her in."

"You showed her in!" I repeated, severely; "an unknown woman, without a bonnet—do you want everything stolen from the rooms?"

The old lady became almost tearful. "I knew you'd be angry, Sir," she said or snuffled; "but when I told her so, she laughed and gave me a look, and I don't know why, Sir, and that's the truth, but I let her in like a lamb and then I shut the door after her, and because I thought she might be after something wrong, Sir, I've sat in the room opposite with the door open, and freezing cold too, watching your door, and she's in there still, and I'm sure I beg your pardon, Sir."

As she spoke, I suddenly heard from my room, indistinct through the outer door, the notes of a song, and I stood back and listened. Evidently the mysterious lady *was* in there still. The voice was a contralto, pure, rich, and full, with the same thrill in it as stringed instruments have for me—something electric, that always moves me to the inmost of my nature. I could catch no words through the door. Suddenly the notes grew fainter, and were silent. Now was the time to act; I quickly inserted and turned my latch-key, and opening the outer door, cautiously flung the inner door back and burst into my room. There was no one there at all!

The candles were alight, as the housekeeper had put them for the visitor. My piano was open—I had left it shut. The armchair was drawn up to the fire, and its cushions disarranged; one was lying on the floor, as if for a footstool. But where was the owner of the voice I had heard? I took up a candle and looked in the cupboards and under the sofa and the tables; nothing at all. Then

I passed into my bedroom and my small study and examined them carefully: again nothing, and no place where even a rat could hide. "There is nobody here, Mrs. Perrin," I said; "perhaps the lady tried the window or chimney while we were at the door." The windows were all shut and fastened inside; two rooms had bright fires in them, and in the bedroom the fireplace was blocked by an ornamental board which had obviously not been disturbed. It was rather uncanny, and I hardly liked to dismiss Mrs. Perrin; but she was so evidently scared and anxious to go, that I gave her leave. Then I sat down to my writing again, but could not fix my thoughts to the story I was working at, and to have something to do I began sorting the loose papers on my desk. Suddenly I came upon a small envelope of a very pretty pink colour, sealed in golden wax with a curious geometrical hieroglyph. I turned the missive over and over before I opened it; it was not directed, and when I cut it at length, I drew out a small sheet of paper, inscribed in gold with the most extraordinary and erratic marks I ever saw. Runic, Chinese, Arabic, were nothing to it; it meandered about the paper in the wildest manner, up, down, left, right, as if traced by a drunken stylograph. I stared and stared, but could not make out one letter of any alphabet I knew. Was I losing my senses? I called up Mrs. Perrin again, and questioned her closely whether she had seen the note before. She had not seen it, and could make no more of it than I. Finally, in despair, I rushed out again, got in at the fag-end of a concert of some kind somewhere, found a friend, went to supper with him, walked half round London to get home, and arrived so dead-beat that I simply flung myself on my bed and slept like a log. I was really afraid to go to my rooms till I had tired myself out of the possibility of being frightened.

I was not troubled again for some time by any intruder; but a fresh annoyance developed itself—a sort of mental trouble, I thought, arising from the late mysterious event. When I was sitting alone in my study, I used to be overpowered by the sense of a presence in the room, as if some one were close to me, breathing on my cheek, looking over my shoulder, pressing close to me, and yet impalpable. Sometimes the sensation was so strong that it drove me from my work; sometimes I conquered it and succeeded in abstracting myself from all thought but that of my subject. But so constant did this persecution become, that one day in February, when I had settled down for a long evening's work, and was once more pestered by this haunting irrational feeling, I laid down my pen, resolved to put an end to my trouble. I said resolutely, though with a consciousness of the ridiculous nature of my words, "If there is any being here except myself, I call upon that being to appear!" and I accompanied the appeal with a strong and sustained effort of my will. There was no sound in the room; and as I sat, I thought that I had only made a fool of myself, to no purpose, but happily, with no hearers. As this reflection passed through my mind, however, I happened to look at my fireplace, and on the broad low bar of the polished brass fender, close to my armchair, I saw something pink, which I could not make out, like a flake of mist clinging there, and lit by the ruddy firelight. I bent forward and glared over my table at the object. Under my glance it seemed to take shape, and I recognised, with a mingled feeling of curiosity and terror, the outline first of one and then of another small and delicate foot, resting lightly on the fender, and apparently warming their dainty toes at the blaze. When I recovered my senses sufficiently to cast my eyes higher and discover to what these feet were attached, I saw that my armchair was occupied by a sort of white mist, rapidly becoming defined and opaque. A hand dawned out of the mist by the side of the chair, and finally, the top of the cloud was kindled to gold; and before I could utter a sound in my astonishment, a face, crowned by a mass of golden hair, shone on me like a sunrise. There was no mistaking that classic profile, those great grey wondering eyes—it was Seraphita! She sat in the armchair, solid and palpable enough, in an attitude whose careless grace a sculptor would have given his life to catch, looking with a slight smile at my bewilderment; then, when I had recovered a little from my amazement, she opened her lips, and for the first time I heard her speak, and recognised the same thrilling voice I had caught through the door. "You did not expect to see an acquaintance, Frank," she said, using my Christian name in the most natural way possible; "I fear I frightened you!"

"Oh, not at all—I am delighted to see you, Sera—that is, Miss—I don't quite know what you prefer to be called."

She sighed daintily, "I suppose you must call me Seraphita," she said; "it isn't my real name, but only what that wretched Patchoulitchine called me. I have a very nice name, too, one of the prettiest I ever heard; but I don't know quite how, when it is projected the section consists only of consonants and a few Arabic gutturals, and Patchoulitchine used to say it sounded like a man trying to talk Welsh on a Channel steamer. It is such a pity! For it is a very pretty name—and I don't like Seraphita, or any of your names. They are not distinctive enough. Seraphita might have been the section of a whole family of names, and all of them ugly"—and she sighed again.

I felt that my brain was reeling with the attempt to understand her speech, which seemed half sense, half nonsense, like something heard in a dream. "Seraphita!" I exclaimed; "do try to tell me what it all means! What do you mean by *projecting* your name? Am I asleep, or what is it all about? How do you contrive to appear and vanish in this way?"

She smiled, as if greatly amused at my bewilderment. "Why, don't you know, Frank? *I'm in four dimensions!* And when I appear, of course, I have only to project myself into three, and here I am—that is, I used to be able to do so once, but now—oh dear!" and she sighed again deeply.

I was touched by her grief, though I did not know in the least what she was sighing for. I rose from my chair, went round to her seat, and kneeling beside her took one of her hands in mine and kissed it. She did not attempt to withdraw her hand, and seemed pleased by my sympathy. "Dear Seraphita," I murmured, "tell me all about it, please. I should be glad to help you. I am a lawyer, too, and if anyone had been annoying you, or if there is any complication—"

She laughed long and musically—and then, with sudden contrition, threw her disengaged arm round my neck, and bent to kiss me. "Forgive me, Frank," she said; "but you men are so funny! I don't think you need trouble to prosecute Patchoulitchine, for he will be punished soon enough; and I don't think, either, you could plead against one of the Pentarchs"—she broke off suddenly and shuddered. "Oh, no!" she whispered, in a hurried, frightened manner; "I did not mean to mention them. Don't speak of them, please, Frank."

"Never mind, dear," I answered, soothingly; "no one shall touch you while I am here."

"Oh, you don't know!" she answered, still in a whisper, "you could not save me, I could not help you, if *They* were to come. I can't tell you about it now, but when you know—you did ask me to tell you all about myself, did you not, Frank?"

Seraphita's very affectionate demeanour might have seemed rather forward in an ordinary mortal, but in her it was somehow no more than I expected. After all, she must know that though I had only seen her once before, I was deeply in love with her; and knowing this she felt she was bound to acknowledge that she reciprocated the feeling. I passed a protecting arm around her, and she told her story, which I give without interruption—there were interruptions.

"Yes, Frank, I am in four dimensions, when I am in my usual health. What a pity you did not take up mathematics at Cambridge; you would have understood me much better if you had only studied under Professor Cayley at Quaternity College—ah, Trinity, you call it—of course! *We* always reckon by fours. But you have heard of four-dimensional space, dear, have you not? A space in which one can get out of a room without opening the door just as easily as you can walk out of a circle chalked on the floor, by stepping over it without touching it? Frank, when I was well, I could do to your room just what you could do now with the circle. And so I could appear and disappear as I chose—we can all do it—by simply walking into your space, just as you could appear in a world that is all on the surface. But now—oh, dear! It is humiliating to say it—*I have lost control of my dimension*. Among our better classes, Frank, it is thought rather foolish, but not wrong to materialise ourselves, as the Baron called it; and the family spectres, who do it for good ends, are often highly respected. Appearing for a medium even is not blamed very much, and some of the best-connected spooks have done it lately, just as your aristocracy, I heard some one say, are going on the stage. But some spirits go much further; they are always materialising themselves for a low class of mediums, and even when invisible they rap and ring bells and lend themselves to all sorts of disreputable things. We call them habitual materialists, and we have asylums for them. The mediums call them by silly little names—Jim and Jack and Kitty and Fay, and they really like it all, poor wretches. But I didn't as you saw, Frank. I used to go at first just to help Patchoulitchine, for he was poor, and I was sorry for him; and when I tired of it, he had got some sort of horrible influence over me, and I could not help myself without calling *Them* in—the five dimension spooks—the Pentarchs" (this in a low frightened whisper). "But at last it grew too hard to bear, and I asked for help and was freed from the Baron. As for him, *They* have other grudges against him. Would you like to see how he will be punished?" She beckoned, and a white cloudlet appeared in the room, which took shape and dropped as a newspaper. I picked it up and found that it was a *Daily Telegraph* (Seraphita preferred to materialise the *D. T.*), apparently moist from the press, and dated three months ahead. One of the leading articles was framed in red ink, and the journal was folded so as to show that only. It gave the usual polysyllabic inflation of an account of the mysterious death of a medium, calling himself a Baron. He had been tied up in his cabinet as usual, and when the doors were opened, he was found strangled, having apparently wound a turn of the cord with which he was bound, round his neck, and tightened it by his struggles. The most singular fact in the case was, the journalist stated, that though a surgeon pronounced life to have been extinct for some time before the death was discovered, *the performance had been going on as usual up to the moment when the doors were opened.*

"I was rid of him then, Frank, but I had not been free long before I found out a terrible thing. I could no longer control my fourth dimension. At any moment I might become as I am now, and at any moment return to my usual state. It was frightful to feel materialisation coming on, and not to have any place to go to! Happily, I thought of taking refuge with you, Frank. Perhaps you may think I should have gone to a lady, but I knew no one except that Countess and the girl who was with her. I could not have anything to do with that creature again! And as for the girl—Frank, do you know she has been dismissed, and does not know what to do; and, dear, I think she is rather fond of you. You ought to marry her some day."

I started back in mingled grief and indignation. "Seraphita!" I exclaimed, "you know I only care for you, and never can care for anyone else. How can you be so cruel?"

She smiled sadly, and stroked my hair with a caressing hand. "That is all very well, Frank," she said; "and you are good to say so; but I shall be going away quite soon, and you will not see me again, and then you will need someone else—and when you do, dear, here is her address." She extended her hand, signed in the air, and a little card came fluttering down and settled in the frame of the looking-glass over my mantelpiece.

"And now," said Seraphita, lightly checking my protestations, "I will go on with my story. The first time I came here, I got in before I was materialised, and stayed here some hours. I lit your lamp to read by, and I fear I left it too high—I did not expect to vanish so soon. Then some days after, I was caught by the first symptoms some way from your house, and I could not get in before I was materialised, and I had to wait outside till the housekeeper let me in. Oh, how cold my feet were on the stairs, Frank! I thought I should cry with pain. Your fire was so delightfully warm when I did get in! But I am afraid I frightened the housekeeper, poor old soul—and you too, Frank, for the matter of that. I could not help it, dear; I was singing, and when you burst in, the shock or something brought back my dimension in a moment, and I disappeared— it was so silly, just when I wanted to stay and explain. I left a note for you, but perhaps you could not read it." I assured her that I had done my best, but failed. "I don't wonder," she said, laughing merrily; "poor Frank, trying to read a section of *our* writing. I quite forgot in the hurry to use your language. After that, seeing what alarm and trouble I caused you, I didn't wish to show myself, and I used to slip in here before the seizures came, and when I was materialised, I hid in your other room: but when you called for me to appear, I was in here, and thought I would stay; and somehow your will seemed to bring on the change, and I found myself sitting in your chair. That is all my story, and I hope you don't think very badly of me, Frank."

I tried to prove to her, not by words alone, how much I admired and respected her; but there was something more that I wanted to find out. "Seraphita," I asked, "what did you mean just now by saying that you would leave me soon and perhaps not see me again? Why should we have to part?"

"I will try to tell you," she answered; "but not just now, for there is not time. I feel the change—" Her voice faltered and failed. I looked up from the hand I was fondling, only to see a mist drifting from the chair; I looked down again, and I was left in doubt whether I should have another visit. Though I sometimes seemed to feel a presence in my room, I was some days without any manifestations. I stayed in constantly, but in vain: and I began to fear that Seraphita was lost to me. But one evening, as I was sitting writing, I had occasion to take a volume from my revolving book-case, and for that purpose I swung it round. I was then surprised to see the book-case, instead of slackening its pace and stopping, begin to revolve swiftly and still more swiftly, till half my books were flung out on the floor. I instinctively stretched out my hand to stop my erratic piece of furniture; but before I reached it, my fingers met and closed over something warm and soft. I looked at it, and it was a foot; and the next moment, out of a hovering white mist dawned Seraphita, seated on top of the bookcase with her feet dangling over the side, and smiling at me. "Hold my foot for another moment, Frank," she said; "I am going to get down," and she rested a hand on my shoulder, and let me lift her down to the floor. Then, after rewarding me with a kiss, she took her old place by the fire.

"I thought I should never get back to see you and to be seen by you, my dear," she said. "You see, I can't materialise myself when I wish, now. I had not time to tell you then that I had to go in for a course of treatment that is meant to destroy my power of projection altogether. Involuntary materialisation is looked on as an ailment among us; and indeed I wanted to be rid of the tendency myself, for I might have got into all sorts of awkward predicaments if the fit took me suddenly. If I had appeared in the streets, for instance, I should have been shut up as an escaped lunatic; and I could never be sure of reaching you in time, Frank. Still, I shall be very sorry when I can't come any more. I am very fond of you, dear; but *They* would never allow me to stay."

"Seraphita," I timidly suggested, "could you not reverse the treatment and recover your old power of appearing when you liked? Why should not your Pentagons or Pentacles, or whatever you call them allow that? It seems much the fairest course."

She shook her golden head. "No, no!" she answered. "I don't know whether *They* could do it—perhaps they could; but they never would, never. What we are to you, *They* are to us, but they rule us as we never try to rule you. Even if I were in four dimensions now, a Pentarch might be close to me, and I should never know it unless he chose—and they are terribly strict! I dare not offend them."

"Well, then," I persisted, "would you think it very terrible to be materialised for good and all, Seraphita, and be my wife? I would try to make you happy, far happier than you would be in four dimensions, I should think. I am not a jealous, strict, five-dimension spook to rule you with a rod of iron."

"Hush," she whispered, laying a finger on my lips; "they may be hearing you! Don't offend them, if you value your life! Remember how poor Patchoulitchine was punished ten weeks hence—no, how he will be punished ten weeks ago—oh, dear! You know what I mean. I would not mind doing it for you, dear, if I could; though you could not understand—of course not—what a *mésalliance* the other spooks would think it. But I don't mind that, Frank. Only I should have to disobey the Pentarchs, break all their laws, defy their power and surprise their secrets; and if I failed, it would be a long misery for me, and a great danger for you. Don't ask me, Frank; for I should try to do it, if you asked me. Give me up and Forget me, and go and take care of that poor girl, who has no friends now—" and she began to sob.

I ought to have yielded to Seraphita's beautiful unselfishness, I know; but I could not help myself. Her beauty was enhanced tenfold by her grief; her eyes shone deeper for her tears, and the pathetic tremor of her lips made me long to kiss away her trouble. My passion carried me away. I knelt beside her, kissing her hands and pouring out an incoherent flood of words, adjuring her with tears not to leave me, but to stay forever by me as my goddess, my bride—to trust to my love and protection, and cast off and defy the tyranny of five dimensions. I even ridiculed the idea that the dreaded Pentarchs could do much. Four-dimension spooks hardly had any effect, I said, on our three-dimension world; and only superstitious and silly people ever obeyed them in anything. Let the lower dimensions rise in revolt against their tyrants, proclaiming the liberty of individuals and the inalienable right of every free-born spook to choose how many dimensions he would have. Even if anyone wanted to make a man of himself, let him be free to do so! (A spook would use this phrase where we would say "make a beast of himself.")

My energy and passion overcame Seraphita's fear, or her duty. She was carried away by my specious eloquence—fool, miserable fool that I was! I had conquered, she whispered to me, and she would be mine and descend to my world, if she could do it—and she would find out a way. If need were, she would conspire with disaffected spooks, and head a desperate band to free the wretched beings now confined to keep them from willing slavery to mediums. Like a true woman, she was ready to trample upon all laws of all dimensions, and upset the whole social order and established hierarchy of spookdom, if only she could please the man she loved; and I in my selfish madness and conceit was ready to let her do it. I cannot excuse myself, except by saying again that I could not help myself; and how often do we find the man who will deliberately abstain from asking for the woman he loves, because he fears his nature may drag hers down?

The fatal resolution was taken. I will not go into the wild plans we formed for overthrowing all the obstacles to what we deemed our happiness. There is something painful and humiliating in the very thought of them. The time flew by, and Seraphita at last felt the premonitory symptoms of her return to four dimensions. With a woman's caprice, she insisted on vanishing from the top of the book-case. I lifted her up, and we said farewell; and then, as before, her golden hair grew vaporous, her white robe flowed away in the mist, and last of all the little feet seemed to melt away beneath my kisses. I stood looking at the empty space she had occupied, when there was a shriek, and Seraphita seemed to rush back into sight and feeling, as if driven out of the spirit world by some mighty repulsion.

"Oh, Frank!" she gasped, as she clung to me tightly, "save me! There was a Pentarch near us all the while. He has come into four dimensions after me! Oh! Oh! He is coming into *three*!"

It was too true. One of the jealous tyrants whose downfall we had fondly plotted, had been listening to our treasonable talk; and now, for my sins, I saw what no mortal before me ever knowingly saw—the section of a five-dimensional spook. It was terrible beyond all powers of description. Whether Pentarchs in their native state are majestic as befits their power, I do not know; but I do know that their projection is pure monstrosity. I seemed encircled by vague ghastly shapes, writhing, slimy phosphorescent, unspeakably loathsome, coiling, and lashing round me like the tentacles of a Kraken. Then the lamp was overturned, the fire scattered and all was hideous darkness. I was fighting wildly, despairingly, against something that I could not seize, could not wound. I felt Seraphita's arms round my neck still; but suddenly they relaxed—or did their clasp dissolve into vacancy? Yet still I struck at random, till my senses failed me, and I fell.

When I woke from a long swoon, in the chill grey light of early morning, my room was a desolation as if a herd of wild buffaloes or the guests of a bump supper had been let loose there. Every single piece of furniture had been broken in pieces and hurled into a heap of tangled rubbish.

My mirror was shattered, frame and glass alike; but poised on the top of the mound of ruin, untorn, was the card bearing the name and address of the girl that I knew. Was it a chance, or Seraphita's last message to me? I do not know, for I never saw my spook again.

"B."
(1862-1925)

"I rode off rather vexed by Toft and Kingston—but made up a ghost story, 'When the Door is Shut', for the magazine, and enjoyed the sunny day, the fresh wind, the spring scents, the orchard leaf. Then I came home and wrote the story out, quite a good one . . . Monty James to dinner, very lively and cheerful . . . we had a gossipy evening, read my story, played cards . . . "

– Diary of A. C. Benson (14 May 1912)

Between 1911 and 1919 eight short ghost stories appeared in *Magdalene College Magazine* attributed simply to "B." They are all set in Magdalene, all attest to an in-depth knowledge of the topography and history of the college, and all tell of fictional undergraduates or Fellows and their encounters with—usually malevolent—supernatural beings. The previously unpublished extract from Arthur Christopher Benson's diary quoted above confirms the long-held suspicion that he was their author.

Magdalene College Magazine was edited by undergraduates, but from the beginning Benson (first a Fellow, and then, from 1915, Master of the College) was a regular contributor. The first item in the first issue was a sonnet by him, "To Samuel Pepys". And until his death in 1925, poetry, essays and stories appeared regularly under different variations of his name: A. C. Benson, ACB, and on one occasion α. β., his initials in Greek.

The following account by Benson of a visit to Cambridge by ex-US President Theodore Roosevelt appeared in the magazine in June 1910:

> [Roosevelt] did not talk very much . . . but ate a good meal drinking nothing but water. After dinner, when the ladies went out, he turned to the Provost of Kings, and said "You come here, Mr. James, and sit beside me—you are not going to escape." I must add that when he was asked whom he wished to meet at Cambridge, he had said that he particularly wanted to meet Mr. James, because he had written the best ghost stories he had ever read . . . Mr. Roosevelt was in high good humour. He plunged at once into a long ghost story, which he told with much emphasis and in great details, in a hoarse voice and with many Americanisms. The Provost of King's told me afterwards that the story was well told, but I did not myself think that it was skilfully done . . .

Benson could claim some authority as a judge of such things. He'd published two volumes of his own ghost stories by this point—*The Hill of Trouble and Other Stories* (1903) and *The Isles of Sunset* (1904). And he had read aloud a supernatural tale, "The House at Treheale", at the same Christmas gathering at King's College in 1903 at which MRJ had read "Oh, Whistle, and I'll Come to You, My Lad"; this was published posthumously in 1926 as "Basil Netherby" [see *Ghosts of the Chit-Chat*]. Benson doesn't seem to have courted the ghostly muse again, however, until the first "B." story, "The Strange Case of Mr. Naylor", appeared in June 1911.

"When the Door Is Shut" (June 1912) was the second contribution by "B." to Magdalene's magazine. There's no record of MRJ's response to hearing it read to him that April evening, but it seems that he might have offered Benson advice about the fifth in the series; for among MRJ's papers in King's College Archive are two corrected galley proofs, signed "B." in pencil, of pages from "The Stone Coffin", which appeared in December 1913.

The haste with which "When the Door Is Shut" was composed (conceived, written and read out in a single afternoon and evening) is, perhaps, apparent in the story, which leaves much unexplained, and arguably frustrates as much as it intrigues. But the remarkable speed and facility with which it was produced is typical of Benson's literary practice. He was an extraordinarily prolific and fluent writer. The diary that he kept between 1897 and 1925, fills 180 notebooks, and over his life he published over sixty volumes of poetry, novels, essays, biographies, and memoirs.

Benson even wrote in his sleep. The following poem was one of several that he claimed to have composed unconsciously and then scribbled down when he woke in the night:

A bold and cheerful company of Ogres,
    Ghosts, and Ghouls
Attacked and smashed to little bits the City
    of Tomfools:
The Tomfools sailed to Araby, and raised
    another state;
I can't say how refined they were,
    and how considerate.
And now in High Tomfoolery they're very fond
    of telling

> What an almighty hash the ghosts made of their
>   former dwelling;
> They chaunt their great deliverance: they teach
>   and preach and say
> How good it was of God to take their former
>   pride away.

Not all the denizens of Benson's night visions were so jolly, however, and the kind of bad dreams that tormented him throughout his life, find their way into the "B." stories, where nightmares abound.

The second story reprinted in this volume, "Quia Nominor", appeared in June 1913, exactly a year after "When the Door is Shut", and it elaborates upon a striking—and for Benson personally significant—image which is briefly alluded to in the earlier story: that of the bear.

The title means "Because my name is . . . " and comes from Phaedrus's Latin retelling of Aesop's *Fables*, a text that was widely used in public school classrooms from the seventeenth to the nineteenth century. In the fable, which is sometimes given the title "The Lion's Share", the king of the animals goes out hunting with a sheep, a cow and a goat. When the day's spoils are to be divided, he claims everything for himself, because, he says, he is strong, he is brave and *"quia nominor Leo"*—"because my name is Lion". (The fact that he was also the only carnivore doesn't seem to have been raised.)

But while Aesop's lion thrives on the power of its name, the slovenly protagonist in "Quia Nominor" is, inexplicably and terrifyingly, undone by the associations of his own. The name Byron he is told by a "courteous and ingenious philosopher" over dinner one night in Magdalene, derives from the Norwegian word for bear, *björn*. And it is bears, both fleshly and psychic, which do for Mr. Byron in the end.

In fact Benson's unnamed philosopher is wrong. The name Byron comes from Old English and has nothing to do with *björn*. Benson's own name, however, does. In one of his earliest books, a family genealogy published in 1895, he tells us that "Mr. Henry Bradshaw, University Librarian at Cambridge, used to say that . . . [my] family was undoubtedly Scandinavian in origin, and had drifted west from Whitby; he believed that the name was originally, Björnsen, son of the Bear, and used to point to the family crest as a confirmation of this." The frontispiece of Benson's book illustrates just such a crest as that attributed to Byron's family in the story: a bear's head, muzzled in the Bensons' case and accompanied by the motto *"Fay bien, crain rien"* ("Do well, fear nothing"). Benson had this same crest and motto painted above the fireplace of his room in King's College as an undergraduate.

Benson returned to the etymology of his name more assertively in the biography of his father, Archbishop Benson, that he published in 1899. "The name Benson" he writes, "is pre-eminently unromantic; it suggests (quite erroneously) a Hebrew patronymic, being as a matter of fact, as Mr. Henry Bradshaw proved, nothing but the Scandinavian name Björnson, a hunter's appellation 'Son of the Bear'. It has no patrician savour, nor any particular historical associations . . . "

Benson compares himself to a bear several times in his diary, usually as a way of expressing a kind of body dysmorphia. In March 1904, after spending time with the beautiful young Miss Cicely Horner and her brother, he reflected that "at such times I become painfully conscious of my own heaviness, bigness, slowness, ugliness. I feel like Quinbus Flestrin, the Man-mountain; like a dancing bear.

"He appears impish, I like an old bear . . ."
George Mallory and A. C. Benson (December 1906).

It is a curious thing that I should find it, on the whole, easy to make friends—easier than many people—and yet I am so profoundly conscious of unattractiveness both physical and mental." And of a photo taken of him in 1906 alongside the young George Mallory—in whom he was passionately interested—Benson noted that "the results were somewhat grotesque. He appears impish, I like an old bear."

But as well as embodying his physical insecurities, the bear appears in Benson's writings as a symbol of the depression with which he struggled throughout adult life. He was twice hospitalised for what he described as "a neuralgia of the soul", and the memory of these breakdowns haunted him even when he felt mentally settled. In 1904 he spoke of "this shadowy terror [which] lies in wait . . . like a wild beast, moving silently through the forest beside me".

More pertinent to "Quia Nominor" is a passage from Benson's book *Thy Rod and Thy Staff* published in 1912, a few months before the story's appearance in *Magdalene College Magazine*. This memoir was written after a particularly acute depressive episode ("a drying up of the springs of life" as he put it), ostensibly as an encouragement and comfort to readers who might endure similar affliction. In the introduction Benson describes the painful progress through his illness; how he conducted himself "like the abject figure in *The Winter's Tale* of the gentleman pursued by the bear; it was a dolorous and undignified flight, full of miserable indecision and helpless prostration. I showed no fight at all; I simply shuffled despairingly away from the monster which pursued me, murmuring apologies, and pleading for mercy." Which is, almost precisely, what we see happening to the main character in "Quia Nominor". Mr. Byron's unwarranted vanity is amusingly drawn, but there is deep pathos in his unravelling, and he is clearly, in part, a self-deprecatory portrait of his creator.

Magdalene College Magazine ran regular ghost stories by "B." until December 1914 when its tone and contents abruptly changed. During World War I most pages were devoted to lists of college members serving overseas and the obituaries of those who had fallen. But by Christmas 1919 the mood had lightened sufficiently for imaginative fiction to appear once more, and Benson supplied another supernatural tale—perhaps his best under the "B." byline. "The Sparsholt Stone" was not included in the collection of "B." stories published by The Haunted Library in 1986, and it appears here for the first time in print since December 1919.

With its hints at a pagan survival in "the uplands" of southwest Cambridgeshire, it's an enjoyable slice of early folk horror. Like all stories by "B." it leaves plenty unresolved, but the loose ends here chill rather than baffle, and the tale is more polished than most of its predecessors. The amusingly delineated antiquarians; the knowing but inarticulate rustic; the perilous ancient artefact; the wild-eyed, hairy antagonist; the "accident of curiosity" that springs the supernatural trap: all these place the story firmly in the tradition of MRJ, but it never feels merely derivative. And at the end, Doctor Frend goes further than any of MRJ's characters ever do in articulating, however hesitantly, a theory of the supernatural—his reflections recall those of Algernon Blackwood's adventurers in "The Willows" (1907):

Suppose a blind man, who sees nothing, stumbling along a road, tapping with his stick, walks into a stream of smoke from a pile of burning weeds. He can perceive nothing with the eye, but he is aware that he is in a current of some kind, laden with the scents of a hidden fire. He does not doubt of it, though he has but one sense that tells him. I think the earth is full of these currents, and that you and I stumbled that day upon one of them. There is some secret influence on that upland . . .

When the Door Is Shut

"B."

When the houses in Magdalene Street, beyond the Old Lodge, were recently being demolished, the clearing away of some flimsy lath-and-plaster accretions revealed a large solid chimney-stack of brick, of Tudor workmanship, with some pleasantly designed buttressing and chamfering, indicating that it was a portion of a substantial mansion. It stood a little way North of the new building, a few yards inside the wall. Beyond the chimney-stack, up the slope towards St. Giles' Church, a fragment of ancient wall was discernible, with the base of a mullioned window, and further North still an old doorway. These were undoubtedly the remains of Copped Hall, a house of some size, which stood detached in a little close, called The Green Peele, with an avenue of lime-trees running East towards the Pond-yard, now the Fellows' Garden. The houses on the Chesterton road abutted on the close and overlooked it. It was the property of the College, was partially demolished at the end of the eighteenth century, and became merged in the street. I have no doubt in my own mind that the doorway was the scene of two tragedies which took place in the eighteenth century.

The first incident is purely traditional, but there is an unmistakable allusion to the second event in that curious book, *Things Fleshly and Ghostly*, by Thomas Peck, in the chapter entitled "Of Foul and Lubberly Insecution". The incident is clumsily and obscurely hinted at, and Peck evidently took pains to avoid identification. But there is a singular entry in one of the College record books, which makes the story somewhat plainer. This entry is entitled "Concerning the death of Mr. Richard Mauleverer", and contains a few facts, leanly told, with notes of a conversation. The record is written in the first person, and is signed "Jno Bellamy, Fellow of Magdalene College"; it seems to have been inscribed in the book on the day of Mr. Mauleverer's funeral. Out of these two records I have pieced together the story as far as I can, just bridging one or two gaps by supplying obvious inferences, and I will tell it as a connected narrative, without undue citations.

Mr. Richard Mauleverer came of a good Worcestershire family, and was born in 1705. He entered Magdalene in 1723, as a commoner, where he did not waste much time in study; in 1726, by private influence, he was elected a Bye Fellow on the Spendluffe foundation, on taking his degree. He did not reside very long, and soon after, succeeded to some landed property; nothing is known of his movements until 1756, when he reappeared at Cambridge, and took a lease of Copped Hall; he was then a man of means and kept riding-horses. He was a bachelor, and lived at Copped Hall with a manservant and an old housekeeper. He was cordially received by the Fellows, the Master, Thomas Chapman, being apparently a distant connection; his chief crony, however, was John Bellamy, Wray Fellow, who had been a contemporary of Mauleverer's, and was a man of convivial habits. If Mr. Bellamy had never been seen drunk, it was equally certain that he had seldom been seen what is ordinarily called sober; but he was a civil, witty man, given to harmless expletives, a good raconteur, and excellent company when he was free of the gout, to which he was a martyr. Mauleverer usually dined in Hall at two o'clock dinner, after his morning ride, and spent the afternoon in the combination room. He was a strong and hearty man, of scanty discourse, good humoured enough, but very stubborn when he had once made up his mind.

The front door of Copped Hall was in the street, and admitted you to a small paved hall lighted by two slits of windows on either side of the door. To left and right were two parlours running through the house; behind the hall, entered by a door opposite the front door, was a small study, where Mr. Mauleverer mostly sat. The room had two windows, with a considerable space between them, looking out on the lime avenue. The fireplace was on the right, and to the left was a door which communicated with the garden by a short passage, which seemed to have been taken out of the room. If you went out into the avenue and looked back at the house, you saw the two windows of the study, with a bedroom above it with three windows; between the two windows of the study, and under the centre window of the bedroom, was a curious projection of brick like a large flat buttress.

Mr Mauleverer found the room dark when the summer foliage was out; he got into his head that a window had been stopped up in the centre, and on tapping about the panelling of the room he found that the space between the windows sounded hollow. So he had the panelling removed. In the space an archway appeared, with a strong nail-studded oak door, which had been very elaborately fastened up; the interstices had been plastered; but what at once attracted Mr. Mauleverer's attention were two broad strips of lead, one nailed from the top of the door to the bottom, and one across the door halfway up, on which were traced some curious geometrical figures. Mr

Mauleverer had the external buttress taken down, and the outer side of the door appeared, with similar strips of lead affixed. He decided to have the door reopened, and the lead was torn away.

It seems that the same day on which this was done, Mr. Mauleverer received a note from an old Fellow of Jesus, Mr. Hinde. He went to see him, but soon afterwards returned, asked for the strips of lead, and took them away with him, after which they were never seen again intact. He came back apparently rather troubled; and it seems that the same evening he told Mr. Bellamy a confused story, related to him by Mr. Hinde, of a murder that had been done at Copped Hall some seventy years before. The circumstances were obscure. But it is clear that a woman living at Copped Hall with her husband, a drunken brute, had been attacked by him in the garden, had fled to the house, and had endeavoured to close the door; the ruffian had burst it open, and killed her with an axe, for which he was very properly hanged at Huntingdon. Mr. Hinde, he said, had urgently advised him to have the door closed up again, but that he said he would not do, for it was a convenience.

The first day that the door was opened a curious event happened; a bird flew in at the open door, as if chased by a hawk, with a loud out-cry, and was killed against a mirror in the room, making an ugly splash of blood on the glass, and cracking the mirror; a week later a very inexplicable thing occurred. Mr. Mauleverer opening the door one evening saw something looking round one of the jambs, and perceived that it was a little ape, with white teeth and large eyes; it looked wickedly at him, and tried to dodge into the house; but Mr. Mauleverer was too quick for it, and straddled across the threshold; the little creature ran quickly to the nearest lime-tree, climbed up the trunk, and

Mr. Mauleverer could not discover where it was, though he heard it hiss and chatter in the branches. It was thought that it was one of a pair of apes kept by Dr. Long, Master of Pembroke Hall. Mr. Mauleverer went across to Pembroke to see if it was so, but saw the two apes snug enough, and found little comfort in the sight.

A week later Mr. Mauleverer had a strange conversation with Mr. Bellamy in the latter's room. He told Mr Bellamy that he had awaked at night, and he had heard something moving about in the room below, the dining parlour. He had gone down, and he had there seen and smelt something "which sickened him". "What was it?" said Mr. Bellamy. "I do not know," said Mr. Mauleverer. Then, after a pause, he said, "I do not know, but I reckon it must have been a bear!" "God-a-mercy!" said Mr. Bellamy, putting down a tankard which he was raising to his lips, "Why a bear?" "Well," said Mr. Mauleverer, slowly and painfully, "it was about that bigness and very heavy; it shuffled to and fro; it put its foot softly and lumberingly to the ground, and then there fell a little clattering of claws upon the boards, as it pushed forwards." "God-a-mercy!" said Mr. Bellamy again. "Yes, and worse than that," said Mr. Mauleverer, as though finding some relief in the telling, "it smelt strong and rank like some great hairy beast, and when I came near it puffed its hot breath upon me—Faugh!" said Mr. Mauleverer, with a kind of sickness upon him, and he took up his tankard and drank. Mr. Bellamy sat musing, and then said, "I have heard of a man—indeed he was own uncle to myself—who saw snakes when no snakes were there; but that was under—under somewhat different circumstances; and I do not think he smelled them!" "I have had enough of it," said Mr. Mauleverer suddenly, in a fury; "I will not have quadrupeds, with birds and feathered fowl, to make free of my house and garden. By God, I will not!" "I would not!" said Mr. Bellamy, "but how did the matter end?" "The beast shuffled away," said Mr. Mauleverer, "through the hall, into the study, and was hidden from my sight; the door stood open into the garden, though I am sure I closed it over-night." "I think I would tell the Mayor," said Mr. Bellamy soothingly; and here the notes come to an end.

A week later—it was always on Saturday nights that the events had occurred—Mr. Mauleverer did not dine in hall, but was busy all day in his study, the door being bolted. He had seen Mr. Hinde again in the morning. The manservant was puzzled, because there came a smell from the study of something boiling. Mr. Mauleverer ate a poor meal in haste, and went back to his study at nightfall, and the servant said that his hands were dirty and discoloured.

Late that night the servant was awaked by a sudden outcry in the garden. It was a moonlight night; he got hastily up and went to the window. He saw Mr. Mauleverer flying, as for his life, into the house, screaming horribly aloud. After him ran something big and dusky. Mr. Mauleverer got to the door, slipped in, closed it, and there was a silence of a minute or two while the creature sniffed about the door. Then came a great crash; the servant fled downstairs, and came into the study in great haste. He saw that the door was wide open, and a table had been overset. He made a light, and found Mr. Mauleverer lying, his feet to the door, with a great gash on his forehead, quite dead. There was nothing else inside the room. When the body was examined, the inside of the hands were found all white, as if with chalk; and a lump of chalk was found broken on the carpet. In the orchard was found a little firebucket lying in the grass in the avenue, which seemed to have been bitten and spurned; there were some cinders hereabouts, and some lumps of what appeared to have been molten lead.

The only other thing of note in the room was that on the inner side of the door was found scrawled very hurriedly in chalk some words in Greek which appeared to be:

$$\text{ῥῦσαι ἡμᾶς ἀπὸ τοῦ} \ldots$$

But at the end of the last letter there was a great line, as if the door had been dashed in on the hand of the writer.

Mr. Hinde died on the following day in his rooms at Jesus, of a stroke of palsy. He had been heavily affected by the news of the death, and it was thought to have hastened his end.

There was an inquest held, and the verdict given was that Mr. Mauleverer died of a fall, occasioned by a sudden stroke of apoplexy. I daresay he did! After the apoplexy, the fall, but what did the apoplexy follow after? I hope with all my heart that Mr. Mauleverer was knocked senseless by the blow, when the door was stove in.

Quia Nominor

"B."

I.

Mr. John Byron, who held a John Smith Fellowship at Magdalene until his death in 1788 at the age of sixty-three, seems to have been a man of noted inefficiency. He had gone to the Bar as a young man, where it was certain he had obtained a single brief, given him apparently by the kindness of the College, in an action against a tenant for cutting and selling timber privately. This much, I say, was certain, for Mr. Byron mentioned it very frequently in his talk; but it was held to be no less certain that he had never obtained another brief, for he would assuredly have made mention of it. He subsisted miserably enough in London on his Fellowship, which was poorly endowed; and he then returned to Cambridge, where he was not much welcome. However, the College made him a lecturer, and here he failed again grievously, being quite unable to command the attention, or even assure the silence, of his class. After which experiment, when he was not again appointed, he lived in his rooms the greater part of the year. But, strange to say, this proved incompetence in all practical affairs was accompanied by a most inordinate vanity.

Mr. Byron was vain of his name, of his appearance, which was meagre and slovenly, of his experience, which was small, and most of all of his conversation, which reached a degree of tediousness impossible to describe. He was both voluble and embarrassed in discourse, fond of telling a few very dreary anecdotes, so that his company was much dreaded by all merry men. He was something of a free-thinker, and spoke very scornfully of the intelligence of others; and he was, moreover, a greedy man, eating profusely and in a very slatternly manner, his waistcoat being generally garnished with the drippings of gravy and ale; so that, indeed, he was no ornament to the table. But being a man of no natural affection, he cared very little how distasteful he was to his fellows, and lived a slothful life, walking much about the town in the mornings, and staring at all whom he met; while in the evenings he sat alone in his rooms and was very peevish; and so the years moved on, with but little change.

II.

Mr. Byron sate one day in Hall next a visitor, a courteous and ingenious philosopher, learned in all sorts of curious knowledge; when Mr. Byron, as was his wont, spoke of his excellent handling of the case against the tenant of the College, and went on to talk very lengthily of the ancient family to which he belonged and all the glories of his name; he said to the visitor that no one had ever been able to tell the origin of the name, at which the philosopher laughed and said that it was plain enough. It was a Scandinavian name, he said, of common use in Norway, where it was called Björn, and had the signification of a Bear. The family, he said bore a bear's head as a crest; at which Mr. Byron said that his own arms were three bendlets enhanced gules, and that he had a mermaid proper for his crest. To this the visitor courteously said that Mr. Byron must then be akin to the Lord of that name, to which Mr. Byron said that he took little interest in such vanities, but that he believed that the Lord Byron was an offshoot of an inferior branch of his family. The visitor went on to talk of the strange way in which certain animals and fowls were attached to certain clans and families, and spoke of some curious customs that seemed formerly to have existed in Northern tribes, by which it was forbidden to any tribesman to slay the animal which was the sign of the tribe, "and I daresay, Mr. Byron," he said, "that some of your ancestors had trouble enough with bears which they met in hunting and were not permitted to slay".

"Very like, very like, sir," said Mr. Byron, who was displeased that the talk should pass out of his hands; and Mr. Byron went on to tell stories of his family and of their greatness, and especially of his great-uncle, who in Mr. Byron's description of him became a very notable man, though he had been, in fact, but a tallow-chandler in Ipswich; but this made no appearance in Mr. Byron's talk. The company would have wished to hear more of the philosopher's conversation, but Mr. Byron allowed him no second chance, and talked very wearifully all the afternoon.

III.

A day or two after, Mr. Byron was walking about the town in the morning, and, as was his wont, staring at all those he met, when he saw a little ring of people in the corner of the market-place. He hurried thither to see what the affair was, and, pushing into the gathering, he saw that a circle had been formed round two men, of foreign appearance, who led with them a great brown bear. The bear wore a little coat on his shaggy shoulders, and a cocked-hat on his head, and shouldered a pole, which he held in his long claws. He seemed to be very friendly and obedient to the men, and, at a word of command, danced a little in the ring, lifting up and setting down his flat feet very clumsily. His little eyes and his red tongue, which lolled out of his mouth across his white teeth, seemed very curious to Mr. Byron, and he pressed further into the ring till he was on the inside. The bear came round still dancing, but when he got close to Mr. Byron, so close that Mr. Byron could perceive his strong and acrid odour, he came to a stop, regarded Mr. Byron very curiously, and dropping his pole, came towards him in a decided way, as if recognising an old acquaintance. Mr. Byron was taken with a sudden terror, and cried out faintly. One of the men called the bear off, who picked up the pole humbly enough and continued his dance. But Mr. Byron conceived a great disgust of the whole matter, and slipped out of the throng, feeling sick and shaky and entirely unmanned. He had a sense that he had been in some danger, he knew not what, and that the bear would have hugged him in his arms, if the men had not interfered. He could not get the business out of his head, and for some days after that he was ill at ease, sleeping brokenly, and often dreaming of the little sullen eyes of the bear and the red tongue which lolled out of his mouth. He gave up his usual walk in the town and strolled instead in the College garden.

IV.

It was a week later that in some dumb hour of the night, Mr. Byron woke suddenly up in his bed and wished for day. His rooms were on the ground floor, on the South side of the Court, near the Porter's Lodge. He woke with a sense of great discomfort, feeling as though something had leaned over him and touched his arm; he had felt, he thought, a hot and foetid breath on his face; and what added much to his alarm was that he could discern the heavy scent of a bear, just as he had smelt the one in the market-place. He dared not move at first, but presently he took courage, made a light and looked fearfully round. All was as it should have been; he got up at last with the taper in his hand, and went out into his ugly and comfortless sitting-room, and even so far as his outer door, which was securely closed. He felt clearer now, and opened a little cupboard, where he kept some brandy; he took a dram, and was soon very valiant again. The clock presently struck three, with a very solitary sound; Mr. Byron betook himself to his bed again, but he could not sleep, and he was glad when the light began to filter in among his curtains, and the sparrows fell to twittering in the ivy.

V.

Soon after this the vacation came on; the scholars all departed, and most of the Fellows travelled away. Mr. Byron was left alone in the College, except for the Dean, an old somnolent man, who had no use for talk; and very dull were the dinners for the two. But Mr. Byron could not hold his peace, and bit by bit told the old Dean the story of his meeting with the bear, and his fancy of the night. The old man heard him very inattentively, and said that such fancies were uncomfortable things, and that Mr. Byron had better go off for a visit, and shake all such thoughts out of his head. "It's an ill thing," said the Dean, in his slow and husky voice, "when a man gets to brood upon bears, and such outlandish cattle. It's a disorder of the mind, Mr. Byron; there is an old story of a family, the name of which I cannot call to mind, the head of which is visited on occasions by the sight of a great white bird, poising in

129

his chamber—and it means no good. I would not have any Fellow of this College to tamper with the thought of birds of the air or beasts of the wood visiting them in their chambers at dead of night. That's an ill thing, Mr. Byron, and it's a boding thing. A man should read the Scriptures at such times, and pray a little; for both of which exercises I fear you have but little stomach."

Mr. Byron said that he thought that strong ale and brandy were a more manful cure, but the Dean shook his head and would say no more on that head, or indeed upon any other head at all.

VI.

Mr. Byron was now left quite alone in the College, for the Dean departed soon, and Mr. Byron was in great dudgeon. He parted with his appetite, and could only palter with toast and tea, which he laced with brandy. He gave up going into Hall, and sate much in his rooms, beating a tattoo with his fingers on the table. It was then that he took to writing a good deal in a little notebook, from which the event that followed is closely taken. It appears from this book that he was not at peace with himself, and that he had a sore heart about his wasted and selfish life; he made some entries, too, about the strange doom which befalls certain families; and he wrote down, too, some silly tales of his boyhood and youth, which had no beginning or end, as thus: "When I was in the garden, I remember that Marjorie came to me, and showed me some pears which Mrs. Vickers had given her, and offered me to share them; but I said no, and that I would play her for them at a game we much used, called Pattle-pottle; then I cheated her, and won all the pears, and ate them all and laughed at her, so that she did not contain her tears. I wish I had not cheated

Marjorie. She died April 8, 1748, of a quinsy, but that was long after. I did not like her husband well; he spoke injuriously to me" . . . So the notes rambled on, without any order. Then comes the following entry, written in a very wild hand, the lines sloping every way: "The worst thing I ever saw in my life, but I am constrained to set it down, for fear of I know not what. May God spare me and have mercy on me, and forgive my disbelief. It was thus: I woke very unquiet, I suppose about three in the morning (this was Wednesday, I think—I am not sure of this or of anything), and getting up I heard something go softly to and fro in my outer chamber; something brushed by the door, and it was thrice pushed and rattled, but it held. Then I heard something sniff and blow under the bottom of the door, and the smell, I cannot write of that, for it sickens me . . . Oh dear, how I am undone—Oh dear! Then I heard it pad about again; and again it sniffed and blew beneath the door. All this time I stood amazed and dared not even move, so that I grew stiff and cold. Then the day came in very slowly, and silence fell; and at last I took courage, and opened the door. The room was grey and dim, but—Oh dear! how can I write it—God be merciful; for the bear sate as I feared, all hunched up opposite the door, and looked at me out of its little eyes, and I saw its teeth and the redness of its tongue. It was there at last—Oh dear, what can I do? I shut to the door and I fainted after that, and crept to my bed; but now I cannot put the smell away from my nostrils: was ever man in such a horror—Oh dear!"

This passage is followed by some unintelligible scrawls, which appear to be fragments of Psalm xcv., "Whoso dwelleth," etc., very imperfectly remembered.

There is but one more entry, two days later. "I have seen nothing further, and the horror is a little abated; but I cannot get the stench of the beast out of my rooms; my clothes seem infected with it, and it hangs about my food. I have sat indoors too much of late. I must go abroad more, and walk more; this and a regular course of life and diet, with prayer, may help me. I dare not go to any physician, and if I went to a clergyman, I know not where I should make a beginning. I cannot rid myself of a burden of thought, and some disaster is awaiting me, I cannot conjecture what. It is too late, I fear, to live differently. Now if it had been twenty years ago! The curse of my house is fallen upon me, through my own great fault. If I had but one friend in the world, I could go forward in hope. If little Marjorie had lived, she would understand."

VII.

The end came very swiftly; but the only record I can find of the event is a brief obituary notice of Mr. Byron, which appears in the *Gentleman's Magazine* of July 20, 1788, about a week later. It was as follows:

"On the 18th of July, at the Fish and Duck Inn, Cottenham, died Mr. John Byron, Fellow of Magdalene College, Cambridge, a facetious and well-respected man. His death was occasioned by a singular accident. The deceased gentleman, who was in excellent health, was accustomed to take long walks in the neighbourhood of Cambridge, where he resided. On the morning of July 18, two Norweyan sailors, known as Swain and Burn, were showing a trained bear in the street at Cottenham, when Mr. Byron turned suddenly out of a side street. The bear, for some cause not explained, broke loose, and made as if it would embrace Mr. Byron, who stood by as if irresolute. He turned to run, with the bear close upon him, but collapsed to the ground, and the bear took hold of him. He was at once extricated, but he seemed to be in a fit, occasioned by terror, from which he did not rally, and died the same afternoon. At an enquiry which was held, Swain, the bear-guard, gave the bear a good character, and said that it could be trusted safely with the smallest child. He said, indeed, that the behaviour of the animal seemed to shew that he recognised in Mr. Byron an old friend, and wished to testify affection rather than any enmity. It had been intended that the bear should be destroyed, but the man Swain pleaded very earnestly for it, as an old favourite and as his means of livelihood; and as the doctor said that Mr. Byron had received no hurt from the bear, Mr. Cutlack, the magistrate, decided in Swain's favour, and let the Norweyans go. Mr. Byron will be buried in St. Peter's Churchyard at Cambridge, and is sincerely regretted by all who knew him."

The Sparsholt Stone

"B."

I.

The year was 1817, the month October, the time the fore-noon, when two old friends and cronies, Mr. Duquantoy and Dr. Frend, went out for a long walk, an exercise of which they were very fond. It was a still rather cold day of autumn, the trees turning yellow and the leaves drifting down into the tangled grass. A little bluish mist hung lightly over the fields and fallows. They walked up Madingley Hill and presently took a path among the meadows.

A word or two about each. Duquantoy was an old Huguenot name of which the owner was proud, and it was commonly pronounced Decanter by the gyps, though with no untoward application, for he was an abstemious man. He was Spendluffe Fellow of Magdalene and the gentlest of men, looking like a faded angel, blond and long-haired. He was a sort of antiquary, but he had no ostensible occupation. It had never occurred to him to wonder what exactly he was paid to do, though if the good Spendluffe, the founder of the Fellowship, had endowed the post to keep a man out of mischief, he had certainly for once succeeded. Duquantoy was the least mischievous of mankind; he never said a harsh word or framed an injurious thought, and was greatly beloved. Dr. Frend was a very different person. He lived in an odd little house in Chesterton Lane, which was full of curiosities. He had been a Fleet-Surgeon and had knocked about the world a good deal. He was connected with no college, and was generally deemed eccentric. His manner was abstracted and his speech was scanty and rough. He was a tall dusky man, who walked fast, swinging his arms; he looked as though he had been hung up in a chimney-corner, like bacon, to be smoked, and as if he had been left hanging a little too long. What had brought the two friends together it is hard to say, but they spent much time in each other's company with obvious enjoyment. Dr. Frend was never rough with Mr. Duquantoy, but spoke to him indulgently as to a child.

As they walked, a distant sound, the baying of a pack of hounds, broke on their ear. The hounds of the old Childerley hunt were at that time kennelled at Madingley Hall and hunted by Squire Cotton.

Mr. Duquantoy had certain ancient phrases which amused Dr. Frend. He spoke of a gun as a "musket" or a "fowling piece"; and to-day after standing for a moment to listen, he said "It seems as though the hunt were up." "Yes, the Childerley," said Dr. Frend. By this time they were almost in sight of the pack, which was, however, concealed from them by a hedge. Something very odd was going on. The hounds were howling and yelling as if their fox was full in view. The whips appeared mixed up with the pack, shouting and slashing at the dogs. No riders were visible. "They have got on to a rabbit, I dare say," said Dr. Frend. The sounds soon died away and they continued their walk; but presently they heard the howling of a dog at intervals, a very peculiar cry. Mr. Duquantoy after a little said "that sounds as if a dog had been hurt—let us go and see what is the matter?" Dr. Frend assented, and guided by the sound, they came at last to a deep wide ditch, almost dry. In it was crouching a fox hound, holding up a front paw, dripping with blood, head in the air, uttering lugubrious moans. "Poor beast," said Mr. Duquantoy. "Very odd," said Dr. Frend; and he slipped down into the ditch and approached the dog, which took no notice of him. "Frend!" said Mr. Duquantoy in a tremulous tone, "I implore you not to go near him—he must be mad, I am sure; he will certainly bite you—I beg you will not touch him!" "Pshaw!" said Dr. Frend, "I would like to see the dog that would bite me!" He went to the dog, and took hold of the wounded paw. The dog ceased howling and looked at him. "Hello!" said Dr. Frend, "there has been a *spear* here! Most extraordinary!" "A spear!" said Mr. Duquantoy. "Yes, a spear, I tell you," said Dr. Frend in a very fractious voice—"Look you here—this was where it went in—it was a broad spear with a central ridge—see how the skin is strained here in the centre—it is a bad thrust, but the point was stopped by the bone—the peripetal bone, to be exact. Good God, how it bleeds— but the dog is more frightened than hurt—he has had a real scare, and no mistake." He took out his handkerchief, and began to wind it carefully around the hurt paw. The dog licked his hand once or twice, when it hurt him. "A spear wound!" said Mr. Duquantoy again, "out on these uplands." "What do I tell you?" said Dr. Frend rather loudly. "These are things that I know and you do not. This is a wound from a spear—I have seen dozens like it." Mr. Duquantoy said no more till the wound was tied up. Then he said gently, as if to soothe Dr. Frend, "They say that they cut the hedges out this way with a sword instead of a bill-hook. It may be that perhaps?" "It is a spear wound I tell you," said Dr. Frend loudly. "How often am I to say it? Here, come on, boy!" he said to the dog; which crept out of the ditch, and followed him. "To heel, sirrah!" said Mr.

Duquantoy—it may be noted that he always called a dog "sirrah", just as he always called a cat "Poor Pussy".

They went across the fields in the direction of a little hamlet to the left, the dog following them, much dejected, shuffling along on three legs, and holding up the wounded paw.

II.

They entered the hamlet, which consisted of four white-walled and thatched cottages, round a triangular bit of rough grass. There was an aged villager standing there. Dr. Frend spoke to him about the dog. "Oh I know all about 'im," said the old man. " 'E's from the Childerley—they've bin along 'ere this morning, for exercise. I'm Strutt, sir, that's my name, and I was second 'unstman for ever so long to Squire Frost down to Childerley." "Well, the dog's got a bad cut," said Dr. Frend, "and he'd best lie up for a bit." "I'll take him in," said Strutt. "It'll be like old times—and I'll take him down to Squire Cotton's, that'll amoose me, will that!" "Well, there's a shilling," said Dr. Frend. "But mark me," he added, "it's a very odd sort of cut." The old man looked at him in a curious way, and said, "I think I know sir, about that—like a wound from a spiked railing, I dessay. Yes, it'll be that. They got out of 'and, those dogs to-day. I seed it all. They couldn't whip them off. Bless you, it always does 'appen about now. I've seen it a dozen times." "What do you mean?" said Dr. Frend. "Why, it's like this, sir," said Strutt. "It's always about now. All the whips know it well, and old Squire Frost, 'e used to cuss himself into a fine passion over it. But it's no use of cussing, tha' it isn't! One way and another, it is always about now it comes over them. It's always on the Portway, as we call it, that bridle track across the fields that go by Hardwick and on down

137

to Bourn. The dogs seem to view something, and most run it down; they seem in a sort of a fury-like. No shouting or whipping does any use; they run it right down 'ere, to Sparsholt Green; and then it goes to earth, wherever it be. And the dogs seem ashamed of themselves—and there are always two or three as get a wound like—that's why Squire Frost used to cuss so 'eavy—it's a queer business, all told; and the less said about it the better, say I."

Dr. Frend shook his head darkly; then he said, "Well, you'll take the dog down the kennel when he can travel? We must be getting on, Duquantoy, eh? By the way, what do you call this place?"

"Sparsholt Green, sir," said Strutt.

III.

"Humph!" said Dr. Frend, "that's odder still, you know."

It was at this moment that Mr. Duquantoy, who had been looking curiously about him during the talk, made his great discovery. "One moment, Frend," he said, "I must look at this."

It was a big stone of a reddish colour, of very smooth grain that lay in the centre of the little Green. They walked up to it. It was square, and looked as if it had been roughly shaped. There were things like rude shafts at the four corners. The top of the stone was flat, but a ledge had been cut out of it at one end, in which were two roughly-shaped holes like basins, and a little channel led from the top of the stone down to them.

"What is this?" said Mr. Duquantoy to Strutt. "Oh, just an old stone, sir," said Strutt, "that lie there many a year. The children have their games there."

"It looks to me distinctly Gothic," said Mr. Duquantoy—"like the base of a font. Frend, this would be the very thing for the rockery at Magdalene. Quite a curiosity! Would it be possible to purchase this, Mr. Strutt?"

"I dessay so," said Strutt, "but my advice to you gentlemen is to leave it lying. There's an old rhyme hereabouts—

> "Best leave alone
> A big old stone."

"That's very quaint, you know," said Mr. Duquantoy. "But I have taken quite a fancy to this stone. What do you say, Mr. Strutt? Four houses here—that might be half-a-crown apiece, ten shillings—and another shilling and a pint of beer to anyone who will bring it down to Cambridge for me. How does that seem?"

"Oh, you could 'ave t for that, sir," said Strutt, "I make no doubt—but I'd leave it, if I were you!"

"Yes," said Dr. Frend, "better leave it, Duquantoy. There are nasty things under old stones, you know."

But Duquantoy was not to be persuaded. He would walk up next day and see it taken up. It could be wheeled down in a wheelbarrow,—and Mr. Strutt would perhaps arrange it.

True to his word, Mr. Duquantoy walked up next day alone. Strutt and another willing inhabitant prised up the stone and the money was handed over. There seemed to be a little edging of the stones underneath, which had supported the bigger stone. There was a hollow in the ground, in which lay the antler of a deer, and another bone, which Mr. Duquantoy did not like the look of. He pushed it down into the earth as far as it would go. The money was handed over. Mr. Duquantoy directed the men to Magdalene, and walked on ahead. Strutt reported that the dog was better, but seemed to have no spirit. " 'E sit shivering all day, wouldn't eat or drink. A bad scare, that's what it is, let alone the cut." But Mr. Duquantoy was too much interested in the stone to listen.

It arrived in Magdalene in due course; it was hauled into Mr. Duquantoy's room, on the ground floor of the front court, and deposited in a little sitting-room, opening out of the study, where Mr. Duquantoy kept his hats and coats and a few bulkier curiosities, such as a gargoyle, and a purbeck shaft from Biggin Abbey.

IV.

It was soon after this that Mr. Duquantoy's long illness began. He had caught cold, he thought, on his walk with Dr. Frend. The worst part of it was that he suffered from extremely vivid and alarming dreams. One dream in particular haunted him night after night. It always began in the same way. He used to dream that he was walking in a place full of thorn-thickets. Then he used to be aware of something sinister and hostile drawing near. He described it to Dr. Frend thus, "I walk on, I turn a corner, and I see a man standing or sitting, who appears to be watching me. He is like the line in Shakespeare—

"A wretched ragged man, o'ergrown with hair."

He is clothed in a rough tunic, which is blue, I think—yes, the prevailing colour is blue—much patched. Then his hair sprouts out everywhere—beard and long straggling locks over his forehead, all tangled; it grows on his arms and on his legs—but his legs are wound round with strips of cloth, I think; and he had boots, shapeless boots, of skin. His eyes look at me out of his hair—fixed and angry, like the eyes of a wild-beast; and he carries a pole in his hand. I

140

run from him, Frend; it is horrible! I go in and out among the thickets. Sometimes he follows me; but worse still, sometimes he disappears, and then he is waiting for me. I awake all in a sweat . . . "

"Pshaw" said Dr. Frend. "Mere nightmare! Take regular walks, and drink a pint of mulled beer the last thing. These are mere fancies, Duquantoy! You mustn't yield to them!"

But for all that Mr. Duquantoy got worse. He sate all day shivering over his fire. Dr. Frend was often with him, and was alarmed to see how he lost flesh. He sometimes persuaded Mr. Duquantoy to walk, but Mr. Duquantoy used to turn faint, and return leaning on Dr. Frend's arm.

V.

It culminated at last on a cold December morning. The Porter, going through the court, heard Mr. Duquantoy shouting for help. He ran upstairs, but Mr. Duquantoy was not in his sitting-room. He heard a smothered cry from the little lumber-room, and going in he found Mr. Duquantoy half lying, half crouching, in a corner, with his hands out before him as if he was pushing something away. He was deadly pale and streaming with sweat. The Porter assisted him into the other room and on to a sofa, went out and sent for Dr. Frend and returned, not liking to leave him alone. Mr. Duquantoy lay on the sofa, his face a leaden colour, faintly moving his hands, and muttering a little. While the porter waited, a faint rhythmical tapping was heard by the sofa; and the Porter going up to see what it was, was horrified by seeing blood flowing out of his shoe and dropping to the ground in a pool. Then he observed that in his trouser by the thigh was a long ragged gash. He went to get a towel, when Dr. Frend appeared like a whirlwind, took in the situation at a glance, sent the Porter flying to get some lint, and hurriedly disrobing his friend, found a long ugly gash in his thigh. This he contrived to bind up, administering restoratives, and after a little time contrived to get Mr. Duquantoy to bed, and installed himself as nurse. Then he waited and was relieved to see the colour come back to his friend's face and hands, though he still muttered at intervals and even cried out sharply.

VI.

The next morning Mr. Duquantoy was better. He could talk a little, but he could not bring himself to say exactly what had occurred. He had dreamed persistently about "the man", and had lain in bed feeling too ill to get up, falling into heavy stupors of sleep, unable to distinguish imaginations from realities. He had got up at last and dressed—but he could eat no breakfast, and had fallen asleep again at his table, his head on his hands. On awakening and looking up, he had seen "the man" standing near him in a menacing attitude— he had rushed into the little room—something had pursued him—hacked at him—thrust at him. He did not know what had happened. Some complication was introduced into the story by Dr. Frend finding in the little room a carving knife from the breakfast table lying on the ground stained with blood. "Yes, I recollect," said Mr. Duquantoy, "I caught it up to defend myself." Dr. Frend persuaded him at last to believe that the wound had been accidentally self-inflicted, and told a precise story to that effect to the Fellows of the College.

But one thing he did not tell. When Mr. Duquantoy had done telling his tale, he was silent for a little then he said—

"Frend!"

"Yes" said Dr. Frend, nodding, "I know what you mean; it shall be taken back this very afternoon. My man shall come here and sit with you, and I will see it replaced. You are quite right, Duquantoy."

"I think," said Mr. Duquantoy faintly, "that the antler had better go too."

"What antler?" said Dr. Frend.

"You will find it on the stone," said Mr. Duquantoy.

The antler was there; and stranger still, it was stained and discoloured in an unpleasant way. Dr. Frend bundled the whole up in a sacking, hired a cart, drove out to Sparsholt, and with Strutt's help replaced the stone. When it was replaced, as they stood looking at it, Strutt said "The little gentleman should 'a let it alone; it's poor work meddling—" he broke off suddenly.

"What was that?" said Dr. Frend looking pale under his dusky complexion.

"It'll be someone shouting down by Homelands," said Strutt.

"Good God, I thought it came from the stone," said Dr. Frend.

"Well, so it do, sir," said Strutt. The two men stood and looked at each other, and a thin cry, half-stifled rose upon the air.

"There's something in there!" said Dr. Frend struggling with a sense of sudden sickness.

"Oh, let it be, sir!" said Strutt, "it ain't a troublesome cry. Someone's pleased, sure enough!"

"Good God!" said Dr. Frend, and walked off without a word.

VII.

It was some three months after the events here recorded when Dr. Frend and Mr. Duquantoy were sitting on each side of the fire in the parlour of a snug little inn at

Weymouth, to which Dr. Frend had carried his convalescent off for change of air. Mr. Duquantoy had never alluded in the remotest degree to the circumstances attending his illness, and Dr. Frend had begun to wonder if they were indeed but the impressions of sickness and hoped that they had faded from his friend's mind.

Suddenly as they sate in a comfortable silence looking at the fire, Mr. Duquantoy said—"Do you know, Frend, there seems to be something very mysterious about the whole business which ended in my illness. May I say a few words to you about it? I have striven to think that it was all a mere disordered dream; but I cannot so regard it, because the events which caused the illness stand out so clearly in my mind, and the illness seems to me the result and not the cause of them. What do you really think? The strange hunting scene, the removal of the stone—I was then to the best of my knowledge in perfectly tranquil health—but after that my recollection is still disordered. What do you think of it all?"

"Well," said Dr. Frend very gravely, "since you ask me, I will speak. I think that you, who have lived so carefully and so quietly, are more surprised at coming across this streak, if I may so call it, of strange affairs, running counter to all ordinary experience, than a man like myself who has gone about the world and seen iniquity. Mind!" he went on, with uplifted forefinger, "I do not claim to be better or wiser because of my experiences—I think that a man who has lived, like you, a sober and godly life, is happier in all ways. Yet to have lived otherwise gives a man a kind of strength—that is perhaps all he gains together with many shadows."

"Now," he went on presently, "let me tell my thoughts in an image. Suppose a blind man, who sees nothing, stumbling along a road, tapping with his stick, walks into a stream of smoke from a pile of burning weeds. He can perceive nothing with the eye, but he is aware that he is in a current of some kind, laden with the scents of a hidden fire. He does not doubt of it, though he has but one sense that tells him. I think the earth is full of these currents, and that you and I stumbled that day upon one of them. There is some secret influence on that upland, setting from that stone we know of, along the old roadway. The dogs without doubt come across it; and are full of rage because they know it to be something evil and fatal to life. Evil befalls them. We have seen it: though I know of no agency that can inflict an outward wound by a stroke that can neither be heard nor seen."

Dr. Frend sate silent for a minute. Then he said, "I have been in a house, very far away, in which I felt, as I set foot, that there was some evil at work. There were spirits there, busy together, that whispered on the stairs and in dark corners, that had an enmity to men. That is a worse case: for in our adventure there was no particular enmity to you or me! But when by accident of curiosity we disturbed the source of the stream, as we might disturb a nest of wasps or a hill of ants, we were instantly assaulted. I do not pretend to understand these things, because to be plain, I am not a man of any great knowledge in religion—which is nevertheless, I believe, a saving force. That is all I can say—that we stumbled, you and I, in all ignorance, across a certain line of powers and have felt the pinch of it. I would like to hunt out the brood, if I could, as I would hunt out a haunt of tigers; but I have not the means. And I doubt, with all my love for you, which is great, if you have quite the stomach for it, sir."

"Indeed I have not," said Mr. Duquantoy hurriedly.

"I will tell you but one thing more," said Dr. Frend. "I learned late from that old retired huntsman, Strutt, that once a year, on a particular night, a cock is killed at Sparsholt, by one of the villagers; and set upon that stone, to bleed into the hollows of it. Why it is done, I know not; but Strutt said 'It is the custom.' It seems to me a devilish business altogether. And I would add . . . "

"Pray add no more," said Mr. Duquantoy, with a sudden pallor. "Let us be thankful to have escaped with so little hurt. I am not the man for all this, dear sir; let us forget about it, and take our walks in gentler regions. It is all too dark for me, and I would not willingly speak of it again."

"Yes, sir," said Dr. Frend, "you are right! There are secrets enough in the world, and we are not bound to affront them. It is enough to live soberly and penitently for what harm we have ourselves done—though I think you are a man of cleaner conscience than I—and to commit these devilries—for that is what they are—to larger hands than ours."

E. G. Swain
(1861-1938)

"CANON SWAIN FOUND DEAD IN A CHAIR
PEACEFUL END OF LONG HAPPY LIFE
Priest, Antiquarian, and Friend of Children"

– The Peterborough Standard (4 February 1938)

Edmund Gill Swain is best remembered today as the author of *The Stoneground Ghost Tales*, an entertaining collection of supernatural short stories, published by Heffers, the Cambridge booksellers, in 1912. The volume was dedicated to "Montague Rhodes James . . . the indulgent parent of such tastes as these pages indicate" and, like MRJ's collections, it was directed at a broad, adult readership. Swain's earliest published work, however, was aimed more squarely at schoolboys.

He had entered Emmanuel College, Cambridge in October 1880, on a scholarship from Manchester Grammar School, to study Natural Sciences. The urge to write was strong upon him, however, and as an undergraduate he composed humorous accounts of varsity life for his old school magazine, *Ulula*. These sketches—amiable, self-deprecating anecdotes about misadventures on the Cam, or travels on the Continent with a chum—were signed "Ova", Latin for "eggs", a play on his initials, EGS. This was not to be the last punning Latin alias that Swain published under.

His final undergraduate year coincided with MRJ's earliest at Cambridge, but they were at different colleges, reading different subjects, and don't seem to have met until Swain arrived as Junior Chaplain of King's College in 1892. He moved into rooms next to MRJ near the chapel and the two became friends. Swain was a regular attendee of the Christmas gatherings at which MRJ read many of his early ghost stories in the 1890s and early 1900s. But it was their mutual interest in the college chapel and choir school, that bought them into closest contact—and that inspired them both to write for the stage.

In 1903 Heffers issued, for 2/6, a slim volume entitled *Three Merry Comedies for Schoolboys and Such* by "C. A. Pellanus". Illustrated with comic black and white drawings, it collated three short play scripts intended for performance by children aged twelve to fifteen: "Too Clever by Half", "The First Day of the Holidays", and "A New Start". In my copy of the book, the handbill for a fourth Pellanus play, "What a State We're In", has been inserted, which lists the members of the cast and records that it was performed at "King's College Choir School December 22, 1903".

"C. A. Pellanus" is to be read as "*capellanus*", Latin for "chaplain". And the *capellanus* most closely associated with King's Choir School at the time these plays were produced was E. G. Swain.

The scripts in *Three Merry Comedies* are dedicated to the boys "who first acted [them]" and one of these young actors, Gordon Carey (part of the original 1898 cast of "Too Clever by Half"), recalled Swain's theatrical years later, in his memoir, *Nobody's Business* (1966). "I dare say, that some of my schoolfellows were happy in the role of performers . . . [but] for me acting was always a hateful ordeal," he confessed, while noting that Swain's scripts were "less scurrilous" than those written by MRJ, "in which certain

Nobbler the policeman from The First Day of the Holidays *by "C. A. Pellanus", illustration by James McBryde (1903).*

College notables were . . . identifiably guyed". These latter entertainments included "The Dismal Tragedy of Henry Blew Beard Esq." and "Historia de Alexandro Barberia et XL Latronibus" ("The Story of Ali Barbar and the Forty Thieves"). The dialogue for these was written by MRJ, the songs by Swain; both men also took leading roles in the performances, the chaplain appearing in drag.

In 1905 Swain left King's to take up the vicarship of the Fenland village of Stanground, on the south bank of the River Nene, near Peterborough. With a burgeoning brickworks close by, this once isolated, rural area was rapidly losing its old-world identity, and Swain's ambivalence to the changes that industry had wrought upon his parish is expressed in a poem that he wrote in August 1910 in the visitor's book of Newhaven Court in Cromer, Norfolk, the home of his friend Hannah-Jane Locker Lampson:

> O Stanground—brickfields, smoke, and slime
>   & clay and earthy men.
> I left you half-a-week since, and today come
>   home again.
> I view your noisome trade with small good-will
> Yet could men raise a haven on a hill
> Without your bricks and you?
>
> This hospitable roof, these happy guests,
>   This smokeless air
> This Hostess dear, whose kindness never rests
>   from cheerful care,
> The treasure here which humble bricks encase

Make me the debtor to your strenuous race.
Hence then! To pay my due.

The same regret at industrialisation is expressed in the opening sentences of the first Stoneground ghost tale, "The Man with the Roller".

Before being collected in 1912, the earliest of *The Stoneground Ghost Tales* were published individually in Swain's local newspaper, *The Peterborough Standard*. "The Man with the Roller" appeared on Saturday, 23 December 1911, as part of a special seasonal edition that offered "Fact, fiction and fun for the Christmas fireside". Fact was offered in an article that examined the question "Why plum pudding?" Fun was provided in a column entitled "Christmas Mirth"—a sample joke: "Will you carve, Mr. Brown?" asked the landlady, as she set the turkey on the boarding house table. "No, thank you," replied the facetious boarder, "Let Mr. Grind. He is a stone-cutter." Swain provided the fiction, under the name "S. Wain", an alias as transparent as the one used for the village in which the stories take place. Indeed, the identification of Stoneground with Stanground is even more explicit in the newspaper version of "The Man with the Roller" than that issued by Heffers, and it is this earlier version that is republished here for the first time since December 1911.

With its focus on a past crime being re-enacted within a picture in the present day, "The Man with the Roller" clearly owes a large debt to MRJ's "The Mezzotint" (first published in 1904, but written and read to an audience, of which Swain might have been a member, in the mid-1890s). Like MRJ, Swain has his supernatural event unfold in familiar, contemporary surroundings, and has fun sketching the supporting cast—the motherly landlady,

Mrs. Rumney, and her lodger, the scientifically inclined young clergyman, Mr. Groves.

But Swain was more than a literary mimic. The final paragraph of "The Man with the Roller" in which the narrator muses upon scientific advancement and the attendant dangers of "seeing more than is good" almost touches on science fiction, and offers the kind of reflection that MRJ himself never indulges in. And, solitary and antiquarian though he be, Mr. Batchel stands apart from MRJ's cloistered and haunted academics. There's an interested acceptance of the supernatural in the Stoneground ghost tales, which does not clash with their central character's religious faith, or that of his creator. The Reverend Roland Batchel is a calmer, more well-balanced figure than many of MRJ's protagonists, more at ease with the existence of psychic phenomena. Though often baffled, the Vicar of Stoneground never swoons or bellows or screams with the voice of an animal in hideous pain.

This is due largely, perhaps to his parish's ghosts being, on the whole, tamer than MRJ's—less muscular, less hairy, less violent. But it would be wrong to overstate Swain's gentleness. And if the final revelation in "The Man with the Roller" lacks the shock of infanticide that we get in "The Mezzotint", it still acknowledges the existence of human pain; there's an arresting pathos in the description of the apparition, the dead criminal with his stricken face, and "indescribable look of suffering . . . [that] seemed to be appealing now to the spectator for some kind of help".

Batchel is keen, also, to distance himself from sententiousness. He is faintly embarrassed by Mr. Groves's bland reflections upon the "good men" who must have trod his lawn in the past. Always personable and humane, the Vicar of Stoneground and his creator are never sentimentalists. And as the next story printed here shows,

E. G. Swain was well capable of imagining, and describing, violent supernatural death.

In February 1916, after eleven years at Stanground, Swain was appointed as Rector of the Church of the Holy Cross in Greenford, Middlesex. This parish was under the patronage of King's College, Cambridge, and as Provost at the time, MRJ must have been closely involved with the appointment.

Now entirely absorbed into Greater London, Greenford Magna was then a rural village with a population of less than one thousand, pleasantly situated on a bend in the River Brent, and surrounded by farmland and ponds.

The rectory itself—a sizeable brick building built in 1875—had substantial land attached, which included several older farm buildings and a long-neglected pigsty. According to the philosopher Mary Midgley, whose father succeeded Swain as Rector of Greenford in 1923, "Mr. Swain . . . had let it all fall gently into decay . . . [F]or a long time he did no repairs, merely moving his bed when the rain came in on top of him." And rain was not the only thing to disturb Swain's sleep: in September 1922 the local newspaper reported that he had written "a strongly worded letter" to the local council "on the subject of the alleged pollution of the stream in Oldfield Lane with sewerage. Mr. Swain wrote that the smell kept him awake at night."

But, despite its leaky rectory and pungent surroundings, Holy Cross Church, with its ancient porch, wooden bell tower and skull and crossbones gravestones, must have appealed to the antiquary in Swain. Though extensively restored in 1882, parts of the building date from the thirteenth century; there are fragments of fourteenth-century glass in the windows; and there are several sixteenth- and seventeenth-century stone monuments attached to the interior walls, carved in memory of local worthies. One of these honours Michael Gardiner, rector of Holy Cross from 1584-1630, who is shown kneeling in prayer, in white ruff and black robes, opposite his almost identically dressed wife. More curious and elaborate, however, is the monument to one Bridget Coston.

Bridget is shown, like Gardiner, kneeling at a prayer-desk, holding her baby, John. Behind her kneel her five daughters, in descending order of age: Frances, Mary, Jane, Anne and Philadelphia. An inscription below praises Bridget as a wife and mother, and explains that she died aged thirty-four on 2 July 1637.

These kneeling figures, seen in profile, are largely expressionless, their clothes the colour of the pale alabaster in which they are carved, and their skin tones only lightly touched in. In contrast, above them, much more vividly depicted, Bridget's husband Simon Coston stares abstractedly out of a window, at a point some way above and behind the viewer's head. His brown hair, blue eyes and red lips are painted in; his skin is comparatively swarthy; he wears a sombre black tunic. His right hand supports his head, while in his left he holds a handkerchief inscribed: "*providentia Dei*"—"by the providence of God'. He is a vision of melancholy.

It's a striking and intriguing monument. The depiction of mourners kneeling alongside their deceased relatives is conventional on funerary monuments from this period, and records show that most of Simon Coston's children survived him. But, so starkly separated is he from his wife and children here, that the casual, Latin-less viewer could be forgiven for thinking that Coston has been left alone to mourn his entire family. And if that is so, one

Monument to the memory of Bridget Colston (d. 1637), Holy Cross Church, Greenford. Photograph courtesy of Bob Speel.

can't help wondering what kind of tragedy might have deprived a rich merchant like him of his wife and their brood in one fell swoop? The Bridget Coston memorial invites speculation, and the piece of local folklore that Swain elaborates in the second story printed here, might well have been partially inspired by the imagery of the monument in his church.

The story was published as the work of "E. G. Swain" under the title "Coston House" in an undated pamphlet printed by the *Middlesex County Times*. But it also appeared as "The Greenford Ghost" in the 11 and 18 December 1920 editions of that newspaper, where it was attributed to "S. Wain", the same light alias that had first been used for *The Stoneground Ghost Tales*. This is its first appearance in print since then.

Like Swain's earlier tales, "The Greenford Ghost" makes use of a real-world village setting and attested historical figures—like, for instance, the Rector Michael Gardiner. But while the adventures of Mr. Batchel were entirely the products of Swain's imagination, a note at the end of "The Greenford Ghost" explains that the story has been "constructed out of surviving traditions". And one of Swain's sources must have been J. Allen Brown's *Chronicles of Greenford Parva; or, Perivale Past and Present* (1890).

The account in Brown's book is headed "The Legend of Perivale Mill", and it contains the most important incidents from the early parts of Swain's telling: a deadly quarrel between the local miller and a woman suspected of witchcraft; the disappearance of a lad called Simon Coston and his return as a wealthy merchant several years later. But Brown leaves much unsaid. He only hints at "the later destinies of Coston and his family", and gives no firm reason why Coston's ghost is still "said to haunt the grounds of the old house which has long since been levelled to the ground . . . [and] to hover about the old pond which once was included in the demesne".

Doubtless Swain picked up other details from his Greenford parishioners. Brown says that, in 1890, there were still "among the poorer people of that village, persons who have a strong objection to pass through Coston's Lane on a dark night" and Swain was there only twenty-six years later. But he has clearly refined and elaborated upon tradition.

There's much to enjoy in "The Greenford Ghost": the dramatic account of the swimming of Dame Gigs; the increasingly doom-laden atmosphere; the spine-chilling coda which brings the story into the present day. And Swain seems to be enjoying himself, showing off his historical and Biblical knowledge, and his command of Jacobean English. There's the sense, too, of his freeing up a part of his imagination that has so far been held in check. The narrative voice of "The Greenford Ghost" is less warm than that of the Stoneground tales, but the chief difference between them lies in the horror of what is described. The image of Coston's screaming infant daughter being dragged along by an irresistible, invisible force, or that of her drowned brother lying, apparently alive, with one hand in the pool "as if he were feeling for some object that had attracted his interest", are vividly horrible.

There's a grim relish, too, in Swain's descriptions of the mysterious, noxious slime, the "oily, loathsome ooze, which conveyed the idea of decay and putrefaction, and the touch of obscene reptiles . . . [and] smelt of fish scales and sick worms". Did the crumbling state of his own rectory and the stink of the local watercourse feed into his description of the collapse of Coston House and the foetor that surrounded it?

There once was a large seventeenth-century manor in Greenford called Coston House. It burned down long before Swain's arrival in the parish. But the name Coston is still heard locally: as well as the memorial in the church, there is Coston's Lane, a Coston Primary School, a tributary of the river Brent called Coston's Brook. And during Swain's time, there was another, newer building called Coston House, a former farm, about half a mile south of Greenford Rectory. In 1920 it was the constituency home of the then Conservative MP for Harrow, and future leader of the British Union of Fascists, Oswald Mosley.

In September 1923 Swain left Greenford to become Sacrist and Librarian at Peterborough Cathedral. He continued to write and research, publishing a guide to the cathedral in 1932; and he was closely involved with the local museum. But the obituary quoted at the start tells the reader that he "was never happier than when he had children around and . . . his collection of toys and games was a wonder and a delight . . . "

Apart from those early plays for the King's choir school, it seems that Swain didn't write anything else specifically aimed at children. But he retained a firm belief in the importance of imaginative fiction, and its power to positively influence the minds of the young. Early in 1925 he delivered a lecture "copiously illustrated with readings, anecdotes and song" in his old parish of Stanground on "Nursery Tales". It was indirectly quoted at length in the *Peterborough Standard* on 23 January, and it offers an answer to the question that is sometimes asked: Why did so many vicars write ghost stories?

> With regard to . . . whether children should be read
> fairytales and other folk tales, Mr. Swain expressed

the opinion that a portion of their time could not be better employed. It was absurd to contend that children took giant and fairy stories for fact . . . We are right in giving children a world to play in other than that into which they are born, and in teaching them that life is full of mystery. They must never cease to look into the unknown, nor lose the sense of wonder that their nursery tales beget, suggesting, as they do, that there is more in life than they can see with their eyes, and inciting them to enquire what it is.

The Man with the Roller

E. G. Swain

Upon the outskirts of Peterborough, but on the other bank of Nene, there lies what was once a picturesque village. To-day it is not to be called either a village, or picturesque. The house of clay in which man's spirit dwells erects other houses of clay for its own shelter and protection, and the material of those other houses is drawn from the earth upon which this and the neighbouring villages stood. The unlovely signs of the industry have changed the place alike in aspect and in population, so much that those who lived in better days have wept at beholding the worse, and even lamented their own survival. The chief habitations, however, have their foundations upon a bed of gravel which anciently gave to the place the name of Stoneground, and upon the highest part of this gravel stands, and has stood for many centuries, the church of the place, dominating the landscape for miles around.

Stoneground, however, is no longer the inaccessible village, which in the Middle Ages stood out above a waste of waters. Occasional floods serve to indicate what was once its ordinary outlook, but in more recent times the construction of roads and railways, and the drainage of the Fens, have given it freedom of communication with the world it once knew nothing of.

The Vicarage of Stoneground stands hard by the Church, and is renowned for its spacious garden, part of which, (and that the part nearest the house, as is natural) is of ancient date. To this original plot successive Vicars have added adjacent lands, so that the garden has gradually acquired the state in which it now appears.

The Vicars have been many in number. Since Henry de Greville was instituted in the year of our Lord 1140 there have been thirty, all of whom have lived, and most of whom have died, in successive vicarage houses upon the present site.

The present incumbent, Mr. Batchel, a solitary man of somewhat studious habits, is not too much enamoured of his solitude to receive visits, from time to time, from schoolboys and such. In the summer of the year 19— he entertained two, who are the occasion of this narrative, though still unconscious of their part in it, for one of the two, celebrating his fifteenth birthday during his visit to Stoneground, was presented by Mr. Batchel with a new camera, with which he proceeded to photograph, with considerable skill, the surroundings of the house.

One of these photographs Mr. Batchel thought particularly pleasing. It was a view of the house with the lawn in the foreground. A few small copies, such as the boy's camera was alone capable of producing, were sent to him by his young friend, some weeks after the visit, and again he was so struck with the picture, that he begged for the negative, with the intention of having the view enlarged.

The boy met the request with what seemed a needlessly modest plea. There were two negatives, he replied, but each of them had, in the same part of the picture, a small blur for which there was no accounting otherwise than by carelessness. His desire, therefore, was to discard these films, and to produce something more worthy of enlargement, upon a subsequent visit. Mr. Batchel, however, persisted in his request, and upon receipt of the negative, examined it with a lens. He was just able to detect the blur alluded to but it seemed to him so inconsiderable that he resolved to neglect it. He had a neighbour whose favourite pastime was photography, one who was notably skilled in everything that pertained to the art, and to him he sent the negative, with the request for an enlargement, reminding him of a long-standing promise to do any such service, when as had now happened, his friend might see fit to ask it.

This neighbour who had acquired such skill in photography was one Mr. Groves, a young clergyman, residing in the Precincts of the Minster at Peterborough. He lodged with a Mrs. Rumney, a superannuated servant of the Palace, and a strong-minded vigorous woman still, exactly such a one as Mr. Groves needed to have about him. For he was a constant trial to Mrs. Rumney, and but for the wholesome fear she begot in him, would have converted his rooms into a mere den. Her carpets and tablecloths were continually bespattered with chemicals; her chimney-piece ornaments had been unceremoniously stowed away and replaced by labelled bottles; the bed even, of Mr. Groves, was, by day, strewn with drying films and mounts, and her old and favourite cat had a bald patch on his flank, the result of a mishap with the pyrogallic acid.

Mrs. Rumney's lodger, however, was a great favourite with her, as such helpless men are apt to be with motherly women, and she took no small pride in his work. A life-size portrait of herself, originally a peace-offering, hung in her parlour, and had long excited the envy of every friend who took tea with her.

"Mr. Groves," she was wont to say, "is a nice gentleman, *and* a gentleman; and chemical though he may be, I'd rather wait on him for nothing than what I would on anyone else for twice the money."

Every new piece of photographic work was of interest to Mrs. Rumney, and she expected to be allowed both to admire and to criticise. The view of Stoneground Vicarage, therefore, was shown to her upon its arrival. "Well may it want enlarging," she remarked, "and it no bigger than a postage stamp; it looks more like a doll's house than a vicarage," and with this she went about her work, whilst Mr. Groves retired to his dark room with the film, to see what he could make of the task assigned to him.

Two days later, after repeated visits to his dark room, he had made something considerable; and when Mrs. Rumney brought him his chop for luncheon, she was lost in admiration. A large but unfinished print stood upon his easel, and such a picture of Stoneground Vicarage was in the making as was calculated to delight both the young photographer and the Vicar.

Mr. Groves spent only his mornings, as a rule, in photography. His afternoons he gave to pastoral work, and the work upon this enlargement was over for the day. It required little more than "touching up", but it was this "touching up" which made the difference between the enlargements of Mr. Groves and those of other men. The print, therefore, was to be left upon the easel until the morrow, when it was to be finished. Mrs. Rumney and he, together, gave it an admiring inspection as she was carrying away the tablecloth, and what they agreed in admiring most particularly was the smooth and open stretch of lawn, which made so excellent a foreground for the picture. "It looks," said Mrs. Rumney, who had once been young, "as if it was waiting for someone to come and dance on it."

Mr. Groves left his lodgings—we must now be particular about the hours—at half-past two, with the intention of returning, as usual, at five. "As reg'lar as a clock," Mrs. Rumney was wont to say, "and a sight more reg'lar than some clocks I knows of."

Upon this day he was, nevertheless, somewhat late, some visit had detained him unexpectedly, and it was a quarter-past five when he inserted his latch-key in Mrs. Rumney's door. Hardly had he entered, when his landlady, obviously awaiting him, appeared in the passage: her face, usually florid, was of the colour of parchment, and, breathing hurriedly and shortly, she pointed at the door of Mr. Groves' room. In some alarm at her condition, Mr. Groves hastily questioned her; all she could say was "THE PHOTOGRAPH! THE PHOTOGRAPH!" Mr. Groves could only suppose that his enlargement had met with some mishap for which Mrs. Rumney was responsible. Perhaps she had allowed it to flutter into the fire. He turned towards his room in order to discover the worst, but at this Mrs. Rumney laid a trembling hand upon his arm, and held him back. "Don't go in," she said, "have your tea in the parlour."

"Nonsense," said Mr. Groves, "if that is gone we can easily do another."

"Gone," said his landlady, "I wish to Heaven it was."

The ensuing conversation shall not detain us. It will suffice to say that after a considerable time, Mr. Groves succeeded in quieting his landlady, so much so that she consented, still trembling violently, to enter the room with him. To speak truth, she was as much concerned for him as for herself, and she was not by nature a timid woman.

The room, so far from disclosing to Mr. Groves any cause for excitement, appeared wholly unchanged. In its usual place stood every article of his stained and ill-used furniture, on the easel stood the photograph, precisely where he had left it; and except that his tea was not upon the table, everything was in its usual state and place.

But Mrs. Rumney again became excited and tremulous, "It's there," she cried. "Look at the lawn."

Mr. Groves stepped quickly forward and looked at the photograph. Then he turned as pale as Mrs. Rumney herself.

There was a man, a man with an indescribably horrible suffering face, rolling the lawn with a large roller.

Mr. Groves retreated in amazement to where Mrs. Rumney had remained standing. "Has anyone been in here?" he asked.

"Not a soul," was the reply, "I came in to make up the fire, and turned to have another look at the picture, when I saw that dead-alive face at the edge. It gave me the creeps," she said, "particularly from not having noticed it before. If that's anyone in Stoneground, I said to myself, I wonder the Vicar has him in the garden with that awful face. It took that hold of me I thought I must come and look at it again, and at five o'clock I brought your tea in. And then I saw him moved along right in front, with a roller dragging behind him, like you see."

Mr. Groves was greatly puzzled. Mrs. Rumney's story, of course, was incredible, but this strange evil-faced man had appeared in the photograph somehow. That he had not been there when the print was made was quite certain. The problem had ceased to alarm Mr. Groves; in his mind it was investing itself with a scientific interest. He began to think of suspended chemical action, and other possible avenues of investigation. At Mrs. Rumney's urgent entreaty, however, he turned the photograph upon the easel, and with only its white back presented to the room, he sat down and ordered tea to be brought in.

He did not look again at the picture. The face of the man had about it something unnaturally painful: he could remember, and still see, as it were, the drawn features, and the look of the man had unaccountably distressed him. He finished his slight meal, and having lit a pipe, began to brood over the scientific possibilities of the problem. Had any other photograph upon the original film become involved in the one he had enlarged? Had the image of any other face, distorted by the enlarging lens, become a part of this picture? For the space of two hours he debated this possibility, and that, only to reject them all. His optical knowledge told him that no conceivable accident could have brought into his picture a man with a roller. No negative of his had ever contained such a man; if it had, no natural causes would suffice to leave him, as it were, hovering about the apparatus.

His horror to the actual thing had by this time lost its freshness, and he determined to end his scientific musings with another inspection of the object. So he approached the easel and turned the photograph round again. His horror returned, and with good cause. The man with the roller had now advanced to the middle of the lawn. The face was stricken still with the same indescribable look of suffering. The man seemed to be appealing to the spectator for some kind of help. Almost, he spoke.

Mr. Groves was naturally reduced to a condition of extreme nervous excitement. Although not by nature what is called a nervous man, he trembled from head to foot. With a sudden effort, he turned away his head, took hold of the picture with his outstretched hand, and opening a drawer in his sideboard thrust the thing underneath a folded tablecloth which was lying there. Then he closed the drawer and took up an entertaining book to distract his thoughts from the whole matter.

In this he succeeded very ill. Yet somehow the rest of the evening passed, and as it wore away, he lost something of his alarm. At ten o'clock, Mrs. Rumney, knocking and receiving answer twice, lest by any chance she should find herself alone in the room, brought in the cocoa usually taken by her lodger at that hour. A hasty glance at the easel showed her that it stood empty, and her face betrayed her relief. She made no comment, and Mr. Groves invited none.

The latter, however, could not make up his mind to go to bed. The face he had seen was taking firm hold upon his imagination, and seemed to fascinate him and repel him at the same time. Before long, he found himself wholly unable to resist the impulse to look at it once more. He took it again, with some indecision, from the drawer and laid it under the lamp.

The man with the roller had now passed completely over the lawn, and was near the left of the picture.

The shock to Mr. Groves was again considerable. He stood facing the fire, trembling with excitement which refused to be suppressed. In this state his eye lighted upon the calendar hanging before him, and furnished him with some distraction. The next day was his mother's birthday. Never did he omit to write a letter which should lie upon her breakfast-table, and the pre-occupation of this evening had made him wholly forgetful of the matter. There was a collection of letters, however, from the pillar-box near at hand, at a quarter before midnight, so he turned to his desk, wrote a letter which would at least serve to convey his affectionate greetings, and having written it, went out into the night and posted it.

The clocks were striking midnight as he returned to his room. We may be sure that he did not resist the desire to glance at the photograph he had left on his table. But the results of that glance, he, at any rate, had not anticipated. The man with the roller had disappeared. The lawn lay as smooth and clear as at first, "looking", as Mrs. Rumney had said, "as if it was waiting for someone to come and dance on it".

The photograph, after this, remained a photograph and nothing more. Mr. Groves would have liked to persuade himself that it had never undergone these changes which he had witnessed, and which we have endeavoured to describe, but his sense of their reality was too insistent. He kept the print lying for a week upon his easel. Mrs. Rumney, although she had ceased to dread it, was obviously relieved at its disappearance, when it was carried to Stoneground to be delivered to Mr. Batchel. Mr. Groves said nothing of the man with the roller, but gave the enlargement, without comment, into his friend's hands. The work of enlargement had been skilfully done, and was deservedly praised.

Mr. Groves, making some modest disclaimer, observed that the view, with its spacious foreground of lawn, was such as could not have failed to enlarge well. And this lawn, he added, as they sat looking out of the Vicar's study, looks as well from within your house as from without. It must give you a sense of responsibility, he added, reflectively, to be sitting where your predecessors have sat for so many centuries and to be continuing their peaceful work. The mere presence before your window, of the turf upon which good men have walked, is inspiration. The Vicar made no reply to these somewhat sententious remarks. For a moment he seemed as if he would speak some words of conventional assent. Then he abruptly left the room, to return in a few minutes with a parchment book.

"Your remark, Groves," he said as he seated himself again, "recalled to me a curious bit of history: I went up to the old library to get the book. This is the journal of William Longue who was Vicar here up to the year 1602. What you said about the lawn will give you an interest in a certain portion of the journal. I will read it."

Aug. 1, 1600—I am now returned in haste from a journey to Brightelmstone whither I had gone with full intention to remain about the space of two months. Master Josiah Wilburton, of my dear College of Emmanuel, having consented to assume the charge of my parish of Stoneground in the meantime. But I had intelligence, after 12 days' absence, by a messenger from the Churchwardens, that Master Wilburton had disappeared last Monday sennight, and had been no more seen. So here I am again in my study to the entire frustration of my plans, and can do nothing in my perplexity but sit and look out from my window, before which Andrew Birch rolleth the grass with much persistence. Andrew passeth so many times over the same place with his roller that I have just now stepped without to demand why he so wasteth his labour, and upon this he hath pointed out a place which is not levelled, and hath continued his rolling.

Aug. 2—There is a change in Andrew Birch since my absence, who hath indeed the aspect of one in great depression, which is noteworthy of so chearful a man. He haply shares our common trouble in respect of Master Wilburton, of whom we remain without tidings. Having made part of a sermon upon the seventh Chapter of the former Epistle of St. Paul to the Corinthians and the 27th verse, I found Andrew again at his task, and bade him desist and saddle my horse, being minded to ride forth and take counsel with my good friend John Palmer at the Deanery, who bore Master Wilburton great affection.

Aug. 2 continued—Dire news awaiteth me upon my return. The Sheriff's men have disinterred the body of poor Master W. from beneath the grass Andrew was rolling, and have arrested him on the charge of being his cause of death.

Aug. 10—Alas! Andrew Birch hath been hanged, the Justice having mercifully ordered that he should hang by the neck until he should be dead, and not sooner molested. May the Lord have mercy on his soul. He made full confession before me, that he had slain Master Wilburton in heat upon his threatening to make me privy to certain peculation of which I should not have suspected so old a servant. The poor man bemoaned his evil temper in great contrition, and beat his breast, saying that he knew himself doomed for ever to roll the grass in the place where he had tried to conceal his wicked fact.

"Thank you," said Mr. Groves. "Has that little negative got the date upon it?"

"Yes," replied Mr. Batchel, as he examined it with his glass. "The boy has marked it August 10." The Vicar seemed not to remark the coincidence with the date of Birch's execution. Needless to say that it did not escape Mr. Groves. But he kept silence about the man with the roller, who has been no more seen to this day.

Doubtless there is more in our photography than we yet know of. The camera sees more than the eye, and chemicals in a freshly prepared and active state, have a power of affecting the eye, which they afterwards lose. Those who turn the instruments of science upon nature will always be in danger of seeing more than is good. There is such a disaster as that of knowing too much, and at some time or another it may overtake each of us. May we then be as wise as Mr. Groves in our reticence, if our turn should come.

The Greenford Ghost

E. G. Swain

It was in the latter days of October—so long ago that Queen Bess had been gone but six months—when Abel Reed trudged stolidly over the Middlesex clays between Northolt and Greenford. Few men would have envied him the task that had taken him abroad that day, for he had been collecting his debts; many, however, might have envied him his success, for he was a man not easy to refuse, and his pouch was well filled. Nor had hospitality been wanting; he was one with whom it was well to be on good terms, and he had filled more than his purse before setting out for home, though it was beyond the power of good cheer to make him cheerful.

They were the times of what people are now pleased to call the good old winters. October had still a few days to run, yet the ground was hard with frost, and a full moon enabled the traveller to see his way clearly. But for that, and the frost, the way must have been made longer by some two or three miles. Field paths in Middlesex are not for all seasons. But Abel took this good fortune ungratefully; his scheme of things contained no place for sentiment. He was the miller of Perivale, a man who lived alone in his mill, brooding alternately upon his rights and wrongs, and though millers are jolly by tradition there was nothing jolly about this one. It was a quality with which no one would have credited him, and he would have scorned it if they had.

He had just crossed the stile at the high-road, by the Greenford Pound, when an unexpected sound bought him to a halt. He heard the cry of a child close at hand. In another minute he had found a little woollen bundle from which the cry issued, and was holding an infant between his hands for the first time in his life. Looking this way and that, he called aloud, using alternate entreaties and threats, but no answer came. Even the cries of the child ceased, and there was no sound but the echo of his own voice. So he carried the babe, which he held at arm's length, to Parson Gardner at the rectory desiring only to be rid of it, and to continue his journey homewards. It was a disagreeable adventure that had befallen him, and he cursed his luck with all the fluency of an expert.

The Rector's household had gone to rest, leaving him at his studies, and when the miller's knock disturbed him, he came to unbar the door, carrying his candle. An exclamation of surprise escaped him as the light fell on Abel Reed and on the bundle he held before him.

"Why, Abel, what brings thee here at such an hour?"

"Marry, sir, that which would ha' pleased me better had it brought another. 'Tis a child I picked up by the pond."

"And art afraid of it biting, that thou must hold it thus? Bring it within to the fire, and let us examine it. 'Tis some trollop's babe, I fear," added the Rector, as he took in the child and uncovered it, "but a hearty boy, none the less. Well, wilt thou take it for thine own, being the finder?"

"Take it for mine own, forsooth," said Abel, in some haste, "I want none such; I did but take it up for safety, being too pitiful a man to leave a babe on the ground this frosty night."

" 'Twas well done," answered the Rector, "and thou must do it the further kindness to carry it across to Salathiel Penny, who is overseer, and to tell him to put the babe with Goody Brandon at the charge of the parish. What sayest thou to a draught of ale?"

"Nay, and thank you," said Abel, "for I must get me towards home, and, indeed, I have tasted overmuch already, so I give thee good-night."

"Goodnight, then," replied the Rector, "and God-speed," upon which he closed the door and returned to his studies.

"A pox on all children," muttered Abel, as he trudged across the road to the overseer's house. " 'Tis enough to make any man mind his own affairs, and leave pity to others." But he delivered the foundling, and the Rector's message, to Master Penny, and set his face finally towards Perivale, his connection with this child, for all he knew to the contrary, being finished, and done with for ever. The overseer on his part, carried the babe to Goody Brandon, whom he roused from her bed, hastening thereafter to his own, and when midnight struck, the new-found infant, and every other person concerned in the night's work, unless we are to except the mother, were sound asleep.

Parson Michael Gardner, albeit a devoted student of the New Learning, was none the less a devoted pastor; his first thought next morning was of the child picked up by Abel Reed, and his first anxiety centred upon the mother who had deserted it—perhaps some outcast who was suffering such misery as she could not allow her child to share, for of course, she had herself laid it in the miller's path. Master Gardner went to the constable only to find that he had already searched the parish, and found no trace of a wandering woman. Nor—to conclude that part of the story—was any trace ever discovered. So the Rector went on to the overseer and had the child brought in to be made a Christian.

"How shall we name the boy?" said the Overseer.

"He was found on the Feast of St. Simon and St. Jude," replied the Rector, "so let him be called Simon. As for his surname, I leave it to you. How was the last foundling named?"

The overseer turned to his book. "The last was left by a Lincolnshire woman, who died on her journey; she came from Boston, and we gave the child that name not knowing how the mother had been called."

"Then," said the Rector, "let this one be Coston, since C follows B."

The foundling was accordingly written down Simon Coston, and the Rector, after giving him Conditional Baptism, returned to his books. Goody Brandon carried him back to the cottage in which he spent the rest of his boy life. And there we may be content to leave him, while we pass in one stride over fifteen years, and place ourselves again with the miller at Perivale, who has somewhat more to do with our story in its next stage.

From what has already been said of Abel Reed, it will be evident that he was little concerned to make his conversation pleasant; as the years grew upon him, indeed, he showed a growing determination to make it unpleasant, and, as people would say thereabouts, to jump down the throat of anyone who spoke to him. More grey and more dour than when we last saw him, he stood upon the platform of his mill one day in the early part of the year, looking upon the land about him, which he had gradually made his own.

A little old woman emerged from a thicket, carrying a bundle of wood; a person, if it were possible, less liked and more feared than the miller himself. It was the day of witches, and Dame Gigs was reputed to be one of them, and indeed, she looked the part. The miller shouted to her as she passed beneath him, "Whose wood art carrying away, now, Mistress?"

She answered him without looking up. "Since when is a poor woman upbraided for gathering a few sticks?"

"The sticks are mine, and not thine," called out the miller; "lay them down."

"Dost grudge me then, an armful of firewood?" she responded.

"My grudging is no concern of thine. It is enough that I gave thee no leave, lay them down."

"Wooding is for them that will, and always has been. Am I to go fireless because thou'rt a miser?" The dame raised her thin voice, and spoke no less angrily than the miller himself.

"Lay them down," shouted Abel, "or I'll take the longest and lay it about thy back and have thee put i' the stocks."

The old lady threw her bundle upon the ground, and turned her wrinkled face to the miller; "Have me i' the stocks, forsooth; thou'lt sooner have thyself where 'tis worse; thou'rt the devil's man, and fit for his company and no better; an' thou fall not off that staging and break thy neck, thou'lt drown i' the dam or get thy ugly body 'twixt thy own millstones. Never wilt thou die in thy bed, for thy master's not one to wait for that. I leave thee thy faggots; better be as cold a home as mine is, than as warm as thine is like to be."

The miller made no reply. He spat upon the ground, and turned into his mill, whilst Dame Gigs trudged down the road.

The sturdy whistling lad of fifteen who shortly came within sight was Simon Coston, now grown to be a terror to all who could not take a boy's mischief in good part. Dame Gigs, not without reason, detested all boys.

"Why, Dame!" said the lad, "Hast left thy broomstick at home?"

"Good for thee, I have," was the answer, "or I might have laid it about thy back."

"Surely thou wouldst not beat a little boy," said Simon, cheerfully, "being not more than twice thy own size."

"I would beat thee till thou didst cry for mercy, thou imp of mischief. Hast no respect for age? I'll tell on thee to Master Gardner when I see him next."

"Nay, Dame, I have such respect for thy age that it pains me to see thee going afoot when thou mightest sail aloft on thy broomstick; thou knowest thou'rt a witch, and witches all go thus."

"Rule thy tongue, thou graceless lad, or 'twill make thee trouble; and I be indeed a witch, this shall prove an ill meeting for thee."

"Thy grandame was a witch, and thy mother was a witch, and thou'rt the naughtiest witch of all," said Simon glibly, "but I fear thee no more than I fear a toad; I killed two an hour a-gone."

With this he slipped deftly behind the dame, put his arms under hers, and, clasping his hands across her breast, lifted her from the ground, and whirled her five or six circles round. Setting her down giddy and breathless. She staggered to a tree for support, whilst Simon resumed his journey towards the mill, still whistling.

"Thou graceless loon," piped the old woman, "thou'lt come to no good; thou comest into the world amiss, thou'rt going through it amiss, and amiss wilt leave it."

The boy waved his hand in reply as he passed out of ear-shot, and the dame went unsteadily on to her cottage.

It was an ill day for each of them, and no less for the miller. The boy and he repeated to each other as much as Dame Gigs had said, and perhaps somewhat more, all of which, within a few days, Simon had circulated freely in three parishes, the boy enjoying his tale so much that he failed to observe the seriousness with which others received it. Witches were held in great fear, and it was an unwelcome thought that there might be one at work near at hand, so a grave and sinister turn was given to this prattle of Simon's.

Within a few days of her encounter with the miller, Dame Gigs found herself in need of a hoe for the weeding of her bit of garden, having broken the shaft of the tool she had used for many years; she made her way, therefore, to a kindly neighbour, who had done her many little services. The neighbour opened his door in answer to her knock, but had no sooner set eyes upon the old woman than he hastily shut the door again and barred it, making his way to an upper window from which he bade her begone.

"Since when," asked Dame Gigs, "have old neighbours lost their welcome?"

"Since they have laid curses upon honest folk," said the man, "and trafficked with the devil to do them hurt."

Upon the same day it happened that Simon Coston took his rod to angle in the Brent. It was Candlemas, and a holy day, and as he set out, he looked for company in his sport. Two sons of a shepherd living near the stream had often shared his pastimes, and to the shepherd's house he betook himself. Their mother stood near her door, and called loudly and hurriedly as Simon approached, "Come not near; away wi' thee; there is nought more to be between us and you."

"Nought more?" replied Simon, halting, as he called out the words; "am I out of favour on some account?"

"Ay, that thou art," was the answer; "Dame Gigs hath laid her spell upon thee, and my lads shall be drawn into no such doings; get thee gone!"

It was a day or two later when the miller turned into the "Coach and Six" for a draught of ale; two or three men sitting by the tap made a hurried exit before Abel reached the door, at which the landlord met him. "I'd as lief not have thee under my roof, Abel," he said, "thou may'st take thy drink outside."

"Outside," said Abel, angrily, "what possesses thee to talk thus?"

"Nay," replied the landlord, " 'tis thou that art possessed, as all the world know; I'll have no more neighbouring wi' thee."

From this it will be seen that Dame Gigs was being taken seriously, and giving rise to fearful talk.

The cruelties practised upon witches in former days are matters of common knowledge. Some of these were sanctioned by law, and others sanctioned only by usage, and condoned. All of them, however, were familiarly known, and came to be frequently suggested by one and another as fitting treatment for Dame Gigs. The gentler minds would have her weighed against the Church Bible; the ruder sort spoke of trying her by water, or having her hanged without more ado. As yet, however, there was nothing laid to her charge but words, and words were not a hanging matter, even with witches. The threats she had uttered against the miller and the boy remained part of the common talk, and frequent repetition multiplied and embellished them, by no means to the dame's advantage. Of consequences, however, there were none; Simon was still as lusty as ever, and as careless, and the miller, to the general wonder, went about his usual business without coming to harm. None were willing to believe that Dame Gigs had no alliance with the Prince of Darkness, but some were beginning to allow that she had failed in practice.

☙

It was at this juncture that Abel Reed disappeared. The door of the mill stood barred, and day after day passed without any sight of him. He was not one with whose concerns it was well to take liberties, but when one after another came for flour and could get none, it became necessary to obtain entrance to the mill, and see what was doing. It fell to the lot of an active young carter to climb to the upper stage and explore. A cry, piteous to hear, followed his entrance, and some of those who waited were soon by his side. What they saw was described with morbid satisfaction at many a fireside next day, when the children had been sent out of hearing. We have no wish to dwell upon the horrible details. Bruised fragments of the miller's body had been found entangled with shreds of his clothing; he had been ground in his own mill with such completeness as hardly permitted of a decent burial, and no one doubted that Dame Gigs was the cause of it. Her very words had come true.

There was a great funeral; Abel Reed's death had procured him more friends than he had ever made in his life. As soon as he was laid in the churchyard, they became his avengers, and set out there and then in a great company, to find Dame Gigs, and deal with her as the manner was with witches.

The Dame was in her cottage, sitting over the remains of a fire. She looked up at the crowd that entered the door, "Who are ye that press into a woman's house, unasked?"

"Who we are is no concern of thine," said the leader of the party. "What we are come for thou shalt soon learn."

"Look how she sitteth in her black thrumb'd cap," said another, "She looketh as witches ever do."

"Thou art as naughty a witch as ever was," said a third. " 'Tis thy work hath bought us out today, and now 'tis our work to bring thee out."

"I am as much a witch as ye are men of sense, and no more," replied Dame Gigs.

"As for that," said the leader, "we shall make a trial of thee, thou shalt be swum."

" 'Tis a noble sport, surely," said the Dame, still outwardly calm, "if I sink not, I am a witch, and if I sink, I am a corpse: call you that a trial or an execution?"

"Trial and execution are all one for such as thou," replied the leader. "Let's bind her and ha' done with it."

The Dame made no resistance; what resistance, indeed, of her feeble body would have availed her? The men stripped her of her poor clothing, and with her garters bound her right hand to her left foot, and her left hand to the other. This done, they wrapped her in a sheet, to which they tied a length of cord, and bore her to a deep pool at no great distance from the place. Their leader made a knot on the cord's end, and held it in his hand, and when he gave the word to throw, two others set the sheet swinging and flung it forward. There was a horrid scream, succeeded by a splash, and the Dame fell into the water a good cord's length from the shore.

"She sinks."

"She swims."

"No, she sinks."

As these cries were uttered it was hard to say which was true. But as the sheet lost its air, the poor creature undoubtedly disappeared beneath the surface. This being a proof of innocence, was disconcerting to the crowd. They awaited her re-appearance in vain. They grew uneasy, and at last called upon the leader to haul in. And then occurred a new mishap. The sheet had been imperfectly bound up, and the cord drew it in by a single corner, empty.

There were cries for drags, poles, and other things not to be had. The pond was very deep, and no man proposed to enter it. There was no reappearance of the Dame's body, and after much idle clamour, the men gradually dispersed, none of them willing to be found upon the scene.

It does not concern us to describe the manner in which their leader was formally but leniently tried for homicide; the public opinion of the day condoned his offence, and he scaped with an insincere reprimand and a trifling penalty.

Our concern is now rather with Simon Coston, who got wind of the sport, as he called it, only as some of the men returned. He ran over the fields towards the now deserted pond, which it was almost too dark to see, and sat upon the last stile to recover his breath and decide whether or not he should go farther. Of what occurred we have but his own account; there were no witnesses, and the darkness gathered quickly. His story, in his own words, was this:—

"My master would give me no leave to attend Abel Reed's burial saying that I had been remiss of late, and that 'prentices were better at their tasks. For this cause I had no news of the design to swim Dame Gigs, or would have escaped from my task to see it, for swimming a witch is lawful sport, as everyone knows, and not like swimming a Christian. But when I was set free and heard of the matter, I made all speed to the pike-pool, and found no man there, for the daylight was almost gone, so I could not learn whether the Dame had withstood her trial.

"Being in a great heat with running, I sat by the stile, looking upon the pike-pool, which lies half-way down the field, and felt great anger towards my master who had caused me to be late for the swimming. It was just growing dark, but there was light enow to see the pool, all still and quiet, and I sat and looked upon it without drawing near, being minded to get me home again, where my supper waited.

"But methought it would be a pleasant thing to cast one stone into the pool from where I was. It was a long cast, and I sought for a good round pebble to make it more surely, for it is a delight to disturb still water; and when I had found my pebble and poised it for the throw, I saw the water moved without the pebble leaving my hand. It seemed that some living thing had risen in the middle of the pool, and then moved slowly to the land; although 'twas large for a dog, methought it must be that, and I poised my stone afresh, and waited.

" 'Twas becoming too dark to see afar off, but methought the animal was climbing out of the pool in my direction. I was not without dread, but was ashamed to flee, and so held my stone poised, and stood peering into the gloom. That which came into sight anon, within a little of where I stood, turned me sick and cold. It was no other than Dame Gigs, with her limbs bare, and her body overhung with slime and weeds from the pool.

" 'Art alive, Dame?' I called out, though she was now close at hand. She gave no answer, but looked at me as she came along, and I saw that her face was dead, whereupon I dropped the pebble from my hand and leapt the stile, and then ran my fleetest towards home."

This was Simon's account as he delivered it to the Rector, and as the latter put it down in writing at the time. The lad delivered it, no doubt, to many others, with more emotion and less propriety of language, but Mr. Gardner was careful to secure the facts before they could become distorted by hard use, and the result is what we have just related. The one addition which we have to record, and which caused Mr. Gardner to shake his head solemnly as he put away his manuscript, is that Dame Gig's body was vainly sought in the pool upon the next day to be given the Christian burial to which the terrible issue of her trial had entitled her. The most determined attempts were made, and all failed. As for Simon's story, there were few who believed it.

The mill at Perivale, meanwhile, stood idle. Abel Reed's lands had passed to a cousin, who was no miller, and he failed in every attempt to find a tenant for the mill, which soon fell into disrepair. There began to be stories about it, such as made men unwilling to live and work there. They said that it was cursed and haunted and doomed, and as time passed its appearance came to match its reputation. By day, even in the softest wind, there were creakings of loose woodwork, and by night the noises of bats and owls were added. Unless in broad daylight, wayfarers of the more timid kind would avoid it, and there were few others who did not hasten their steps as they passed by.

The mill came to be occupied, nevertheless, not with any consent of the owner, but at the time without his interference. An aged Jew out of London, contemptuous of the superstitions of country-folk, took up his abode there, well content that the mill should be in ill-repute, since the reputation afforded him an inexpensive lodging.

This man was called by no name. People knew him only as the Jew, and the stories which soon became current about the Jew eclipsed even the stories about his abode. None of them omitted to describe him as a miser of enormous wealth, and many of them contained lurid accounts of the manner in which his wealth was obtained. It served his purposes to be an object of awe to his neighbours, and though the bolder amongst the youth, one of whom was Simon Coston, would throw stones at his shutters, he was mostly feared and let alone. One day, however, to Simon's astonishment, as he passed by the mill, the Jew stood upon the platform and accosted him.

"Prithee, boy," called out the Jew.

"What's your will?" said Simon, as he halted, and looked up.

"Can'st get me a coney?" asked the Jew.

"Wouldst have a live coney to play with, or a dead coney to eat?"

"Bring me a coney to eat, dead or living, and thou shalt have its value," said the Jew.

"Such as get conies from me," answered Simon, "must trust me with their value before I entrap them."

"Thou'rt a sagacious youth," said the Jew, "and I love thee for it." With that he threw two groats at Simon's feet. It was generous payment, and Simon took a rabbit to the mill the next day, and went to Hammersmith with the groats on Lammas Day to see a bear baited.

It was the beginning of a sort of friendship with the Jew, which destroyed the remnant of Simon's reputation. The boy was never admitted into the mill, but he became the Jew's provider, and soon acquired great skill in bargaining, and no small profit in coin. But such friends as he retained regarded him as lost, and since neither warnings nor threats moved him, he was, in no long time, as much shunned as the Jew himself. Those who felt kindly towards the boy, regretted that the mill had not been burnt to the ground, and done with. This, it may be mentioned, was the fate commonly predicted for the old mill. The Jew was no niggard in candles, and the bright light he kept about him was visible from long distances up to a late hour; all nights were alike, and no matter how late a traveller might be abroad, the Jew would be reported as "still at his mischief", long after most honest folk had gone to their beds. After months of regularity, his lights came to be as little remarkable as the stars themselves. What caused a great deal of remark and conjecture was the absence of the Jew's light upon a certain night in the autumn of the year 1620. A second night of darkness led to further excitement and surmise, and when that was followed by a third, the general curiosity reached bursting point, and a crowd of the bolder sort gathered round the mill on the next morning.

Those who lived near at hand, and were well acquainted with the Jew's movements, were sure that he remained in the mill, but none of the men who gathered round it showed any inclination to go within. They invited and challenged each other without result. It had come to be regarded as the most unholy ground. All manner of suggestions had been made and scouted, when some one said, "Fetch Simon Coston." There was no dissent from this, and Simon was sent for.

He came willingly enough. He had seen nothing of the Jew for a week or more. "Wilt go up into the mill, lad?" asked one of the men.

"That will I," answered Simon, and, suiting the action to the word, he rapidly ascended the ladder, whilst the crowd waited below.

Simon did not keep them waiting long. In a minute or so the upper door was opened from the inside, and with a scared look, he appeared upon the platform, "Away, quick," he shouted, "the man who stays is lost. Get you far away." Upon this, to use the language of a tragedy then becoming popular, "they stood not upon the order of their going but went at once". One of them was positive that upon looking back he saw the face of Dame Gigs looking over Simon's shoulder, but none who had heard his cry wished to remain or to return. That same night a grazier who lived hard by heard a strange voice outside his shutters, and these were the words it uttered:

> *Bury me bury me, 'ere you sleep,*
> *In Perivale churchyard, ten feet deep.*

The grazier who heard this did not sleep that night, but neither did he venture out to find the speaker. In the morning the body of the Jew was discovered not far from the door, and as for Simon Coston, he was no more seen or heard of. It was commonly allowed that he had been made away with.

The reader, however, shall be informed of facts unknown to any of the people of that day. Simon had found the Jew seated lifeless at his table, upon which was outspread a wealth of coins—Jacobuses, laurels, angels, crowns, and smaller money. Wishing to be master of such a situation, he had secured the flight of his company in the manner described already and had carried out the body of the Jew, which done, he had made his way to St. Katherine's Dock and took his passage in the next hoy for Holland, with a heavy leathern bag at his waist.

There was then a thriving linen trade with the Low Countries, into which Simon found his way; and, to summarise this part of the story, within four or five years, he became a fairly prosperous merchant; before a score of years had passed, he found himself master of a considerable fortune, with a wife and an increasing family, and then he determined to return to England and settle in his native place. About the manner of his reception by his old acquaintance he thought little, and might as well have thought nothing at all. Those who were his own age were humble folk, and of the elder who remembered his name, there were few who remembered it with any further interest.

After an absence, therefore, of some twenty years, Coston took ship to London with his family and his goods, and having lodged the former without difficulty in the city, where his name was well known, he was not long in taking horse to Perivale. He road along the well remembered lanes, chuckling over the adventures of his boyhood, as the once familiar scenes brought them to mind. The mill stood no longer, but the place in general was little changed; he drew rein and laughed aloud in the place where he had laid hold of Dame Gigs and whirled her round him. He recalled his adventure at the pond, and allowed that it was "mighty curious", but many eventful years had passed since then, and he somewhat mistrusted his recollections. The reminiscence, however, served a more practical purpose; he meant to build a house, and the field about the pike-pool, as he remembered it, was an excellent site, so he made up his mind to ride there and see it again. The field lay in the parish of Greenford, a bare mile away; and he turned his horse westwards and cantered over the meadows. He was enjoying his ride, being a good horseman, and having discovered that he rode a good horse, borrowed though it was. He cantered easily over the level fields to Greenford, and was soon within sight of the pike-pool. He observed with pleasure that his recollection of the place had not deceived him. The land lay as conveniently as anyone could wish for the building of a house, and the pool could be left within its enclosure for the storing of fish. He rode on, measuring the ground with his eye, when suddenly his horse began to show signs of waywardness, and then stopped; a touch of the whip sent him on a few yards forward, and then he stopped again, and reared, doing his best to turn around. Losing his temper somewhat, Simon used his spurs, and so got the horse another dozen yards forward, and then found himself pitched over the animal's head, and lying on the ground.

He was not long in picking himself up, but he then saw his horse galloping away towards Perivale, and its distance showed him that he had lain for some little time. There were no bones broken; he had pitched upon a soft place, and was no more than bruised, but there was a curious sensation of icy coldness about his left hand. The hand was resting on the ground, and he did not at once look at it, but when he did, its appearance filled him with astonishment and disgust. It was covered with slime—an oily, loathsome ooze, which conveyed the idea of decay and putrefaction, and the touch of obscene reptiles; and as he brought it nearer to his face, it smelt of fish scales and sick worms. He could not bring himself to touch the slime; he kept it at arm's length, and scraped it off with a chip that lay near him. Simon was no philosopher, and was little apt to concern himself with the causes of things, yet he could not forbear looking about him for the hole into which chance had thrust his hand. He looked, at first, only with curiosity, but soon with impatience, and something not far removed from fear, for the turf about him, although soft and yielding, was nowhere broken and nowhere wet. He trod all over the place of his fall, and tried every inch of it with his whip. It proved to be sound everywhere alike. He was left with the preposterous conclusion that his left hand had become cold and slimy while it lay upon the warm and clean surface of the grass.

As we have intimated, however, he was not the man to concern himself with much speculation; he valued a conclusion chiefly because it bought the matter to a close, and in the present case, after another rapid examination of the site upon which he hoped to build his house, he set of in the direction taken by his horse, the more anxiously because it was not his own. In that matter fortune favoured him; he soon came upon a labourer who had caught and fastened up the animal, and in this man's cottage he obtained the means of washing his hand clean, which done, he mounted and set off towards the city.

The horse was still excited, and called for continued soothing and coaxing; it regained confidence only as they neared its home and stable in Bishopsgate, where the owner stood awaiting it, perhaps with the anxiety which may be excused those who lend their horses to friends.

"I trust the nag hath carried thee to thy liking, friend Coston," was his greeting.

"Carried me as far as he would," answered Simon, "and pitched me over his head, when he would no farther."

"Say not so," replied the owner, "that horse has never been other than gentle with man, woman, or child."

" 'Tis the last time thou can'st say so much," was Simon's reply, as he dismounted, "for he has turned vicious today."

"If he hath," said the owner, "he hath been bewitched, for vice is beyond his nature."

"Have it as though wilt," said Simon, "I give thee hearty thanks for the loan of him," and, shaking hands with the citizen, he took his leave, and rejoined his wife and children at their lodging.

It had not been a propitious visit to his native place; there are people who would call it ominous, but Simon was not greatly concerned at his adventure. He described the site of the house to his family, and promised them an outing to the place; he told his boys how they should learn to catch pike in the pool, and entertained them with stories of English country life as he had formerly known it. He was, in point of fact, sure of obtaining the land; he had learned at Perivale to whom it was that the field belonged, and that the owner was not only willing to sell but anxious to be rid of it. There seemed to be no reason why they should not be installed there in a new house before the winter.

The negotiations, when the time came for entering upon them, were entirely successful, and a substantial and roomy house was designed. In the early spring the materials were conveyed to the site and building began. The house was set with its greater rooms facing southwards, some fifty yards away from the pike-pool, whose overhanging trees would make it an agreeable feature for the gardens in the rear. The enrichment of the house front was secured by a handsome doorway, with a portico in the Italian style, and a short flight of marble steps, which Simon had purchased from a thriftless nobleman who had begun to build, and was not able to finish. It promised to be a house worthy of a man of consequence, and Simon was well content, and his wife and children impatient for its completion and the commencement of their country life in England.

Meanwhile the day arrived upon which they were all to visit the place; a coach was obtained and well horsed, in which they drove out of Cheapside under a blazing sun, with Simon in advance, on horseback. He took the children upon his saddle by turns, and they made a merry party, upon which the passers-by looked with envy. They went at such speed as the road allowed, through the villages of Kensington, Acton and Ealing, and reached Greenford at noon, overjoyed, after a winter spent in the city, to be out in the open fields. With strict injunctions to the little ones about the dangers of the pool, and a caution to the waiting woman who attended them,

Mistress Coston dismissed these to roam about at their pleasure, while she herself listened to Simon's discourse upon the house.

"I like not to have the pool so near," said the lady, as they turned to the rear, and stood to look over the garden. "It hath the look of deep water."

"Thou'lt like the fish well enough," answered Simon; "as for the pool, they shall set a strong paling about it."

"We'rt thrown from thy horse on this side?" his wife asked as her eye wandered towards the farther part of the field.

"Come and see," said her husband. He had been no more there, but had ridden along the road upon his subsequent visits to Greenford. Having led her to the place, he described his former struggle with the horse, and the unaccountable slime upon his hand, and together, having no other employment for the moment, they examined the ground for a wet hole, but found the turf, as Simon had found it before, sound and unbroken. It seemed a matter of no great importance, and they soon desisted, but the recollection of the slime upon his hand, and of its putrid smell, revived the feeling of disgust, and associated itself unpleasantly with his new house—"Coston House", as he determined, somewhat magnificently, to call it.

At this moment, a shrill scream startled both parents alike. They turned hastily in the direction of the sound, to see their little daughter Phillippa partly running and partly sliding, at a great pace, towards the pool, in the direction of the deepest water. There was no such slope of the ground as would account for her speed, and yet her shrieks proved it to be beyond control; a few moments, and she must be over the edge. Simon and his wife darted forward—a useless movement at that distance—whilst the child rushed unaccountably to her destruction.

"Go back," shouted both parents together, and with a cry of relief they saw the waiting woman dart across, and pull the child on to the ground, within five yards of the water's edge, and there lay both of them panting and trembling when Coston and his wife reached the spot.

"What is it, child?" said Simon. "What are you doing?"

"My hand went cold," said the sobbing Phillippa, "and it pulled me along." Her mother took the hand as the child drew it from under her, and hurriedly dropped it.

Simon saw and smelt the slime he would have liked to forget, and again he searched in vain for its source. Mistress Coston meanwhile, with all the grimaces of one performing a nauseous office, wiped the child's hand and soothed her as best she could.

The day's pleasure was, of course, at an end; the return to the city was no longer delayed, and Mistress Coston broke the silence at intervals by the repetition of her first remark: "I like not that pool. I like it not."

If the building of the house had not proceeded so far, perhaps Simon would have pleased his wife by changing the site; his portico, however, was erected, and also the southern front of the house up to its level—it was too late to change.

Phillippa's fright was more than a child of nine could bear without injury, and she needed careful nursing for many days. Sleeping or waking, she continually rehearsed her flight towards the pond, crying out, "I cannot stop" or "Let me go" or "My hand is bitter cold." And yet before this trouble was over, there came another.

The builder arrived one morning in the City, greatly distressed, to report that his foundations had failed. The marble steps had first begun to sink and slide backwards, and then the whole of the southern front. Simon chafed both at the delay and the expense, but after considering the matter, despatched his builder to Huntingdon, bearing a letter to a certain Dutchman whom Stephen knew to be engaged in draining the Fens, and skilled in building upon unstable soil. A week later, this Dutchman, one Cornelius van Hoogh, came to London, and was conducted at once to Greenford. He made light of the difficulty, showing the builder how to relay his foundations upon elm-trunks laid in the clay; he gave assurance that they would remain immovable under any weight whatever. After some rebuilding, therefore, and no great delay, the house proceeded, and by the end of the summer was near completion.

It was ready by Michaelmas. The autumn had been fine and dry, and the family took up their abode in it in early in the month of October. It was indeed a noble house, spacious and beautiful. Simon beheld it with satisfaction, and no little pride, and when the furniture and fittings required no more attention, set himself to consider the garden, in which very little work had yet been done. His first step was to summon one Peter Dwight, who had been commended to him on account of his skill as a gardener. A hale and vigorous man of some sixty years presented himself to learn what was wanted of him.

"Can'st undertake it?" asked Simon, when he had unfolded his plans.

"Being where it is, 'tis no work for a decent Christian man," was the reply, "and I cannot."

"Being where it is," Simon rejoined, "what mean'st by that? I take it my garden is as good as that of another man,"

"No other man's garden stands by the bottomless pit," replied Master Dwight, "which folk have shunned this twenty years or more; not without good reason, either. Thou'rt a bold man, Master Coston, and, as some among us know, thou wert a bold lad, but boldness avails little among the powers of darkness."

"What old wives' tale are bemusing thy wits with now?" said Simon, in some heat. "One would take thee for a mindless thing, with thy bottomless pits, and thy powers of darkness."

Peter Dwight coloured with anger at the taunt, but continued to speak respectfully, and without any other show of resentment. "Can'st remember Dame Gigs, Master Coston?"

"I remember her well enough," Simon answered, "she was swum for a witch."

"Ay," said the other, "and in that pool yonder—and clutched out of her sheet or ever she touched the water."

"What mean'st by clutched? Who clutched her?" said Simon.

"Who? Why those who inhabit the waters under the earth, else why was not her body found?"

"Doubtless it lies at the bottom of the pool," said Simon, "what remains of it."

"I tell thee the pool hath no bottom," rejoined Dwight, "it is but the neck and mouth of the lower waters, where lives the beast that in the end shall ascend out of the bottomless pit, as Revelation saith, and go into perdition. Dame Gigs lives with the lost, as all witches must, but her threats overhang thee and thine, and thou'rt playing with worse than fire to come near her."

"This is no talk for grown men," said Coston, "let me hear no more." Notwithstanding he could not but recollect what crawled out of the pond, after the swimming, and he was less easy in his mind than he had been.

"Well," answered Dwight, "I have said my say. Thy garden is like to the vale of Siddim that was full of slime pits, and thy pool goes down to the same under-world. If thou'rt seeking a gardener thou must find another than me, but it will be a hard thing to do."

The man took his leave, but he had uttered a word of ill-savour for Simon.

The recollection of slime troubled him, as Dwight's last speech revived it, and for many a day he could not shake off the disquieting impression this conversation had left.

A large house, however, is a solid object, and unaffected by impressions. With such a sign of his power and stability to encourage him, Coston soon recovered his confidence; as for the pool, he decided, if need should seem to arise, that he would fill it up. It would destroy his fish-store, but it would be some compensation to end the talk about it having no bottom, and to show his contempt for the dangers of which Peter Dwight had warned him. Mistress Coston and the children, the local talk had not reached, and Simon was too wise to mention it.

It was the middle of November that he rode one day into Uxbridge, and returned to find the house in confusion and sorrow. His son, Henry, a boy of eight, had tired of his play indoors, and slipped away from the other children to go out upon some pursuit of his own. He had been missed and sought by his mother and the children's maid in the dusk of the afternoon, not at first by the pool, which was forbidden him, but in such other places as were frequented by the children. Only when these had failed did the searchers come to the pool. The boy was there, sprawled upon the ground by the water's edge, with one arm round the trunk of a young willow and the other plunged into the water as if he were feeling for some object that had attracted his interest. His mother called to him, loudly and cheerfully so that he might not think her angry, but he paid no heed. Only when they came near did they first suspect, and then discover, that the boy was dead and cold. His face lay just beneath the surface of the water, and when they drew out the arm that was immersed, they found it covered with unnatural and odious slime which Mistress Coston had seen once before.

The death of a boy must needs be pitiful to no matter whom. To parents it is a most grievous sorrow at its best, and so it was to Simon, but he said nothing to his wife of the cause he had for feeling a measure guilty. To himself he said that though he feared not a rat, it was not amiss to stop its hole, and with great sorrow and self-reproach that he had not sooner done it, he began to collect material for filling up the pool. The loss of his boy was irreparable; but he would at least protect the others against such a fate. The bereaved family, therefore, greatly overcast by the loss of one of its brightest members, impatiently awaited the filling up of the pool, and in the meantime avoided it, both on account of its bitter memories, and its present dangers, Mistress Coston continually blaming herself for not having at first shown greater firmness in protesting her dislike.

Otherwise the house proved to be a pleasant habitation, and not so far from London as to prevent the interchange of visits. Simon's stout carriage, with its pair of smart horses, was often upon the road, and the hospitality of his new house was attractive to his friends. The loss of Henry had quite disposed them to spend a very quiet Christmas at home, but upon the last day of the month they agreed to entertain two merchant friends of Simon's with their families, who were to spend the night at Coston House and return to the City on the following day. They enjoyed at least something of the mirth of the season. Simon was hospitable almost to prodigality and

The massy bowl, to deck the jovial day
Flashed from its ample round a sun-like ray

At the parting of the years they wished each other joy with the happy ceremonies sanctioned by custom, and thereupon retired to their chambers with a general "Good-night."

The night, however, was less good than they had hoped for. It proved, in fact, to be a strange night for everyone. After a bare hour of sleep, Simon awoke with a sense of movement that left him clutching at his curtains—at least with the hand that his wife was not clutching in her turn. At the same time, the crockery on the washing-stand fell to the floor, and there followed the sound of breaking crockery, the whinnying of the horses in the stable, and the cries of children from various parts of the house. In little more than a moment, Simon was out of bed and out of his room, Mistress Coston with the intent to reach her children, being close upon him. They found their guests all at their doors, some having lighted candles, and all in a state of alarm. So they all stood, with faces blanched, saying little, and awaiting what might follow. At last one of the merchants, who had travelled in the Levant, was certain of an earthquake, and counselled them all to leave the house and make for the open.

"Methinks it will prove somewhat too open for our ladies," said Simon, "the climate of Greenford in January is not that of the Levant; let it suffice that we return to the lower rooms and mix another bowl."

The advice was taken; the fires were revived, and the anxiety of everyone wore off, as the night advanced without further signs of danger. Finally the household and guests returned to their chambers. The assemblage at a late breakfast on the morrow showed that nobody was the worse, and the guests took the road, in better spirits, at eleven of the forenoon.

There had been no earthquake, of course. Simon's thoughts had reverted at once, as will be supposed, to the elm-trunks laid down by the advice of Cornelius van

Hoogh, and he had but to walk around the house, to find that it had indeed slipped backwards without moving from its foundation, over some two feet of ground.

The matter was serious enough, and Simon had spent so much of his capital in building the house, that he was annoyed at the prospect of having to spend more. He debated with himself whether he should leave things as they were, or seek the advice of van Hoogh again. The house appeared to be none the worse for its slide, and threatened no further movement. In the end, he decided to take horse to Huntingdon, and lay the matter before his friend, to be dealt with or left alone, as he might suggest, summoning his own builder in the meantime to inspect the place. He said nothing to alarm his wife, but only announced a few days' absence, such as was not unusual, and gave rise to no more than commonplace questions.

The journey to Huntingdon took three days, and van Hoogh listened to the story on the next day following. He heard it with surprise, and when Simon had convinced him of its truth, declared that they must ride back together. He would examine the ground and structure for himself, and decide what should be done. The two friends therefore set out next day, and on the next but one afterwards, had reached St. Alban's, within a day's ride of Coston House. And there at "The Crown", Simon found his builder, who had come out in the hope of meeting him. Now that he had succeeded, however, he seemed to have no words.

"Is it by chance that we meet thus, or by design?" said Simon.

"As it chances, by design," answered the builder confusedly. "I had somewhat to say about the house, I know not where to begin."

"Begin at the beginning, of course," said Simon. "How dost thou account for the movement of it?"

"It is the work of the devil and nought else," said the builder, crossing himself piously.

"From a sensible man," answered Simon, "it is not the answer I looked for."

"Hath the house moved again?" asked van Hoogh.

"It is past moving any more," said the builder, and buried his face in his sleeve, quite overcome with emotion.

"What folly is this," cried Simon, "that a man weeps because his wall have shifted? I lay no blame to thee man, nor ever did."

The builder looked up again, but not at Simon. "Tell him," he said to van Hoogh, "that the house is gone."

"Gone," cried Simon, now thoroughly alarmed, "gone where? Talk reason, man."

The builder made no reply but crossed himself once more.

"But the wife and children?" shouted Simon.

The builder shook his head.

It was van Hoogh who patiently extracted the builder's story. He had made his way to Greenford upon Simon's summons, to find the house, according to a group of bystanding villagers, had disappeared in the night, with all that were in it. A portion of a wooden bedstead, bearing Simon's and his wife's monogram, floated on the pool; a few foundations were left round the site; all else had vanished— the villagers said, "sucked down into the bottomless pit". The builder, therefore, had set off to break the news.

The travellers bespoke fresh horses, and rode in haste to Greenford; they found only what confirmed the builder's story; the whole site was pulpy, the few heaps of brickwork lay at its edges, the bedstead, Simon's own, floated on the pool, and nothing else was to be seen.

"Come away," said van Hoogh to Simon, "it's an evil place."

"Go where you will," he answered, "I stay here."

He would yield to no persuasion, and the darkness was coming on.

They told him of an inn at Kensington, where they would await him with a supper prepared, and with a last injunction that he should not fail them, rode away.

Left alone, Simon paced to and fro on the ground, and about the pool.

The last of the villagers left the spot while it was still light, and finished the day in the safer region of the "Load of Hay", but Simon noticed their departure no more than he had noticed their presence. "My wife! My children! My house!" he repeated again and again, as he paced about in the darkness.

What was that which startled his horse, tied by a bridle to a willow? The constable averred the next day that he heard the animal shriek, and then saw it leap the ditch, and pass him at a gallop down the lane. He had gone as near to the scene of the disaster as he had dared, and that is what he heard and saw.

Early next morning, however, Peter Dwight and another, saw a man prone upon the ground, and feeling for something, as it seemed in the pool. They went up to the place, and found Simon Coston, cold and dead, with one arm round a young tree, and his face in the water. The hand which seemed to be feeling in the water, came out, as they drew his body away, covered with a quivering oily slime, so offensive to the sight that neither would touch it; they let it fall upon the turf, and stood away. They were met, soon afterwards, running down the lane as if for very life, and would stop to answer no question. Later on, after some days had passed by, and the memory of the adventure was softened, they told how the slimy hand had reached again towards the pool, and how the body, now that the other arm was disengaged from the tree, had followed it, until it had gone rapidly under with a sucking noise, which was the last sound they heard as they turned their backs and fled.

❦

The story now takes a great leap of not less than two centuries. The "Coach and Six", albeit a new building in these days, is still the favourite resort of idlers, and a group of these, upon a certain summer afternoon, are teasing and questioning the village idiot, a young man of five-and-twenty, carrying a coloured whip.

"Come here, Billy," says one of the group, "and tell us when you went to bed last night."

"Billy went to bed last night when the cock crew this morning," he gravely answers.

"Where did you go?" asked another, "before you went to bed?"

"Billy went down Coston-lane to see Simon and the Witch."

"How often have you seen them?"

"Ten times, twenty times, hundred times," says Billy.

"Tell us what they do," says another. It is evidently a well-known catechism.

"Simon walks about like this, and says 'My wife, my children, my house.' Witch comes dripping wet, and laughs at him like this," and Billy imitates a weird and horrible laugh.

The story is attested by others than the idiot, but in their case cautiously and fearfully. What the vacant mind of Billy accepts as entertainment is to the occasional benighted wayfarers a horrible experience. The pool remains unfilled, and perhaps has defied many attempts to fill it. The small remains of Coston House lie on the ground overgrown with turf.

But on dark nights, even when Billy has been beguiled to his bed with sweetmeats, and fear has kept the lane free of wayfarers, there will rise suddenly a noisy commotion of owls and nightbirds, which proclaim to the villagers as they turn in their beds that the presence and voices of Simon and the witch have broken the stillness.

The half-awakened sleepers well know the scene that is being enacted, and rejoice that they are safely abed. Some there are who cross themselves, and pray for the repose of the two wandering souls; the more part, as they compose themselves to sleep again, vaguely wonder how long the ghosts will walk.

It is agreed that they must walk until the pool is filled in, but when one or another asks how a pit may be filled when it has no bottom, the question remains unanswered.

[The foregoing story is constructed out of surviving traditions.]

R. H. Malden
(1879-1951)

*"[R. H. Malden] was known to his contemporaries as
'Ginger' from the colour of his hair, 'Lord Howard'
from the forcefulness of his character, and 'Pompey'
from the impressiveness of his manner, which he always
used with excellent effect, as for example in delivering
one of the only really supreme jokes which I ever heard
at the Chetwynd Society . . . "*

– Sir Charles Tennyson
Basileon, 1900-1914

Richard Henry Malden went up to King's College,
Cambridge, in 1898 to study Classics, on a
scholarship from Eton. Clever, sociable and funny,
he would have been a natural candidate for membership
of the University's Chit-Chat Club, of which MRJ was
the *de facto* leader, and to which he'd read his two earliest
published ghost stories. The Chit-Chat, however, had
folded the year before Malden's arrival ("from inanition"
in MRJ's words) and so the new undergraduate had to find
other outlets for his wit. It wasn't difficult. The Chetwynd
Society was, like the Chit-Chat, a forum in King's for late
night conversation and debate, and Malden's joke, referred
to above, was delivered during a discussion of the question
"Should Dons Marry?" It was made at the expense of the

famously fat (and homosexual) Fellow of King's, Oscar Browning (1837-1923), and was to the effect that, in the unlikely event that Browning should ever take a wife then, whatever other qualities that lady might possess, "she must at all costs be *concave*".

In 1900 Malden set up a college magazine, *Basileon-a* (Greek for "The First Book of King's", a pun on the college's name and the title of the eleventh book of the Old Testament; it was followed in subsequent years by *Basileon Beta, Gamma, Delta*, etc). Malden and Charles Tennyson (grandson of the great poet) jointly edited this between 1900 and 1902, and were responsible for publishing early work by, amongst others, E. M. Forster, Percy Lubbock, and MRJ's friend and illustrator, James McBryde. As the title suggests, the contents were learned and facetious. Malden himself wrote poems, editorials, and essays with titles like "The Business of Pleasure" and "On Wasting Time", while Tennyson contributed, amongst other things, a comic dialogue, "Historiae Pater" ("The Father of History") in which an undergraduate meets the ghost of the Greek historian Herodotus in modern Cambridge.

Malden and Tennyson also collaborated on a comic play, *The Dean's Dilemma*. This was to have been performed at the ADC Theatre in November 1901, but was banned at short notice by the University's Vice Chancellor (the disappointment caused by this censorship is alluded to in Malden's story "A Collector's Company", reprinted in this volume). No trace of *The Dean's Dilemma* has survived, but the official of the title might have been MRJ, who was Dean of King's himself during the 1890s, and who was well known for his friendly relations with the junior members of the college. Years later Tennyson drew a vivid picture of a gathering in MRJ's rooms at the time:

Almost every evening would find half a dozen men sprawling in his armchairs or leaning against his mantelpiece. Most of them would be undergraduates from the college . . . The host lay back in his chair, smoking. He seemed to have no fear of silences, but spoke low and intermittently, turning from one to another and presenting to each in turn the friendly transparency of his large round spectacles. Now and then he would throw back his head and laugh with a sharp barking sound at some quip or anecdote. Sometimes he would let fall a dry witticism as he padded softly across to the mantelpiece to fetch a spill or fill his large curving pipe at the tobacco jar.

– Stars and Markets (1957)

Malden was undoubtedly sometimes among this privileged half dozen, and his friendship with MRJ survived his leaving Cambridge in 1904, for Manchester, where he was ordained. As well as sharing identical educational backgrounds, he and MRJ had in common an interest in mediaeval manuscripts and Biblical Apocrypha, and A. C. Benson recalled that Malden was one of those friends who, even after moving away from King's, "would come naturally back to see Monty". In 1907 Malden took up a lectureship at Selwyn College, Cambridge, and it's then that he seems to have begun his occasional habit of writing ghost stories.

"A Collector's Company" was originally titled "A Reclusive Rector" and (according to a letter once owned by another ghost story writer, David Rowlands) it was written to be read aloud to friends in Cambridge in 1909. The chief narrator Arthur Harberton, a self-effacing cleric with antiquarian leanings and a detached interest in his fellow man, is clearly an authorial self-portrait. His early career as a Cambridge lecturer (and his undergraduate experience of having a play banned by the University's Vice Chancellor) mirrors Malden's own. And the relaxed tone, the frequent asides, the authenticity of the details, the assumption of knowledge on the part of the reader/listener: all give the impression, as MRJ's work does, of a senior university man talking to his peers.

We don't know the occasion of Malden's reading the story aloud, but given its Advent setting, a Christmas gathering seems likely, and MRJ could well have been present. If so, he'd have had every right to feel flattered that his own techniques and style had been so cleverly assimilated, for there is in "A Collector's Company" everything that distinguishes MRJ at his best: a vividness of description (the charismatically evil face of Melrose, the eponymous rector/collector, is superbly evoked); plenty of scholarly, antiquarian detail (we sense that the Abney-like Melrose is to be treated with caution early on when we're told that he's made a careful study of Philostratus' *Life of Apollonius of Tyana*, and is a collector of "Gnostic gems"); and some marvellous shifts in tone, from not-quite-light-heartedness to unmistakeable menace (the descriptions of Harberton's waking in the night and what he sees out of his window are superbly creepy).

It's true, perhaps, that outright terror is missing; there is not the abrupt, shattering eruption of dread that occurs in MRJ's best work. But there's something just as effective: an uncanny atmosphere, a strangeness, made all the more unsettling by the narrator's inability, or unwillingness, to fully describe what he sees. Harberton's "I could not help thinking that [Melrose] knew more than he ought about a great deal which was very undesirable" strikes a distinctly Jamesian note.

"A Collector's Company" eventually saw print in 1943 in Malden's collection *Nine Ghosts*. The book's publisher

Edward Arnold had issued all of MRJ's collections, and the marketing for *Nine Ghosts* made much of its Jamesian qualities: "How many readers have regretted that there were no more of M. R. James's ghost stories to come? Yet Dr. James has found his successor in [Malden] . . . No more need be said than that the connoisseur will find in these stories a draught of the genuine vintage with its own subtle flavour."

But for all this positive influence, there's evidence that Malden was, at one stage in his ghost story writing career, keen to assert his independence from MRJ.

The fourth story in *Nine Ghosts*—"The Sundial", reprinted here—had first appeared in the 1930 Christmas edition of the *Leeds Parish Church Magazine*, with the following note appended: "As this story might be regarded as somewhat of a plagiarism of "The Rose Garden" in *More Ghost Stories of an Antiquary*, I may mention that it was written a good many years ago; before that admirable volume had been published – RHM."

Is there a tetchiness, here? A defensiveness? Is Malden anticipating the accusation, which has been aimed at him often since, that in "The Sundial" he was simply copying MRJ? Was he claiming precedence in using the ideas that are common to both stories? It's notable that he doesn't mention MRJ by name; his Leeds parishioners are presumed to know who the author of *More Ghost Stories of an Antiquary* was.

That there are strong resemblances between Malden's tale and "The Rose Garden" is undeniable. As well as the shared central image of the staked ghost and several verbal echoes, there are appearances by noisy night birds, bad dreams, a mask-like face seen in the bushes, wise vicars with antiquarian leanings, and the curious, almost identical cries heard, or imagined, from under the earth: "Pull, pull;

I'll push, you pull," in "The Rose Garden" and "If you pull, I'll push" in "The Sundial".

With its comic by-play between Mr. and Mrs. Anstruther, and Miss Wilkins's fine dramatic monologue, MRJ's story is perhaps the more entertaining of the two. But the most effectively spine-chilling moment in either tale is surely the chase around the yew hedge in "The Sundial" in which the hunter gradually, and terrifyingly, becomes the hunted.

"The Rose Garden" was first published in *More Ghost Stories of an Antiquary* in 1911, so, if Malden's note is to be believed, "The Sundial" was likely written between 1909 (after "A Collector's Company" which he says is the earliest of the stories in *Nine Ghosts*) and late 1910 (when he left his post at Selwyn). And if, like "A Collector's Company", Malden first read it aloud in Cambridge, then MRJ could have heard it. Did he draw inspiration from Malden rather than, as is usually assumed, the other way round? Is there a teasing reference to the author of "The Sundial" in the name of the Essex town that Mrs. Anstruther sends her husband to at the beginning of "The Rose Garden"? Did MRJ himself go to Malden/Maldon to get the materials that he needed for his ghost story?

Whichever came first, neither James nor Malden could in good conscience accuse the other of plagiarism, because both draw clear inspiration from Danish folklore, in particular the works of Evald Tang Kristensen (1843-1929), whose work MRJ had read in the late 1890s. The phrase "You pull and I'll push"—or variations thereof—spoken by a staked ghost recurs several times in the tales that Kristensen collected from his fellow Jutlanders. And in these Danish folk tales the ghost that is set free by the moving of the stake can take the form of a noisy night bird.

By the time "The Sundial" was republished in *Nine Ghosts*, MRJ was seven years dead, and Malden had cut his concluding note and added the preliminary paragraph about finding the story in manuscript in a Charing Cross Road book-shop. And in the preface he openly acknowledged MRJ's influence: "It was my good fortune to know Dr. James for more than thirty years. Among my many debts to him is an introduction to the work of Joseph Sheridan Le Fanu, whom he always regarded as The Master."

But that Malden's debt to MRJ was intellectual—spiritual even—as well as literary, is suggested in one of several theological works that he published in his lifetime. *Religion and the New Testament* appeared in 1928 with a dedication from the author to the Provost of Eton (MRJ) as "*doctori discipulus*"—"a pupil to his teacher". Malden must have sought permission to publish so intimate a tribute, and in his book we can perhaps get an idea of MRJ's own religious beliefs—a subject he seldom directly addresses himself in his published academic work or fiction. Malden's book was based on a series of public lectures that he gave at the University of Leeds in Spring 1925 which sought to bridge the gap between academic theology and the knowledge of "the ordinary church-goer, or newspaper-reader". It's a clearly written, thorough account of the origins of the New Testament and its place in history, and an up-to-date plea for the recognition of its importance in contemporary national life. In the preface he acknowledges MRJ as his "single largest creditor".

Malden had significant literary talent and knew how to deploy it, but like his mentor, he also had a strong Anglican sense of duty, and this drove him to expend his professional energies elsewhere. He left Cambridge for good in 1910 to become Principal of Leeds Clergy School. During World War I he served as a Royal Navy Chaplain, and was on board *HMS Valiant* during the Battle of Jutland on 31 May 1916. (Two years later he published a frank and dramatic account of his experiences during the action to raise money for naval charities.) In 1919 Malden returned to Yorkshire as Vicar of Headingley, and was appointed an honorary Canon at Ripon Cathedral. His clerical career reached its peak in 1933 when he was appointed Dean of Wells Cathedral, and he spent the last eighteen years of his life like a minor character in a MRJ story, preaching, writing history and theology, enjoying the comfort of his official residence, and leading an ostentatiously old-fashioned lifestyle: he always went about town, it was said, in a frock coat and top hat.

A Collector's Company

R. H. Malden

The story which follows was told to me rather more than thirty years ago. The narrator was elderly then. He died very soon after the end of the last war with Germany, so there can be no harm in repeating it now. His name, if you want to know, was Arthur Harberton. As he was a young man when it happened to him I suppose it must be dated not long after the year 1870. I made notes of it at the time, and reproduce it now as nearly as I can in his own words.

"Three years after my ordination I was offered a post as a college lecturer at Cambridge. That was the kind of work which I had always thought that I should like, at any rate for a few years, so I accepted the offer very gladly. I have never regretted that I did so; nor that I did not devote the rest of my life to academic work.

"I was not dean of the college, and as in those days the number of Fellows in Holy Order was much larger than it is now, it was very seldom necessary for me to be in the Chapel on a Sunday. Accordingly I used to go about the diocese a good deal, visiting the country churches. I don't think that I was under any illusion as to my powers as a preacher, even then. But I thought, without, I hope, undue vanity, that it might be good for village congregations to hear a fresh voice occasionally, and even for the incumbent if he were present. That was not always the case, for I was always willing to take the whole duty of the day if I were asked, so that the incumbent might secure a short holiday.

"As a rule I enjoyed these expeditions thoroughly. They began with a short train journey, followed by a drive from the station, sometimes of as much as ten miles. Country lanes were country lanes then. They had not been blackened with tar macadam and motor-cars were, of course, unknown. An occasional traction engine, preceded by a man on foot carrying a red flag, was the only disagreeable object likely to be encountered. From a dog-cart, which was usually the vehicle which came to meet me, it was possible to see over the hedges and to get a very fair idea of the country as you went along at eight to ten miles an hour.

"My hosts were generally interesting. For the most part they were country-bred men who belonged naturally to their surroundings. Many of them had a wide variety of interests (and sometimes a store of real knowledge) on which they were ready to discourse to a stranger. When I had the house to myself it was amusing to try to deduce what manner of man the owner might be from his books and pictures.

"Most of the churches and a good many of the houses presented features of architectural interest, which appealed to me strongly. Besides, I used to enjoy such conversations as I might have with rural churchwardens, sextons and other parish officials. I remember one churchwarden (a farmer, I think) who had heard that Huntingdon was a fine town. Personally he had never penetrated farther than St. Neots. When I told him that I lived at Cambridge I might as well have said Pekin or Timbuctoo.

"In another place the village school-master was opposed to elementary education in the abstract: not merely to the particular form of it which he was required to administer. He thought it unsettled children and took them off the land. There was, no doubt, something to be said on behalf of his views; but I couldn't help wondering whether he were quite the right man in the right place. Well—no doubt the countryside is more sophisticated now, and I won't bore you with speculations as to whether the gains outweigh the losses or not.

"So, as you see, I had good reason to look forward to these excursions. In fact, I only once got to a place which I should not care to visit again, and that is the one which I am going to tell you about now. All the same, I don't entirely regret that I did go there. Anyhow, it was a unique experience.

"Towards the end of one October term I got a letter from the bishop's chaplain, asking me if I could preach twice on the following Sunday at a village about twenty-five miles from Cambridge—I don't think I will tell you in what direction. The incumbent, it appeared, was not very well, and having no curate was doubtful of his ability to get through the day single-handed. As it would be the second Sunday in Advent it would not be difficult for me to preach at short notice. The collect and epistle for the day provided me with a subject ready-made: a subject, moreover, which I have always found particularly congenial.

"I discovered that there was a convenient train to the nearest station on the Saturday afternoon and from it on the Monday morning, so I telegraphed 'Yes', and wrote to my prospective host to say when I might be expected.

"It was a little after three when I got out at a wayside station. I was met by a groom with a dog-cart who brought a note from his master apologising for not having come in person. As I had understood that he wasn't well I hadn't expected him. I will call him Melrose.

"As we drove away from the station I said to the groom,

" 'I hope Mr. Melrose has nothing serious the matter with him?'

" 'No,' he replied, 'but he du come over all queer-like at times—so he du. When he have one of his turns—well, it's not for me to be explaining of it, if you take my meaning, sir.'

"I was not at all sure that I did, but thought it would be ill-bred on my part to ask for details. Also I was inclined to suspect that they might be copious rather than enlightening. However, as my companion seemed inclined to talk I did not feel bound to try to suppress him.

"I gathered that Mr. Melrose was wealthy and a bachelor. He had 'travelled furren', which was regarded locally as a hazardous proceeding, on the ground that all foreigners are well known to be black, and that they blackamoors might be up to anything. He was much took up with reading: also in my companion's opinion a dubious proceeding. For if there was good in some books, there was bad in others, and how'd you know which till arterwards, and then it was done.

"The general impression left on my mind was that while Mr. Melrose might be loved by his parishioners he was certainly feared. I thought that I might look forward to an unusually interesting week-end. As it turned out this expectation was not unduly sanguine, as I think you will agree when you have heard the rest of my story.

"After a drive of about seven miles we arrived. The light was failing, but I could see that the house was an old one. It was rather larger than the average, and I judged that there was probably a considerable garden behind it. I looked forward to examining both more closely between services on Sunday.

"Mr. Melrose made me very welcome. He was a tall man who stooped a little. I set him down as about seventy;

probably over rather than under. He had abundant white hair and very prominent white eyebrows. His eyes were dark and his nose aquiline. The general effect was scholarly and striking. He would have been noticeable in any company, and once seen would always be remembered. My first impression was that he was very handsome."

Here Mr. Harberton paused for a minute or two and then said rather abruptly, "Did you ever see Thompson (W. H. Thompson, 1866-86.), the Master of Trinity?"

"No," I said. "He was some years before my time. But I know the portrait; by Richmond, I think."

"No, of course you didn't," he went on. "Stupid of me. But one forgets how time passes. I don't think the portrait really does him justice. However, if you know it you'll understand what I am going to say.

"I knew him very well by sight and he was one of the most distinguished-looking men I have ever seen. He was handsome if you like, and you couldn't doubt his ability or force of character. You had only to look at him to see that he was a great man. Yet somehow I never could think his face a pleasing one. It always seemed to me to contain great possibilities of evil. I could believe him to be capable of absolutely diabolical conduct."

"Well," I said, "I believe that when Richmond painted Lightfoot he declared that he had never had a sitter whose jaw was so obviously and unmistakably that of a murderer. And I have been told by people who knew the Bishop well that they could believe that he had a naturally violent temper, and that his complete mastery of it was part of his greatness. The same may have been true of Thompson."

"Yes," said Mr. Harberton, "it may. Anyhow, this was the effect which Mr. Melrose produced on me. However, I tried to dismiss it from my mind as foolishness.

"After tea, which we had in a square hall by a log fire, Mr. Melrose asked me to excuse him until dinner-time as he had some letters to write and the post went out at six-thirty. He had a small study on the first floor opening out of his bedroom to which he proposed to betake himself. The library, which was on the ground floor and opened out of the hall, was at my disposal and there were writing materials there if I wanted them.

"The library was a large room, completely lined with bookcases. A cursory inspection of these showed that my host was a man of wide and miscellaneous reading. He seemed to be particularly interested in the later Neoplatonists and to be well supplied with Orphic literature. On a glass-topped table by the window was a collection of Gnostic gems. An Egyptian mummy-case stood upright in a corner. On a table by the fire was a book which he had presumably been reading when I arrived. I picked it up and found that it was Philostratus's *Life of Apollonius of Tyana*. It had been interleaved and was copiously annotated. I should have liked to read some of the notes, but thought that would be impertinent.

"Evidently I was in the house of a scholar whose interests were out of the common run, and the possessor of means which enabled him to indulge them freely.

"At dinner he proved very good company. He had travelled widely and had visited places which were then very much off the beaten track, such as Sicily and Transylvania. He had spent some considerable time in the latter country and had made a careful study of its grim folklore.

"The dinner was good, and my host exerted himself to be pleasant. Interesting he undoubtedly was, but I was not at all sure how much I liked him. I had a vague feeling that in some way he was playing a part. But I could find no rational ground for my suspicion. And, after all, why should he think it worth while to try to impress anyone so much younger than himself?

"It struck me as curious that a man of his calibre should be content to bury himself in so obscure a place. Of course the country was much more prosperous then than it is now and rural life offered more interests than I fear it does to-day. But this particular neighbourhood was not specially attractive in any way. Most of the land had belonged to the See of Ely and was now administered by the Ecclesiastical Commissioners. I believe that they are always considered to be good landlords, but naturally there are seldom any country-houses other than farms on their estates. I could hardly see my host at ease in the society of farmers, nor could I imagine that they would be able to make much of him. (I had discovered that he did not shoot or hunt, and in those days a man who did neither was very much out of it in the country.)

"When he told me that he had been rector of the parish for more than thirty years I could not help expressing surprise—rather clumsily, I fear, and perhaps not too politely, but I was very young then—and saying something about the solitariness of the life which he led.

" 'Yes,' he said; 'I don't wonder that it strikes you like that. The road from the station is rather desolate. But I have plenty of occupation and interests here; and do you know I find some of my neighbours more companionable than you would expect.'

"The last sentence struck me as rather odd, not only in itself but in the way he said it. I felt that there was more behind the remark than I was meant to understand, and did not like the feeling. I liked the laugh which followed it even less. However, there was obviously no more to be said about that. Perhaps he thought I had been rather impertinent, and perhaps he was right.

"After dinner we went into the library for coffee, and somehow our talk drifted to witchcraft, necromancy and kindred topics. I had always taken an interest in such matters, if not a very serious one, and have often wondered what foundation, if any, there is or was for the belief that the powers to which witches lay claim have any real existence.

"At this distance of time I do not mind admitting that as an undergraduate I had once made an essay in Invultuation. The object was the Vice-Chancellor of the day, whom I did not know by sight. He had annoyed me by refusing to allow a play which I had written to be acted publicly by the A.D.C., on the ground that it was disrespectful to authority. I adopted the only method of retaliation which seemed to be open. I made a waxen image and placed it on my mantelpiece. After some incantations which I thought appropriate ('*Flectere si nequeo superos Acheronta movebo*' [*Aeneid*, vii. 12.] is the only line which I remember now) I inserted a pin into one leg. The very next day I heard that the Vice-Chancellor had slipped going downstairs in his lodge and had sprained one of his ankles. I felt that my cause had been vindicated and took no further steps. But, as you will understand, I had not been serious in the matter. I never pretended to think that the accident had been more than a coincidence for which I need not reproach myself. The story leaked out somehow, and one comment on it which came to my ears was 'Whole religions have been founded upon less evidence.' I will not name the author, but I still think he ought to have known better.

"Mr. Melrose's discourse seemed to me to be a very different story. I could not help thinking that he knew more than he ought about a great deal which was very undesirable. And he spoke with an air of inside knowledge which I found disquieting. His tone was that of a lecturer on a subject which he had really made his own, and he gave the impression of having verified at least some of his knowledge by experiment. I felt that there was something malign about him, as well as creepy.

"Finally, I came to the conclusion that he was like an evil caricature of Dr. Hans Emmanuel Bryerley, the Swedenborgian teacher in *Uncle Silas* (by Joseph Sheridan Le Fanu). Altogether I was extremely glad when he suggested a move bedwards, and was at pains to lock the door of my room. Perhaps that would not avail much if it came to the point. But the illusion of security which it produced was comforting.

"I do not know how long I had been asleep when I awoke with the impression which one sometimes has of having been disturbed by a loud and sudden noise. Probably the church clock, I thought, though I had not noticed its strike earlier in the evening. I was just disposing myself for a renewed period of slumber when it struck me that although my fire had burned low the room was curiously light; not with firelight either. I had drawn back the window curtains before going to bed, as I usually did, and the light was coming from the window.

" 'Moonlight,' you will say. But I knew that it was not. In the first place, the moon was several days short of full, and in the second, the light was not coming from a particular point. It was evenly diffused, like daylight on a cloudy day; and no moon could have produced so much light from behind clouds. It seemed to me to have a bluish tinge which was unnatural and unpleasant. I went to the window and looked out. It commanded a view of a good-sized lawn flanked by dark shrubberies of some sort—rhododendrons, I found out subsequently.

"This lawn sloped slightly upwards away from the house, and at the farther end was a low wall with a gateway in it leading to the churchyard. This and the church itself were as plainly visible as if it had been midday instead of just after midnight in December. But everything to right and left was in darkness. I felt as if I were looking down an illuminated tunnel, and it seemed obvious that something would appear at the upper end. I took my courage in both hands and waited. I did not have to wait long. Through the gate in the churchyard wall came my host. He seemed to be wearing a cassock with a long black cloak over it. On his head was a high-pointed cap, something like a mitre, and he carried a short rod in his right hand. He came straight down the lawn towards the house. I wondered whether I was as visible to him as he was to me; and hoped not.

"Anyhow I felt bound to see the performance through. He was followed by a number of figures: I think about twelve, but I could not be sure.

"Although there seemed to be plenty of light they were somehow curiously indistinct. They may have dodged behind each other from time to time in some odd fashion. Anyhow I found that it was no use to try to count them. They were dressed in long black cloaks with hoods, which prevented their faces from being seen. On the whole I felt glad of that. They moved rather stiffly, like marionettes. Of course their feet made no sound upon the grass. But I was conscious of a faint creaking, the source of which was not easy to determine. It might have been produced by the breeze in the shrubbery; but I did not think that it was.

"The procession advanced until it had reached the middle of the lawn. Then the leader stopped and the others formed a circle round him. Still I could not be sure how many they were. Every time I tried to count them I became confused and arrived at a different result.

"Then they began to dance while he beat time or conducted, however you like to put it, with his wand. They moved more quickly than I should have expected, though they still suggested marionettes. The faint creaking which I had heard before was more audible. There could be no doubt now that it came from the dancing figures.

"Do you remember a story told by one of the minor characters in Stevenson's *Catriona*? About Tod Lapraik, the warlock weaver of Leith. He used to fall into a dwam in his house and once while he was in that state he, or something in his likeness, was seen dancing alone on the Bass Rock 'in the black glory of his heart'. Those words rose in my mind now. The performance which I was watching seemed to be inspired by an unholy—well, *joie de vivre* I suppose I must call it, though I don't know how far the dancers could be considered to be alive. The whole effect was abominably, indescribably evil. Yet, curiously enough, I did not feel afraid. I have never considered myself a particularly courageous person, and have not had many opportunities of discovering whether I am or not. But anyhow I was not conscious of any fear then. Partly perhaps I was too deeply interested in what I was watching to think of anything else. Also, youth and a good digestion will carry their possessor securely through many of the changes and chances of this mortal life.

"The dance grew faster, and the ring of dancers contracted. As it did so the mysterious light contracted too. I could no longer see the church, or the greater part of the lawn. Only the tall stationary figure with his black-shrouded companions whirling—it had come to that now—whirling round him. The group was illuminated as a particular figure sometimes is upon the stage (spotlight, I think they call it), but as before the light did not seem to be coming from any particular direction. Perhaps this was why I could see no shadow upon the grass.

"In another minute the dancers seemed to have closed in and then (as was perhaps to be expected) the light went out. I could neither see nor hear anything. The garden seemed to be as dark and deserted as you might expect between midnight and one a.m. on a moonless night in December. As I turned away from the window I heard the discordant cry of a night-jar (at least that was what I thought it sounded like) very loud and apparently very close to my window. Immediately afterwards I heard a low chuckle. It was not a pleasant one. I felt pretty sure that whatever the joke might be I should prefer not to meet the author of it. I made certain that my door was locked, made up my fire to last until daylight, got into bed and rather to my surprise fell asleep almost immediately.

"It was getting light when I woke. I got out of bed and unlocked my door. As I waited to be called I naturally thought of my experience of a few hours earlier. The more I considered it the less confident did I become that I had not dreamed the whole thing. I have always been an active and vivid dreamer, but have never had a vision of my head upon my bed worth taking seriously; even by the most nasty-minded psycho-analyst who ever came out of Vienna or anywhere else.

"At eight o'clock the butler brought me tea and hot water. On the tray was a note from Mr. Melrose saying that he regretted that he was unable to leave his room. The clerk would show me where everything was in the church. Would I make myself at home in the house and ask for anything I wanted, etc. etc.

" 'Is your master seriously ill?' I asked the man. 'Ought a doctor to be sent for, or can you look after him?'

" 'No, sir, not serious. But he don't come down as a rule, after one of his nights, not for a day or two.'

"For a moment I thought he was going to say more, but he turned away and began laying out my clothes. So I said something to the effect that old people often slept badly and that no doubt a wakeful night was very exhausting.

"To this he merely replied, 'Yes, sir,' and left the room.

"While I was drinking my tea I thought I would look at the lessons for the day, as I should probably have to read them myself. There was a Bible beside my bed and I opened it at Isaiah (the first lesson was Chapter 5, as you probably remember), and it so happened that the first words which caught my eye were from Chapter 8, verse 19:

Seek unto them that have familiar spirits and unto the wizards that peep and that mutter.

"No doubt a coincidence. But as I dressed I became more and more inclined to think that I had not been dreaming.

"The day passed uneventfully. Evensong was at three, as was not unusual in the country then during the winter months; I must confess that I was glad of this as I did not relish the prospect of coming down the lawn from the church in the dark. Of course it was getting dark by the time service was over, and as I went through the gate leading from the churchyard I had an uncomfortable feeling that my movements were being watched by some person or persons whom I could not see—and not with any amiable solicitude for my welfare.

"However, nothing untoward happened then or during the evening. I went to bed early and slept soundly all night. Next morning the butler brought another note from my host, expressing his regret that he would be unable to see me before I left, the disappointment which he felt at having had so little of my society, and a hope that I had been made comfortable.

"I replied to the first two heads of this communication as politely as was consistent with the truth. As regards the third I could reassure him honestly. I left the house soon after breakfast. The butler had not seemed disposed to be communicative, nor was the groom who drove me to the station. Three days later I went down for the Christmas vacation."

Mr. Harberton was silent for a minute or two, so I asked—I must admit with a feeling of disappointment—"Is that all?"

"Not quite," he replied. "But for the conclusion of the story you had better read this."

He handed me a cutting from a newspaper, probably a local weekly, which he took from a large old-fashioned pocket-book. I had seen the book before, as it was his practice to carry it with him. The cutting was from the bottom of a column, so no date was visible. I judged it to be about thirty years old. It ran as follows:

RECTOR'S STRANGE DEATH

A painful sensation was produced at [the name of the place was carefully erased] on Christmas morning.

As soon as it was light the sexton (Mr. Jonas Day) had gone to the church to make up the fire in the stove. As he approached the south door he was horrified to observe the body of the rector lying face downwards on a flight of four steps leading from the churchyard to the rectory garden. He went at once to the house and summoned the butler (Mr. Thomas Blogg) and the groom (Mr. Henry Meekin). They carried the rev. gentleman to his room, but it was all too evident that the vital spark had ceased to pulsate. Dr. Horridge was sent for and arrived a little before ten o'clock. He reported that the neck of the deceased was broken and that death must have intervened some hours before.

It may be presumed that the unfortunate gentleman had gone to the church at a late hour to satisfy himself that everything was in order for the morrow. The steps were slippery with frost and he did not appear to have taken a lantern.

The Rev. [name erased] had held the rectory for thirty-two years and the sad occurrence cast a deep aroma of gloom over the festivities naturally incidental to the day.

The inquest was held at the Fox and Grapes on the 30th ult., Dr. Horridge presiding as Coroner. Mr. Blogg deposed that his master not infrequently went to the church late at night. When asked by one of the Jury if he knew for what purpose, he replied that he had never demeaned himself to curiosity in his master's business. He was warmly commended by the Coroner for his reply.

Mr. Day deposed that when he approached the body he saw some curious marks on the back of the coat. When pressed to describe them he said "Like muddy claws." Neither Mr. Blogg nor Mr. Meekin had noticed these. The coat was sent for, but it had been brushed. The Coroner thought that they might easily have been made by an owl or some other bird of the night perching upon the body after life was extinct, and by his direction the Jury returned a verdict of Death by Misadventure.

The funereal obsequies were celebrated on the 2nd instant.

"May I take a copy of this?" I asked.

"Yes, if you like," said Mr. Harberton.

And I did.

The Sundial

R. H. Malden

The following story came into my hands by pure chance. I had wandered into a second-hand book-shop in the neighbourhood of the Charing Cross Road and was about to leave it empty-handed. On a shelf near the door my eye fell upon a copy of Hacket's *Scrinia Reserata* solidly bound in leather, which I thought well worth the few shillings which the proprietor was willing to accept for it. It is not an easy book to come by, and is of real value to anyone who wants to understand certain aspects of English Church History during the first half of the seventeenth century.

When I opened the book at home a thickish wad of paper fell out. It proved to consist of several sheets of foolscap covered with writing. I have reproduced the contents word for word.

From the look of the paper I judged that it had been there for at least thirty years. The author had not signed it, and there was nothing to indicate to whom the book had belonged. I think I could make a guess at the neighbourhood to which the story relates, and if I am right it should not be difficult to identify the house and discover the name of the tenant. But as he seems to have wished to remain anonymous he shall do so, as far as I am concerned.

The form of the story suggests that he intended to publish it; probably in some magazine. As far as I know it has not been printed before.

☙

I belong to one of the numerous middle-class English families which for several generations have followed various professions, with credit, but without ever attaining any very special distinction. In our own case India could almost claim us as hereditary bondsmen. For more than a century most of our men had made their way there, and had served John Company or the Crown in various capacities. One of my uncles had risen to be Legal Member of the Viceroy's Council. So when my own time came, to India I went—in the Civil Service—and there I lived for five and twenty years.

My career was neither more nor less adventurous than the average. The routine of my work was occasionally broken by experiences which would sound incredible to an English reader, and therefore need not be set down here. Just before the time came for my retirement a legacy made me a good deal better off than I had had any reason to expect to be. So upon my return to England I found that it would be possible for me to adopt the life of a country gentleman, upon a modest scale, but with the prospect of finding sufficient occupation and amusement.

I was never married, and had been too long out of England to have any very strong ties remaining. I was free to establish myself where I pleased, and the advertisements in the *Field and Country Life* offered houses of every description in every part of the kingdom. After much correspondence, and some fruitless journeys, I came upon one which seemed to satisfy my requirements. It lay about sixty miles north of London upon a main line of railway. That was an important point, as I was a Fellow of both the Asiatic and Historical Societies, and had long looked forward to attending their meetings regularly. As a boy I had known the neighbourhood slightly and had liked it, though it is not generally considered beautiful. There were two packs of hounds within reach, which could be followed with such a stable as I should be able to afford.

The house was an old one. It had been a good deal larger, but part had been battered down during the Civil War, when it was besieged by the Parliamentary troops, and never rebuilt. It belonged to one of the largest landowners in the county, whom I will call Lord Rye. It generally served as the dower-house of the family, but as there was at that moment no dowager Countess, and as Lord Rye himself was a young man, and both his sisters were married, it was not likely to be wanted for some time to come. It had been unoccupied for nearly two years. The last tenant, a retired doctor, had been found dead on the lawn at the bottom of the steps leading up to the garden door. His heart had been in a bad condition for some time past, so that his sudden death was not surprising; but the neighbouring village viewed the incident with some suspicion. One or two of the older people professed to remember traditions of "trouble" there in former years.

This had made it difficult to get a caretaker, and as Lord Rye was anxious to let again he was willing to take an almost nominal rent. In fact his whole attitude suggested that I was doing him a favour by becoming his tenant. About five hundred acres of shooting generally went with the house, and I was glad to find that I could have them very cheaply.

I moved in at midsummer, and each day made me more and more pleased with my new surroundings.

After my years in India the garden was a particular source of delight to me; but I will not describe it more minutely than is necessary to make what follows intelligible. Behind the house was a good-sized lawn, flanked by shrubbery. On the far side, parallel with the house, ran a splendid yew hedge, nearly fifteen feet high and very thick. It came up to the shrubbery at either end, but was pierced by two archways about thirty yards apart, giving access to the flower-garden beyond. Almost in the middle of the lawn was an old tree stump, or what looked like one, some three feet high. Though covered with ivy it was not picturesque, and I told Lord Rye that I should like to take it up. "Do by all means," he said, "I certainly should if I lived here. I believe poor Riley (the last tenant) intended to put a sundial there. I think it would look rather nice, don't you?"

This struck me as a good idea. I ordered a sundial from a well-known firm of heliological experts in Cockspur Street, and ordered the stump to be grubbed up as soon as it arrived.

One morning towards the end of September I woke unrefreshed after a night of troubled dreams. I could not recall them very distinctly, but I had seemed to be trying to lift a very heavy weight of some kind from the ground. But, before I could raise it, an overwhelming terror had taken hold of me—though I could not remember why—and I woke to find my forehead wet with perspiration. Each time I fell asleep again the dream repeated itself with mechanical regularity, though the details did not become any more distinct. So I was heartily glad it had become late enough to get up. The day was wet and chilly. I felt tired and unwell, and was, moreover, depressed by a vague sense of impending disaster. This was accentuated by a feeling that it lay within my power to avert the catastrophe, if only I could discover what it was.

In the afternoon the weather cleared, and I thought that a ride would do me good. I rode fairly hard for some distance, and it was past five o'clock before I had reached my own bounds-ditch on my way home. At that particular place a small wood ran along the edge of my property for about a quarter of a mile. I was riding slowly down the outside, and was perhaps a hundred yards from the angle where I meant to turn it, when I noticed a man standing at the corner. The light was beginning to fail, and he was so close to the edge of the wood that at first I could not be sure whether it was a human figure, or only an oddly shaped tree-stump which I had never noticed before. But when I got a little nearer I saw that my first impression had been correct, and that it was a man. He seemed to be dressed like an ordinary agricultural labourer. He was standing absolutely still and seemed to be looking very intently in my direction. But he was shading his eyes with his hand, so that I could not make out his face. Before I had got close enough to make him out more definitely he turned suddenly and vanished round the corner of the wood. His movements were rapid: but he somehow gave the impression of being deformed, though in what precise respect I could not tell. Naturally my suspicions were stirred, so I put my horse to a canter. But when we had reached the corner he shied violently, and I had some difficulty in getting him to pass it. When we had got round, the mysterious man was nowhere to be seen. In front and on the left hand lay a very large stubble field, without a vestige of cover of any kind. I could see that he was not crossing it, and unless he had flown he could not have reached the other side.

On the right hand lay the ditch bounding the wood. As is usual in that country it was both wide and deep, and had some two or three feet of mud and water at the bottom.

If the man had gone that way he had some very pressing reason for wishing to avoid me: and I could detect no trace of his passage at any point.

So there was nothing to be done but go home, and tell the policeman next day to keep his eyes open for any suspicious strangers. However, no attempts were made upon any of my belongings, and when October came my pheasants did not seem to have been unlawfully diminished.

October that year was stormy, and one Saturday night about the middle of the month it blew a regular gale. I lay awake long listening to the wind, and to all the confused sounds which fill an old house in stormy weather. Twice I seemed to hear footsteps in the passage. Once I could have almost sworn my door was cautiously opened and closed again. When at last I dropped off I was disturbed by a repetition of my former dream. But this time the details were rather more distinct. Again I was trying to lift a heavy weight from the ground: but now I knew that there was something hidden under it. What the concealed object might be I could not tell, but as I worked to bring it to light a feeling began to creep over me that I did not want to see it. This soon deepened into horror at the bare idea of seeing it: though I had still no notion what manner of thing it might be. Yet I could not abandon my task. So presently I found myself in the position of working hard to accomplish what I would have given the world to have left undone. At this point I woke, to find myself shaking with fright, and repeating aloud the apparently meaningless sentence—"If you'll pull, I'll push."

I did not sleep for the rest of that night. Beside the noise of the storm the prospect of a repetition of that dream was quite enough to keep me awake. To add to my discomfort a verse from Ecclesiastes ran in my head with dismal persistence—"But if a man live many years and rejoice in them all, yet let him remember the days of darkness, for they shall be many." Days of darkness seemed to be coming upon me now, and my mind was filled with vague alarm.

The next day was fine, and after Church I thought I would see how my fruit trees had fared during the night. The kitchen-garden was enclosed by a high brick wall. On the side nearest the house there were two doors, which were always kept locked on Sunday. In the wall opposite was a trap-door, about three feet square, giving on to a rather untidy piece of ground, partly orchard and partly waste. When I had unlocked the door I saw standing by the opposite wall the figure which I had seen at the corner of the wood. His neck was abnormally long, and so malformed that his head lolled sideways on to his right shoulder in a disgusting and almost inhuman fashion. He was bent almost double; and I think he was misshapen in some other respect as well. But of that I could not be certain. He raised his hand with what seemed to be a threatening gesture, then turned, and slipped through the trap-door with remarkable quickness. I was after him immediately, but on reaching the opposite wall received a shock which stopped me like a physical blow. The trap-door was shut and bolted on the inside. I tried to persuade myself that a violent slam might make the bolts shoot, but I knew that that was really impossible. I had to choose between two explanations. Either my visitor was a complete hallucination, or else he possessed the unusual power of being able to bolt a door upon the side on which he himself was not. The latter was upon the whole the more comforting, and—in view of some of my Indian experiences—the more probable, supposition.

After a little hesitation I opened the trap and, as there was nothing to be seen, got through it and went up to the top of the orchard, where the kennels lay. But neither of my dogs would follow the scent. When brought to the spot where his feet must have touched the ground they whined and showed every symptom of alarm. When I let go of their collars they hurried home in a way which showed plainly what they thought of the matter.

This seemed to dispose of the idea of hallucination, and, as before, there was nothing else to be done but await developments as patiently as I could. For the next fortnight nothing remarkable took place. I had my usual health and as near an approach to my usual spirits as could reasonably be expected. I had visitors for part of the time, but no one to whom I should have cared to confide the story at this stage. I was not molested further by day, and my dreams, though varied, were not alarming.

On the morning of the 31st I received a letter announcing that my sundial had been despatched, and it duly arrived in the course of the afternoon. It was heavy, so by the time we had got it out of the railway van and on to the lawn it was too late to place it in position that day. The men departed to drink my health, and I turned towards the house. Just as I reached the door I paused. A sensation—familiar to all men who are much alone—had come over me, and I felt as if I were being watched from behind. Usually the feeling can be dispelled by turning round. I did so, but on this occasion the sense that I was not alone merely increased. Of course the lawn was deserted, but I stood looking across it for a few moments, telling myself that I must not let my nerves play me tricks. Then I saw a face detach itself slowly from the darkness of the hedge at one side of the left-hand arch. For a few seconds it hung, horribly poised, in the middle of the opening like a mask suspended by an invisible thread. Then the body to which it belonged slid into the clear space, and I saw my acquaintance of the wood and kitchen-garden, this time sharply outlined against a saffron sky. There could be no mistaking his bowed form and distorted neck, but now his appearance was made additionally abominable by his expression. The yellow sunset light seemed to stream all round him, and showed me features convulsed with fury. He gnashed his teeth and clawed the air with both hands. I have never seen such a picture of impotent rage.

It was more by instinct than by any deliberate courage that I ran straight across the lawn towards him. He was gone in a flash, and when I came through the archway where he had stood he was hurrying down the side of the hedge towards the other. He moved with an odd shuffling gait, and I made sure that I should soon overtake him. But to my surprise I found that I did not gain much. His limping shuffle took him over the ground as fast as I could cover it. In fact, when I reached the point from which I had started I thought I had actually lost a little. When we came round for the second time there was no doubt about it. This was humiliating, but I persevered, relying now on superior stamina. But during the third circuit it suddenly flashed upon me that our positions had become reversed. I was no longer the pursuer. He—it—whatever the creature was, was now chasing me, and the distance between us was diminishing rapidly.

I am not ashamed to admit that my nerve failed completely. I believe I screamed aloud. I ran on stumblingly, helplessly, as one runs in a dream, knowing now that the creature behind was gaining at every stride. How long the chase lasted I do not know, but presently I could hear his irregular footstep close behind me, and a horrible dank breath played about the back of my neck. We were on the side towards the house when I looked up and saw my butler standing at the garden door, with a note in his hand. The sight of his prosaic form seemed to break the spell which had kept me running blindly round and round the hedge. I was almost exhausted, but I tore across the lawn, and fell in a heap at the bottom of the steps.

Parker was an ex-sergeant of Marines, which amounts to saying that he was incapable of surprise and qualified to cope with any practical emergency which could arise. He picked me up, helped me into the house, gave me a tumbler of brandy diluted with soda-water, and fortified himself with another, without saying a word. How much he saw, or what he thought of it, I could never learn, for all subsequent approaches to the question were parried with the evasive skill which seems to be the birthright of all them that go down to the sea in ships. But his general view of the situation is indicated by the fact that he sent for the Rector, not the doctor, and—as I learned afterwards—had a private conference with him before he left the house. Soon afterwards he joined the choir—or in his own phrase "assisted with the singing in the chancel"—and for many months the village church had no more regular or vocal attendant.

The Rector heard my story gravely, and was by no means disposed to make light of it. Something similar had come his way once before, when he had had the charge of a parish on the Northumbrian border. He was confident, he said, that no harm could come to me that night, if I remained indoors, and departed to look up some of his authorities on such subjects.

That night was noisy with wind, so the insistent knocking which I seemed to hear during the small hours at the garden-door and ground-floor windows, which were secured with outside shutters, may have had no existence outside my imagination. I had asked Parker to occupy a dressing-room opening out of my bedroom for the night. He seemed very ready to do so, but I do not think that he slept very much either. Early next morning the Rector reappeared, saying that he thought he had got a clue, though it was impossible to say yet how much it might be worth. He had brought with him the first volume of the parish register, and showed me the following note on the inside of the cover:

"October 31st, 1578. On this day Jn. Croxton a Poore Man hanged himself from a Beame within his House. He was a very stubborn Popish Recusant and ye manner of his Death was in accord with his whole Life. He was buried that evening at ye Cross Roades."

"It is unfortunate," continued the Rector, "that we have no sixteenth-century map of the parish. But there is a map of 1759 which marks a hamlet at the cross-roads just outside your gate. The hamlet doesn't exist now—you know that the population hereabouts is much less than it used to be—but it used to be called New Cross. I think that must mean that these particular cross-roads are comparatively recent. Now this house is known to have been built between 1596 and 1602. The straight way from Farley to Abbotsholme would lie nearly across its site. I think, therefore, that the Elizabethan Lord Rye diverted the old road when he laid out his grounds. That would also account for the loop which the present road makes"—here he traced its course with his finger on the map which he had brought.

"Now I strongly suspect that your visitor was Mr. Croxton, and that he is buried somewhere in your grounds. If we could find the place I think we could keep him quiet for the future. But I am afraid that there is nothing to guide us."

At this point Parker came in. "Beg your pardon, sir, but Hardman is wishful to speak to you. About that there bollard on the quarter-deck, sir—stump on the lawn, I should have said, sir—what you told him to put over the side."

We went out, and found Hardman and the boy looking at a large hole in the lawn. By the side of it lay what we had taken for a tree stump. But it had never struck root there. It was a very solid wooden stake, some nine feet in length over all, with a sharp point. It had been driven some six feet into the ground, passing through a layer of rubble about three feet from the surface. At the bottom the hole widened, forming a large, and plainly artificial, cavity. The earth here looked as if it had been recently disturbed, but the condition of the stake showed that that was impossible. It was obvious to both of us that we had come upon Mr. Croxton's grave, at the original cross-roads, and that what had appeared to be a natural stump was really the stake which had been driven through it to keep him there. We did not, of course, take the gardeners into our confidence, but told them to leave the place for the present as it might contain some interesting antiques—presumably Roman— which we would get out carefully with our own hands.

We soon enlarged the shaft sufficiently to explore the cavity at the bottom. We had naturally expected to find a skeleton, or something of the sort, there, but we were disappointed. We could not discover the slightest vestige of bones or body, or of any dust except that of natural soil. Once while we were working we were startled by a harsh sound like the cry of a night-jar, apparently very close at hand. But whatever it was passed away very quickly, as if the creature which had made it was on the wing, and it was not repeated.

By the Rector's advice we went to the churchyard and brought away sufficient consecrated earth to fill up the cavity. The shaft was filled up, and the sundial securely planted on top of it. The pious mottoes with which it was adorned, according to custom, assumed for the first time a practical significance.

"It not infrequently happens," said the Rector, "that those who for any reason have not received full Christian burial are unable, or unwilling, to remain quiet in their graves, particularly if the interment has been at all carelessly carried out in the first instance. They seem to be particularly active on or about the anniversary of their death in any year. The range of their activities is varied, and it would be difficult to define the nature of the power which animates them, or the source from which it is derived. But I incline to think that it is less their own personality than some force inherent in the earth itself, of which they become the vehicle. With the exception of vampires (who are altogether *sui generis* and virtually unknown in this country), they can seldom do much direct physical harm. They operate indirectly by terrifying, but are commonly compelled to stop there. But it is always necessary for them to have free access to their graves. If that is obstructed in any way their power seems to lapse. That is why I think that their vitality is in some way bred of the earth: and I am sure that you won't be troubled with any more visits now.

"Our friend was afraid that your sundial would interfere with his convenience, and I think he was trying to frighten you into leaving the house. Of course, if your heart had been weak he might have disposed of you as he did of your unfortunate predecessor. His projection of himself into your dreams was part of his general plan: I incline to think, however, that it was an error of judgment, as it might have put you on your guard. But I very much doubt whether he could have inflicted any physical injury on you if he had caught you yesterday afternoon."

"H'm," said I, "you might be right there. But I am very glad that I shall never know."

Next day Parker asked for leave to go to London. He returned with a large picture representing King Solomon issuing directions to a *corvée* of demons of repellent aspect whom he had (according to a well-known Jewish legend) compelled to labour at the building of the Temple. This he proceeded to affix with drawing-pins to the inside of the pantry door. He called my attention to it particularly, and said that he had got it from a Jew whom he had known in Malta, who had recently opened a branch establishment in the Whitechapel Road. I ventured to make some comment on the singularity of the subject, but Parker was, as usual, impenetrable. "Beggin' your pardon, sir," he said, "there's some things what a civilian don't never 'ave no chance of learnin', not even if 'e 'ad the brains for it. I done my twenty-one years in the Service—*in puris naturalibus* all the time as the saying is—and" (pointing to the figure of the King) you may lay to it that that there man knew 'is business."

A Theory of Black Cats

The King's College debate about the existence of ghosts on 9 March 1883 (see "Preface") followed closely on the appearance of an article in the *Fortnightly Review* by Edmund Gurney and Frederic Myers, Cambridge classicists who'd both been instrumental in founding the Society for Psychical Research the previous year. "Transferred Impressions and Telepathy" (1 March 1883) included many, sometimes striking, eye-witness accounts of thought-transference. And it stirred up intense interest in King's.

A few weeks later the same article prompted an earnest, if clumsily argued, think-piece in the *Cambridge Review*, "A Theory of Ghosts" (2 May 1883), which posited that ghosts were "appearances produced by agents once alive and now in some unknown region, expiating their evil deeds and with the thought of the crimes they have committed constantly recurring to them". Published anonymously, this could have been the distillation of one of the more serious arguments put forward at the King's debate. And it in turn elicited the facetious reply reprinted in this volume, "A Theory of Black Cats". Signed αἰλουροφόβος ("ailurophobe", or "cat-fearer"), I propose that this is by the undergraduate MRJ.

MRJ's curiosity about, and knowledge of, witches and their craft is evident from several of his later ghost stories, but it was an interest that he'd cultivated since his schooldays. On 5 February 1881, he'd read a long, detailed paper to the Eton College Literary Society on "Occult Arts"; and in early February 1884, a few months after "A Theory of Black Cats" appeared, he delivered a talk to the Chit-Chat Society entitled "Art Magic".

The author of the letter in the *Cambridge Review* is coy about his source for the story of "ye Ladye of Listone" and "the seyer Joan" and, authentic though the language looks and sounds, it is almost certainly an invention. The creation of spurious historical documents, and a mastery of the language of past centuries, was a speciality of MRJ throughout his career, as is evidenced in many of his later stories—"The Treasure of Abbot Thomas" (1904) and "Mr. Humphreys and His Inheritance" (1911) to name but two. But, again, even before his arrival in Cambridge, he had form in this. In his final year at Eton he was a co-editor of the *Eton College Chronicle* and is undoubtedly the author of an anonymously published article entitled "Days in the Lives of Past Etonians, From Contemporary Authority" (3 February 1882) in which appear diary entries from 1450 ("dyd ryse at fyue of the clok"), 1560 ("I an three more whipt for pelting of the Colledge Barber . . . ") and 1645 ("The Husher did check me right sharpely for singing of 'The Lord Salisbury his Pavin', this day being as he sayde, the Sabbath.")

There are within the "Ladye of Listone" narrative, and the letter as a whole, prefigurements of later ghost stories by MRJ. In his undated story "The Fenstanton Witch", the narrator makes a similar observation to the author of the letter about Germany being a hotbed of stories about witchcraft and the practise of magic. The cat as a nocturnal agent of supernatural vengeance makes a memorable appearance in "The Stalls of Barchester Cathedral" (1911)—though in his diaries Archdeacon Haynes never specifies his persecutors colour. And with its murderous animal emissary entering a bed chamber through an open window at night, the Listone tragedy strongly resembles MRJ's greatest treatment of the witchcraft theme, "The Ash-Tree" (1904).

Like "The Ash-Tree", "A Theory of Black Cats" relies upon the underlying assumption that witches are real and that the stories told about them in times past were true, and is full of specious argument. The author's overconfidence in his own non-logic, his unmerited insistence on having "proved" his points, mark him out as a crank. He is perhaps not quite as absurd as MRJ's Professor Merganser (see the introduction to "A Night in King's College Chapel"), but he is every bit as preposterous in his way. Hopelessly argued, were it not for a certain elegance of expression "A Theory of Black Cats" might have been mistaken for an early work of the Abbot of Lufford.

The abrupt and cryptic introduction of "Selenephany" to the argument also calls to mind MRJ. It's an invented word, coined from Ancient Greek. It should mean something like "the appearance of the moon" but is almost nonsensical in this context; an entirely counterfeit science, like the "Ontography" in which Professor Parkins holds a Cambridge Professorship in "Oh, Whistle, and I'll Come to You, My Lad" (1904).

There were, of course, dozens of other witty, inventive, classically-educated people in Cambridge in 1883, who could coin words from Ancient Greek and parody clumsy arguments. But "A Theory of Black Cats" has all the hallmarks of MRJ's humour, imagination, and enthusiasms. And if he is the author, then the account of ye Ladye of Listone's tragedy, could lay claim to being his earliest published ghost story.

The reader must judge for themself . . .

A Theory of Black Cats

To the Editors of the *Cambridge Review*.

SIRS,—The article on "A Theory of Ghosts", which appeared in last week's number of the *Cambridge Review*, has introduced to our notice a method of argument and research capable of such extended application, that the present writer feels no apology is needed for disturbing a question which has for many years lain dormant. The question is one closely allied to that of ghosts and their actions, and affords an equally fruitful and important field for investigation; it is, in fact, that of witches and their invariable companions, black cats. Of the existence of witches, and consequently of their companions, we may have no doubt, the evidence being found in books of even greater trustworthiness than a "fortnightly" periodical appearing once a month, whose articles may at times be written with a view to afford innocent amusement.

The literature of our subject is extensive and the stories relating to witches very numerous, especially in German. Justice Hales, King James I, Baring-Gould, Lee, and others, have furnished us with many, the authenticity of which is unimpeachable. From amongst these we have selected the following:—"Ye Ladye of Listone then did journeye unto the seyer Joan for counsel for that her infant sone was sore vexed to deth of a siknesse. Her sone being eased of hys pains, my ladye did forget her promised guerdon. Whereat was Joan mightie wroth and voued fierce vengeannce. That night my ladye slombered ill at ease and did see a catte crepe in at ye opened lattice, alacke! in ye mornynge her sone was ded. My ladye's chamberere did eke confirmen ye wordes of her maistresse, sayenge how that she did see a catte flitte acrosse ye sky . . . Then did ye Ladye of Listone bethink her of her guerdon."

The first point which this touching story brings into prominence is that the witch can by means of her familiar cat work any desired mischief *at a distance*, the distance itself being of no consequence, since the evidence of the serving-woman shews that the cat was able to fly. It is hardly necessary to add that the cat must have seen the lady at the same time that the lady saw the cat.

It follows, therefore, that the cat was *no mere phantom*, but that the apparition *was real*, sent there by the powerful concentration of the witch's thoughts.

Lastly, we see how important the cat was in the furtherance of the witch's evil intentions, for we do not learn that the appearance of the animal caused any alarm, the phenomenon being presumably one of no great rarity in her lady's domains. Had the witch come in person, no doubt her terrible aspect would have frustrated her designs. We have shewn, therefore, that cats as well as ghosts form a portion of the subject of "Selenephany", a science which we feel most intensely to be of the utmost importance to all firm believers in the existence of ghosts.

We may now consider "What is the popular opinion about black cats?" We find an almost universal belief has existed that the black cat is the familiar spirit in attendance upon the witch, able and willing to perform any action, not distinctly good, in obedience to command. We have also Shakespeare's authority on this point in *Macbeth* where he introduces three witches to our notice, and since we cannot imagine a witch without her attendant, we have here the very important corroborative evidence of the truth of the popular belief.

But why should not black cats be wicked spirits in disguise, the agents of the evil one, seeing that he has the thought of crime ever before his mind? It would then naturally follow that where crime is most common, there we should expect to find the greatest number of black cats. Now this is precisely what is found to be the case, for statistics conclusively shew that crime is most rife in densely populated districts, the very places where black cats are found in greatest abundance. What a convincing proof have we not here of the existence, of the personality indeed, of the devil and his servants.

In conclusion we would remark that the subject of "Selenephany", though far reaching, has been but little investigated from a scientific standpoint. We venture, therefore, to think that with our much improved methods of research, and widened powers of deduction, many very remarkable results may be looked for. We have, at the very outset, by a superficial examination only, been enabled finally to lay at rest a much vexed question. What may we not expect from a careful study?

In thus recommending the subject of "Selenephany" to the accurate investigation of that society which has devoted itself to the collection of ghost-stories, we feel that we have greatly enlarged its field of research, and placed within its grasp the power of permanently benefitting the human race.

I am, Sirs, yours etc.,
αἰλουροφόβος

Sources

"A Night in King's College Chapel" by M. R. James was written around 1892; it was first published in *Ghosts and Scholars 7*, edited by Rosemary Pardoe (Runcorn: Haunted Library, 1985).

"A Night in King's College Chapel (Early Fragment)" by M. R. James was first published in *Ghosts and Scholars 7*, edited by Rosemary Pardoe (Runcorn: Haunted Library, 1985).

"The Wraith of Barnjum" by F. Anstey was first published in *Temple Bar* (March 1879); it was collected in *The Black Poodle and Other Stories* (London: Longmans, Green and Co., 1884).

"The Breaking-Point" by F. Anstey was first published in *The Strand* (December 1919); it was collected in *The Last Load: Stories and Essays* (London: Methuen & Co., 1925).

"A Midnight Fantasy" by Henry Doone [Arthur Reed Ropes] was first published in *The Reflector 5* (29 January 1888); it is reprinted here for the first time.

"Seraphita: The Story of a Spook" by Henry Doone [Arthur Reed Ropes] was first published in *The Cambridge Review* (3 and 10 May 1888); it is reprinted here for the first time.

"When the Door Is Shut" by "B." [A. C. Benson] was first published in *Magdalene College Magazine* (June 1912); it was first collected in *When the Door Is Shut and Other Ghost Stories* (Runcorn: Haunted Library, 1986).

"Quia Nominor" by "B." [A. C. Benson] was first published in *Magdalene College Magazine* (June 1913); it was first collected in *When the Door Is Shut and Other Ghost Stories* (Runcorn: Haunted Library, 1986).

"The Sparsholt Stone" by "B." [A. C. Benson] was first published in *Magdalene College Magazine* (December 1919); it is reprinted here for the first time.

"The Man with the Roller" was first published in *The Peterborough Standard* (23 December 1911) under the name "S. Wain"; this version is reprinted here for the first time. A slightly revised version was collected in *The Stoneground Ghost Tales: Compiled from the Recollections of the Reverend Roland Batchel, Vicar of the Parish* by E. G. Swain (Cambridge: W. Heffer & Sons, 1912).

"The Greenford Ghost" by "S. Wain" was first published in the *Middlesex County Times* (11 and 18 December 1920). It was later reprinted as a pamphlet by the *Middlesex County Times* (undated) under the title "Coston House" and attributed to E. G. Swain.

"A Collector's Company" by R. H. Malden was first published in *Nine Ghosts* (London: Edward Arnold, 1943).

"The Sundial" by R. H. Malden was first published in the *Leeds Parish Church Magazine* (December 1930); it was slightly expanded and collected in *Nine Ghosts* (London:

Edward Arnold, 1943). This later text is the one printed here.

"A Theory of Black Cats" was first published in *The Cambridge Review* (9 May 1883) under the name αἴλουροφόβος ("ailurophobe", or "cat-fearer"); it is reprinted here for the first time.

Acknowledgements

"A Night in King's College Chapel" and the earlier fragment appear with the kind permission of the Estate of M. R. James; with further thanks to Rosemary Pardoe for the use of her transcriptions.

The extract from A. C. Benson's diary has been transcribed with the permission of the Master and Fellows of Magdalene College, Cambridge.

The diagram of the King's College Chapel window on page 5 is by Dr. Donal Cooper. The photograph of MRJ and F. Anstey in Pressburg on page 29 is reproduced with the permission of King's College, Cambridge. The photograph of the Bridget Coston memorial from Holy Cross Church, Greenford, on page 155 is by Bob Speel.

For advice and help while researching and writing the introductory material for *Friends and Spectres* I'd like to thank the staff of the Archives of King's College, Cambridge; Magdalene College, Cambridge; and Manchester Grammar School. Also the staff of Cambridge University Library MSS and Rare Books rooms; and the West Yorkshire Archive Service. Individual thanks are due to Dr. Donal Cooper, John Coulthart, Dr. Christine Faraday, Malcolm Gaskill, Philip James, Timothy J. Jarvis, Meggan Kehrli, Steve J. Shaw, Helen Murray, Adriaen Baez Ortega, Jim Rockhill, David Rowlands, Brian J. Showers, Dr. Hayley Smith, Bob Speel, Dr. Jennifer Wallis, and Annette Wickham. Particular thanks are due to Peter

Hounsell, Archivist for Holy Cross Church, Greenford, for drawing my attention to E. G. Swain's "Coston House".

This book is dedicated with love to Alban and Carys Lloyd Parry.

About the Editor

Robert Lloyd Parry is a performance storyteller and writer. In 2005 he began what he now refers to as "The M. R. James Project", with a solo performance of "Canon Alberic's Scrap-book" and "The Mezzotint" in MRJ's old office in the Fitzwilliam Museum, Cambridge. The Project has since encompassed seven one-man theatre shows, several films and audiobooks, three documentaries, a guided walk, and numerous magazine articles. For Swan River Press he has previously edited *Ghosts of the Chit-Chat* (2020) and *Curfew and other Eerie Tales* by Lucy M. Boston (2011).

SWAN RIVER PRESS

Founded in 2003, Swan River Press is an independent publishing company, based in Dublin, Ireland, dedicated to gothic, supernatural, and fantastic literature. We specialise in limited edition hardbacks, publishing fiction from around the world with an emphasis on Ireland's contributions to the genre.

www.swanriverpress.ie

"While small publishers often produce beautiful books, few can match those from Swan River Press."

– Washington Post

"It [is] often down to small, independent, specialist presses to keep the candle of horror fiction flickering . . . "

– The Irish Times

"Swan River Press—cutting edge of New Gothic."

– Joyce Carol Oates

"The redoubtable Brian J. Showers [keeps] the myriad voices of Irish fantasy alive there in Dublin."

– Alan Moore

GHOSTS OF THE CHIT-CHAT

edited by Robert Lloyd Parry

On the evening of Saturday, 28 October 1893, Cambridge University's Chit-Chat Club convened its 601st meeting. Ten members and one guest gathered in the rooms of Montague Rhodes James, the Junior Dean of King's College, and listened—with increasing absorption one suspects—as their host read "Two Ghost Stories".

Ghosts of the Chit-Chat celebrates this momentous event in the history of supernatural literature, the earliest dated record we have of M. R. James reading his ghost stories out loud. And it revives the contributions that other members made to the genre; men of imagination who invoked the ghostly in their work, and who are now themselves shades. In a series of essays, stories, and poems Robert Lloyd Parry looks at the history and culture of the Club.

In addition to tales and poems never before reprinted, *Ghosts of the Chit-Chat* features earlier, slightly different versions of two of M. R. James's best-known ghost stories; Robert Lloyd Parry's profiles and commentaries on each featured Chit-Chat member sheds new light on this supernatural tradition, making *Ghosts of the Chit-Chat* a valuable resource for casual readers and long-time Jamesians alike.

"An exquisite reading pleasure."

– Black Gate

"This is a lovely little book . . . there are some fascinating and often rarely seen pieces of writing here."

– A Ghostly Company

GREEN TEA

J. Sheridan Le Fanu

Published alongside "Carmilla" in the landmark collection *In a Glass Darkly* (1872), Le Fanu's "Green Tea" was first serialised in Charles Dickens' magazine *All the Year Round* in 1869. Since its first publication, Le Fanu's tale has lost none of its potency. "Green Tea" tells of the good natured Reverend Jennings, who writes late at night on arcane topics abetted by a steady supply of green tea. Is he insane or have these nocturnal activities opened an "interior sight" that affords a route of entry for an increasingly malignant simian companion? This 150th anniversary edition of "Green Tea", with illustrations by Alisdair Wood and an introduction by Matthew Holness, is the definitive celebration of Le Fanu's masterpiece of psychological terror and despair.

"Even 150 years after it was published,
'Green Tea' has stood firmly against the test of time
as a wonderfully eerie and well-crafted ghost story."

– Ghosts & Scholars

"To paraphrase Little Women, it wouldn't be Christmas
without any ghost stories . . . Swan River Press
has just issued a beautiful keepsake volume
of J. Sheridan Le Fanu's Green Tea."

– Michael Dirda, *Washington Post*

THE HOUSE ON
THE BORDERLAND

William Hope Hodgson

An exiled recluse, an ancient abode in the remote west of Ireland, nightly attacks by malevolent swine-things from a nearby pit, and cosmic vistas beyond time and space. *The House on the Borderland* has been praised by China Miéville, Terry Pratchett, and Clark Ashton Smith, while H. P. Lovecraft wrote, "Few can equal [Hodgson] in adumbrating the nearness of nameless forces and monstrous besieging entities through casual hints and significant details, or in conveying feelings of the spectral and abnormal."

"Almost from the moment that you hear the title," observes Alan Moore, "you are infected by the novel's weird charisma. Knock and enter at your own liability." *The House on the Borderland* remains one of Hodgson's most celebrated works. This new edition features an introduction by Alan Moore, an afterword by Iain Sinclair, and illustrations by John Coulthart.

"A summit of Cosmic horror.
Scary, disturbing and magical."

– Guillermo del Toro

"Swan River Press has produced the best version ever.
There is no need for any other."

– *Dead Reckonings*

www.ingramcontent.com/pod-product-compliance
Lightning Source LLC
Chambersburg PA
CBHW051143190726
48290CB00006B/1966